Felicity grasped his wrist with b[...]
Metal kept a frown off his face as he held her hand, surreptitiously
putting a thumb on her pulse. A thready fifty beats per minute.
Blood pressure very low. They had to get going.

"No...hospitals," she gasped. "Can't...leave a trace."

"No hospitals," he agreed, pulling on latex gloves. She'd already
made that clear, and he'd already factored in that whoever had
sliced her was still out there, looking. The fucker would never get
his hands on her again. "No trace. Now hold still just a second, this
might sting."

Her face scrunched when he disinfected the wound, but she didn't
make a sound. *Good girl.*

"So, Felicity," he said calmly, "it is Felicity, isn't it? That's what
Lauren called you."

*Try to keep the patient engaged, try to ask simple yes or no
questions.*

She nodded.

"That's a pretty name. Felicity. Sort of means happiness, doesn't it?"

She nodded again, huge sky-blue eyes unblinking.

"Well, here's the deal, Felicity. I'm going to apply some coagulating
powder on the wound and then bind it up. I understand you don't
want to go to a hospital. You're afraid the guy who attacked you
might find you. He will not find you. And even if he does, Jacko—
that's the mean-looking guy over there—and I have your back.
You're safe with us, I promise. But we need to take you somewhere
where you can get a blood transfusion because you've lost blood.
Do you know your blood type?"

"A positive," she whispered.

"Good girl," he said. "If we know your blood type we don't need
to use plasma—we can use blood directly. And you know what?
I happen to be A positive, too, so if where we're going is low on
your blood type, I can donate. I'm really healthy. Don't worry about
anything."

She was watching him so very carefully. Listening hard with every
organ she had, it seemed. Not just her ears but through her skin
and eyes. She nodded. "Okay," she whispered. "Gotcha. No
worries." Then she rolled her eyes and tried to grin at him.

Oh God. Beautiful and brave. With a sense of humor.

**Also available from Lisa Marie Rice
and Carina Press**

Midnight Vengeance
Midnight Secrets

**And watch for *Midnight Fire*, the next book
in the Midnight series, coming soon!**

LISA MARIE RICE

MIDNIGHT PROMISES

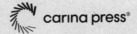 carina press®

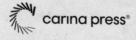 carina press®

ISBN-13: 978-0-373-00289-4

Recycling programs for this product may not exist in your area.

Midnight Promises

www.CarinaPress.com

Printed in U.S.A.

Dear Reader,

I hope you enjoy Felicity and Metal's story.

Felicity and Metal find each other during the course of the story and they become each other's family. Felicity has no family left, and Metal lost his on 9/11.

Felicity grew up in the Witness Protection Program. All during her childhood her parents were looking over their shoulders to scan for the danger they'd left behind. Her parents were distant, frightened people, and she had to find refuge in her computer.

Metal came from a close and loving family of first responders—cops and firefighters. On one awful day, he lost his entire family—father and brothers and then a mother dead of a broken heart a week later.

Felicity and Metal are strong characters, and they found refuge and meaning in their work—Felicity as a computer security expert, and Metal as a medic and navy SEAL. They didn't know that something big, something important, was missing from their lives until they found each other.

Midnight Promises is about these two smart, strong, idealistic souls finding each other and protecting what they have found. Danger and violence stalk them, but they prevail, and their love is stronger than ever at the end.

Felicity and Metal become each other's family. This book covers the intriguing and exciting (and dangerous!) events that bring them together, but rest assured that they will be loving partners the rest of their lives and they will love and protect their children fiercely.

The Midnight books are about just that—about couples coming together and forming a unit within the larger unit of the Midnight team. They will all be lifelong friends. The men work within the company with the same zeal they showed as SEALs, knowing that each teammate is responsible for the well-being of the other teammates and the company.

They will face danger together and they will never let any of their teammates down.

The women are bound by strong ties of affection and form an extended family, everyone willing to offer a helping hand and to stay utterly loyal to each other.

Each Midnight book is a tile in this mosaic of strong and loyal men and women forging bonds that will last a lifetime.

Lisa Marie Rice

Acknowledgments

Immense thanks to
Christine Witthohn and Angela James

This one is dedicated to my son,
starting his life as a creative. Good luck, my love.

PROLOGUE

ONE YOUNG WOMAN could hold the key to a new world order and a resurgent Russia. The daughter of a traitor. All he had to do was find her.

Vladimir Borodin stood at the window of his presidential suite at the sumptuous Court Place Hotel, looking down Fifth Avenue. It was snowing lightly and the streets were thronged with expensively dressed men and women hurrying on their way to dinner or the theater. The shop windows gleamed, filled with expensive items. Though Borodin couldn't hear them through the double glazed windows he knew the streets would be filled with the sounds of rich happy shoppers making dinner plans.

All was well with America.

But twenty-five years ago, when instead of being an oligarch, the CEO of Intergaz, the largest energy corporation in Russia, he'd been *Colonel* Vladimir Borodin of the *Komitét Gosudàrstvennoj Bezopàsnosti*, the feared KGB, he'd been so very very close to destroying this country. It would have taken America a generation, maybe two generations, to come back to a semblance of nationhood, to claw its way back up to a third-rate economy.

And the Soviet Union would have become the most

powerful nation on earth. Right now, if things hadn't gone wrong, Russia would be sending blankets and powdered milk to the teeming masses of poor in America. The Soviet Union would still be alive, strong and rich, bestriding the world.

Instead, the Soviet Union had fallen and a much reduced Russia had risen from its ashes.

They had counted on Nikolai Darin for the means to destroy America. Tragically, Darin died twenty-five years ago before finishing the task. Or so they thought. But he hadn't. He had died a few years ago in America. And he had a daughter who went by the outlandish American name of Felicity Ward.

She held the key to everything. There was still time to implement the plan that had been born a generation ago. Catch the woman and make her talk. Make her tell him where they were.

Borodin checked his watch. It was 5:00 p.m., soon it would be time to call for room service. After dinner, while waiting for word that Felicity Ward was caught and on her way to him, he'd treat himself to an Armagnac. He could taste it already. He'd come to the States with a team of five men, four of them pilots. His assistant, Anatoli Lagoshin, together with a pilot, had been dispatched to intercept the woman at the Portland, Oregon airport. Anatoli was flying cross country in one of Intergaz's corporate jets and he would land before Felicity Ward.

He'd nab her, fly her back to New York with the same plane and with a little persuasion, they'd get what they came for.

And if Felicity suffered it was only fair. Her father had cost Borodin twenty-five years and their motherland, the Soviet Union, had been wiped off the map. If Darin hadn't betrayed his country, they would now be masters of the world.

Felicity, his daughter, should suffer. And she would.

ONE

SAFE. THE WORD kept rolling around in Felicity Ward's head. *Safe. Safe. Safe.* The word seemed odd when she repeated it over and over. Like a sound with no meaning. Like the word itself, really. Safe didn't exist. It never had for her.

But her friend Lauren had used it so often lately. And it sounded as if, after being abducted by a crazy guy for money and saved by her lover, a former Navy SEAL— well, it sounded like Lauren was more or less as safe as you could be in this dangerous world.

Felicity Ward, aka Alina Darin, aka Katrin Valk knew all about the world being dangerous. Her father, Niko- lai Darin, a world-famous Soviet nuclear physicist, had defected to the United States before she was born. He'd defected the night he'd won the Nobel Prize for Phys- ics and the CIA had orchestrated a fake car crash. He'd planned it under the nose of the KGB. If the KGB had suspected his defection, they'd have sent a wet team.

Ironically, her parents really had died in a car crash, only it was nineteen years later in America.

Which just went to show that though most dangers came from other human beings, there were also natural dangers such as accidents and fire and snowstorms. Like the one raging now.

The sky outside the enormous airport skylights was unnaturally dark and snow flurries swirled against the hundred-foot-high windowpanes.

She needed to get to the taxicab stand fast. Her flight from Burlingham, Vermont via Chicago and Denver had been one of the last to land. If the snowstorm continued like this the roads would close down. She didn't want to be stuck overnight in this airport, however pretty it was.

But it was hard to move fast when she was so distracted.

Felicity spent most of her time—well, all of her time—indoors in her apartment. The colors and sounds and smells of the airport nearly overwhelmed her. Shop after shop after shop of bright things—clothes and shoes and electronics and makeup. Felicity never went to shopping malls. She ordered everything online, and this was so distracting and enticing. So much to see.

And the people! When was the last time she'd been in a space with so many people? They were fascinating. You could make up stories about them forever. That was one of the things she did for a living—inventing online and paper personas for people on the run. The crowd milling around the airport wasn't on the run but you could read their stories in their faces, in their bodies.

That man there, in the expensive rumpled suit, frowning and checking his wrist watch for the third time in a minute. Maybe he'd just gotten off a flight from Hong Kong and was waiting for his driver to take him to the meeting he was late for.

And that woman over there in a luxury store, fingering a beautiful cashmere shawl. She had a very sad look on her face. Was she expecting someone who wasn't coming?

But that girl emerging from the exit area Felicity had just come from—she had someone waiting. Tall and lanky with a huge grin on his face and a bouquet of wilted daisies in his big hand.

Fascinating.

She felt like a puppy that had been let out in the garden after a winter indoors. All these colors and shapes and sounds…

And purses! She walked by an upscale purse shop that made her think wryly of her own beige five-year-old canvas bag. For this trip she'd just put documents and keys and lipstick and flash drives in her laptop backpack, not even bothering with her canvas bag. Why didn't she buy herself new purses? Just look at them in the window!

She stopped and all but pressed her nose against the shop window. Such pretty pastel colors—had pastels just come in or had they been in for years and she hadn't noticed? Soft leather, exquisitely fashioned details, shiny brass studs. She sidestepped and stood in front of the open door. A shop assistant in the back who'd been putting away a stack of scarves in every color of the rainbow looked up and smiled. Felicity made an *I'm just looking* gesture and the shop assistant nodded.

She pulled in a deep, delighted breath and smelled leather and newness and style, if style had a smell. Portland was bound to have purse shops. Oh man, she was going to hit every single one and spend some money. It wasn't as if she didn't have any. She had plenty of money, she just never spent it.

Maybe Lauren would go shopping with her. That would be…fun. Shopping with a girlfriend. Something she'd never done before. Her parents had discouraged friendships throughout her school years. At MIT her friends had mostly been men and they barely washed, let alone shopped.

So many things she'd never done. Why hadn't she done them? That was about to change, big-time.

This crazy trip to Portland was sort of a test. A test to see if she could live a normal life. Go out like other people did. Take trips, go to the movies instead of watching Netflix on her seventy-eight-inch curved screen. Go shopping in RealSpace, eat out instead of ordering in. Everyone else did, why shouldn't she?

So this was going to be her new life. Maybe. With luck.

Traveling to see friends, because when you went out you made friends. That was the way it worked, right?

Right next door to the purse shop was a cosmetics shop and heavenly smells came from it. Perfumes and lotions and lipsticks and creams. Another deep breath to pull it all in, then on to the next shop.

Shoes! Oh yes! Just look at those soft ankle boots, a fabulous shade of purple, she'd have to pull up the Pantone scale to discover the exact name, but it was *gorgeous*. Would it hurt to walk in for a few minutes? A glance out the windows told her that the weather—

"Don't move," a voice said. Low, male, vicious. A hard thump on the back made her stagger. One big strong hand held her shoulder, another pushed something sharp against her side, at the edge of her laptop backpack straps. "Don't turn around, don't fucking breathe," the voice said. "You feel this?"

This was a knife, sharp-pointed. It had cut through her coat and sweater and the point was pressed against her skin. Any move she made would result in the knife slashing her side.

"Yes." Felicity tried to keep her voice even. She scanned the hall but there was no help coming. Hundreds, maybe thousands of people, hurrying this way and that and not one paying her the slightest bit of attention. What would they see, anyway? A woman with a man at her back. He could be her husband, her boyfriend, her brother. "I feel it."

"Good. Now, this is how it's going to work. We're going to take the escalators down to the street level. Then head outside. You're going to walk in a straight line the fifty meters to the escalators and be very quiet. You are not going to attract anyone's attention because by the time you have caught someone's attention, I'll have sliced you open. Do you understand me?"

She nodded.

"Say it!"

"I understand."

He spoke English well with a slight British accent and something underneath that. An accent very similar to her mother's only better English than her mother had ever learned. Russian? Ukrainian? And he calculated in meters. Lots of people did, though, including the million and a half members of the US military plus the eight hundred thousand in the reserves. But what did she know? Linguistics weren't her forte. Computers were.

Computers had saved her life, were her life. Maybe….

Another hard thump from behind to propel her forward, the man's hand painfully gripping her shoulder. Felicity started walking as slowly as she dared.

Because in here, in the bustle of the crowd, there was safety in numbers. Once they had gone down to street level and exited the airport, once he'd herded her away from the crowd, any hope of rescue would be gone. Though it was only midafternoon, the sky was dark. The weather outside would make everybody walk around in a little cocoon of self-preservation, eyes slitted against the snow, watching their feet, not noticing anyone else.

If she could make an escape it would have to be here, inside. Outside the doors of the airport, she'd be lost. Whatever this man wanted from her, he'd get. Whatever this was, it might end with her body dumped by the side of the road.

She slowed down slightly, head bowed, dejection in every line of her body. She watched people moving, some fast, some slow, and calculated trajectories. A watch-and-sunglasses kiosk with stand-alone revolving displays was coming up on her right hand side.

Felicity lunged and a line of fire sliced down her side. She was cut, maybe badly, but she was free of the heavy hand on her shoulder, of the knife held in the man's other hand. However badly she was hurt, she'd be in worse shape if he caught her again.

He wanted quiet, he wanted to grab her without any fuss, so he wouldn't shout out.

If he had help—if there were other men around as backup—she was in trouble. There was no way of knowing. She could only implement the crazy plan that had blossomed between the shoe store and the watch kiosk.

The line of fire, as if someone had pressed a hot piece of steel down her side, turned to pain. Hot, searing pain that made her gasp.

Passing the watch-and-sunglasses kiosk she shoved really hard at the two displays, happy they tumbled, scattering watches and sunglasses everywhere.

Felicity didn't dare look around to see where he was. All she could do was run. She took off, dragging her carry-on and realized instantly it would slow her down in the crowd. She abandoned it. She had the only thing she really needed in her backpack—her specially designed laptop, worth over fifty thousand dollars and now worth her life. She barreled forward, pushing and tripping people, leaving as much confusion behind as possible.

Ten feet away was a pillar. Scrambling behind it, she looked back. It was a risk, but she had to know what the situation was like behind her and she had to know what her assailant looked like.

She'd left chaos in her wake, colorful watches and sunglasses littering the floor, several women kneeling on the floor, a couple of college-age students picking up watches with a smile, a couple of crying kids and…there he was! Medium height, dirty blond hair barely visible beneath a wide-brimmed hat, well built, well dressed, cold flat eyes. And—yes—he was holding something in his right hand that was dripping blood. Her blood. He put the knife away almost immediately.

She was dripping too. She put a hand to her side and it came away wet and red. It was a serious wound. It was fiercely painful and impeded movement. She had to do something quick. Another slash like that and she wouldn't survive this.

Well, she'd lived with danger close all her life and was built for this. A fully formed plan had consolidated in her mind and it gave her strength. Ducking and weaving, using every inch of cover available, she headed straight for the bathrooms on the other side of the huge concourse.

Something on the floor caught her eye. She looked

down and froze. Bright red drops. A blood trail, a huge arrow that would lead him straight to her once order was established. Whoever this man was, he would be more than capable of following a blood trail.

A couple passed by with a baby in a stroller, both parents burdened with huge amounts of kid paraphernalia, including a blue baby blanket. And—aha!—a dirty baseball cap. She grabbed the cap and the blanket, pressing the blanket to her side under the coat. She ran to the bathroom, checking to see that she didn't leave bloody footprints.

A small atrium before the doors of the women's restroom gave her a moment's shelter. She stopped, panting, and peeked around the corner, grimacing with pain. She swayed and propped herself up using a knuckle, since her palms were slick with blood.

The man was in profile, scanning straight ahead. The god of nerds was smiling on her because a huge knot of people, most of them young like her, moved across the concourse, perpendicular to the flow of people. Her attacker moved forward as though he'd been sprung out of a cage. The knot of people was exactly the kind of crowd she'd try to hide in and like a bloodhound scenting prey, he shot across the floor, head swiveling to catch a glimpse of her.

But she was behind him now, ducking into the ladies' room, which was—thank God!—empty. In the handicapped stall, she locked the door and sat cross-legged on the toilet lid, pulling out her cell phone and her laptop. She took the battery out of her cell, so she couldn't be tracked and opened her laptop. It was very special and could run for two hundred hours without recharging. A prototype, given to her by China's top hacker while he'd been a Black Hat. It turned on immediately. Her fingers flew over the keyboard. The laptop was very fast and powerful and had a lot of programs it shouldn't have. With the help of one she accessed the airport's security system and initiated a bomb alert. A siren sounded immediately.

Then she hacked into the airport loudspeaker system, overrode the regular announcements and used an app she'd designed to disguise her voice. It turned her natural soprano into a male basso profundo that sounded like God Himself.

"Attention, attention, we have just received a bomb alert. We ask all passengers and personnel to please make for the exits in an orderly fashion. You may use the stairs and the escalators but not the elevators. Attention, attention—"

She put the announcement on a loop.

As if on cue, sounds of screams came from the concourse outside the toilets, the flooring shivering with the vibrations of thousands of feet running.

The laptop screen went out of focus for an instant and Felicity grabbed the stability bar for the handicapped, grateful that she'd chosen this stall. She held it, white-knuckled, until her head cleared. Almost afraid, she glanced down at her side and saw that the blanket she'd wrapped around herself was soaked with blood. Soon she was going to faint and then she'd really be prey. Her attacker wouldn't find her outside and would come back inside and check the place thoroughly. If he found her unconscious on the floor of the bathroom stall, she was done for.

One last thing to do.

Like all large airports, the Portland airport had an

ambulance service on duty 24/7 in case of an airplane crash. Though the letters danced on the screen, she found the emergency service and directed the ambulances to come around to the front of the street level.

Someone would have ordered them out anyway, eventually, but she needed an ambulance *now*.

Hitching her laptop backpack higher up on her shoulders, she planted a bloody hand against the pristine white walls of the stall, realizing that she was leaving DNA and fingerprints. She should go into the outer room, grab some towels, soak them with water and soap, and wipe it down.

But really, she'd need bleach. And she didn't have the strength anyway. Pressing the last dry part of the baby blanket against her side, she put on the baseball cap, tucking her hair in to hide the color, and walked out into utter chaos.

Good. Chaos was good.

Her disguised voice kept booming over the loudspeakers, a deep top note over the screams and cries of the passengers. "Attention, attention—"

She put herself in the middle of a stream of people scrambling down the stairs and made it down almost without her feet touching the ground.

People were pushing and shouting to get out through the revolving door exits, creating bottlenecks so that the exits looked like one huge writhing organism made up of arms and legs instead of terrified travelers desperately trying to get out.

She felt a thump at her back and her adrenaline spiked, cutting off her breath. It wasn't her attacker, though, it was a woman in a knot of people rushing for the exits. Felicity was caught in the middle and carried

forward, her feet barely touching the floor. A strident
alarm signal started up, like an air-raid siren. She hadn't
done that, it must have been an automated system. But
it served to increase the frenzy of the passengers in the
terminal. Only half had made it outside, the others were
mostly clustered at the chokepoints of the exits.

The knot of people propelling her forward dissipated
like a clump of dirt hitting water as they made it out
through the revolving doors, and she dropped to her
hands and knees, head down between her arms, observing running feet rushing by. Sneakers, pumps, tiny
kids' shoes, polished men's shoes, high heels…they all
streamed by while she held herself up on trembling arms.
A few drops of blood stained the concrete pavement.
She'd bled right through the blanket.

The screams, the alarm, the voice booming *attention*,
attention—they all melded into a background blur then
faded. She blacked out for a second but came to immediately when a sneakered foot crushed her hand. The pain
woke her before she could slump to the ground. Grateful that it had been a sneaker and not a stiletto, she rose
on one knee, then the other, then rose up on her feet,
trembling and weak.

Someone else bumped into her from behind. You
don't stand still in a stream of panicking people. Stumbling forward, she tried to scan for her attacker but there
was darkness at the edge of her vision.

Stumbling and bleeding, she made her way through
without attracting attention. People were fighting to get
away, their eyes straight ahead. No one noticed a young
woman, even if she was bleeding and half-dead on her
feet. Panic was excellent camouflage.

The alarm was still whooping and now a thousand

people were outside the airport, blinking in the snow, children crying, men shouting. Some had been injured in the stampede and Felicity could see a woman cradling her arm, but it didn't look broken. She hated the thought of causing injuries but she'd had no choice.

Her attacker was at the other end of the sidewalk, head turning, pushing people out of his way. He was heading toward her, systematically checking faces. Felicity ducked behind a big planter. Moving as fast as she could despite the searing pain in her side she turned and made her way to the far end where ambulances were driving up, sirens wailing. Soldiers with machine guns were trying to establish order, funneling people out toward the parking lots.

Felicity staggered when she got to the first ambulance, stopping a medic with a bloodstained hand.

"Ma'am?" he said, frowning, looking at her hand then down her side. She pulled back her coat, lifted the blanket from the wound and looked at him. She didn't have to playact anything.

"I need help." She wanted to spin a story about how she'd fallen and cut herself but she didn't have the strength. She could barely stand and only those stark words came out in a whisper.

"Right," the medic said, signaling the driver. A gloved hand probed the wound. She gasped in pain, then bit her lips. No crying out, no calling attention to herself. She'd lost track of her attacker but he was out there somewhere.

"Let's get you into the van and start a saline and plasma drip right away," the medic said.

It got hazy after that. The sounds of a gurney being unfolded, gentle but strong hands helping her onto it, the gurney being loaded into the back of the ambulance, the probing as the medic found a vein and started an IV line of something...

She drifted in and out of consciousness, the siren wailing, the IV bag swaying, the medic holding her wrist, a finger on the pulse. The radio on the dashboard would crackle and someone at a central dispatch imparted orders but none of the words made any kind of sense. She lost all sense of time and even of where she was. Her consciousness was reduced to a pinprick of awareness, no past and no future, just an endless now with pain and noise.

The ambulance went up a ramp, fast, and braked to a halt.

The medic and driver were smooth and efficient. She was out of the ambulance and into the ER as fast as possible, the medic giving the nurses a rundown of her condition so quickly she couldn't follow. Maybe it was better that way.

"...the airport?" one of the nurses asked and the medic shook his head.

"Lots of confusion, we should be ready for minor injuries. Lucky that bomb didn't go off."

"Yet. Though they are saying that maybe it was a false alarm," the nurse said. The nurse was standing at the top of the gurney so Felicity couldn't see her face. The nurse came around, probed at the wound, and Felicity blacked out again, just for a second. It was as if her life was being conducted under strobe lights, at every pulse of light she was in a different position, something else going on. The nurse injected something into the IV bag. A painkiller.

The lancing pain—almost electric in its intensity—started to abate, became some dim far-off thing, not really connected to her body. Her head, too, took a trip toward the ceiling.

She was still in the emergency room when passengers from the airport started to stream in. Cuts, lacerations, one woman was limping. Nothing really serious but the influx of panicked passengers created a swirl of chaos. Felicity watched it somewhat dreamily from her gurney, sorry she'd created the chaos, happy she'd escaped her attacker.

Now that she was safely in the hospital she should tell the doctor she'd been attacked. He didn't have to know she'd pulled the alarm, she'd just glide over the fortuitous fact that right after being knifed, the airport announced a bomb alert.

She had solid heavy-duty medical insurance. She could probably have two liver transplants and a nose job while here. When they asked, she had everything in her backpack.

If she needed surgery, no problem, though she hated the thought of being unconscious with her attacker out there somewhere. But she was in a hospital, with guards and nurses and doctors all around her. Her attacker wouldn't…

Felicity froze, her heart suddenly beating painfully hard behind her breastbone. *There he was!* Oh God, at the entrance, scanning the organized chaos of the emergency room, looking for her. She was partially covered by a green curtain, a privacy screen, and he'd have to go down a long line to see if she was on one of the gurneys. Surely he wouldn't…

Yes, he would. Thorough *bastard*. Oh God, she was trapped! She didn't have the strength to get up from the gurney and rush to a hiding place. What could she do?

Her mind was usually quick but now it was sluggish, thoughts slow and unclear. She might as well be dead if she had to think like that.

Dead! God yes! Her attacker was moving forward from the exit, looking sharply at faces, no one stopping him. Maybe at a calmer moment someone would ask what he wanted but right now he had total freedom to move as he pleased. He strode decisively across the room. In a second or two he would be at the foot of her gurney and it would be over.

Dead. She had to get dead quick, before he killed her.

Felicity pulled the IV out of her arm, and blood started seeping out of the needle. Good. She pulled the needle out of the tube and bright red blood spattered the pristine white sheet. She pushed away from the wall, making her gurney isolated, abandoned, and pulled the sheet right over her face.

Dead. Dead. Dead. *Deader'n shit* as a Texan hacker used to say. But she was gasping in panicked breaths and there was no way she could hold her breath. She was absolutely sure the sheet was rising and falling with her heartbeat.

Okay, think. She'd refused to let go of her backpack—her entire life was in her computer—and it was going to save her life right now. She pulled the backpack over her chest and put her pillow over that. What anyone would see was an obese dead person, thick belly unmoving, bloodied sheet pulled up over its face in the universal sign of respect for the dead.

Felicity held herself as motionless as possible, sure that her heart knocking up against her computer case must be audible. It felt like thunder in her ears.

Some of the shouting and confusion in the entrance

had died down and she could make out the sound of deliberate footsteps. Not a patient, they were all waiting for medical attention or receiving it. No patient who was ambulatory would be allowed back here, anyway.

It was Knife Man, Felicity was absolutely certain. The steps were slow and even, though they stopped every once in a while to check the wounded. His steps approached where she lay, terrified, mind a great white glare of panic. However she tried to game out what she'd do if he pulled the sheet off and attacked her again, she couldn't. She was freezing cold, a clear sign of shock and blood loss, and she felt weak. She was a sitting duck.

Lying duck, actually.

Someone gripped the end of her gurney, brushing her foot. By sheer willpower she didn't jump. The hand stayed there, on the footrail, forever. Or at least it felt like forever. Terror gripped her chest and she had to work hard not to wheeze in panic, making her breaths shallow and silent.

Cold sweat broke out all over her body and a liquid rush against her side told her that she was bleeding again. Oh God, if he saw fresh blood he'd know someone was alive under the sheet shroud.

And still he didn't move. She'd have given anything to be able to see him, watch his face. Were his eyes latched on to her sheeted form, waiting for her to show signs of life? Was he still scanning his surroundings, looking for a clue as to her whereabouts? What was he doing?

Finally, the slight pressure on the end of her gurney lifted and the deliberate pace of the footsteps resumed, walking away toward the entrance, the sound of the footsteps soon lost in the confusion.

It was so hard to think straight, to plan. Her ally her

whole life had been her brain. She was used to being able to think faster and more clearly than most. This feebleness, this fog in her head terrified her because if she couldn't think her way out of this, she was lost. There was no way to outgun or outrun the man. She had to out think him.

She tried to time herself by her beating heart. She usually had a standing pulse of sixty beats per minute. A beat a second, a reliable touchstone. Instead of *one Mississipi two Mississippis* she'd always had her heart to go by. But now her heart was pounding wildly, erratically, no longer a touchstone.

Two competing imperatives—wait for the man to leave, but move soon because she was losing blood and energy by the second.

It had to be done. She eased the sheet slowly and carefully to the side. You'd have to be looking straight at her to see the movement. Finally she exposed an eye, tried to look as carefully as she could without moving her head. No one was looking in her direction.

It was now or never.

Slowly, very slowly, she pulled the sheet off, sliding her feet to the floor. Thank God for the painkillers—it felt as if the pain was in another room. The moment the painkillers wore off, she was going to be in big trouble.

She could barely stand, her legs frighteningly weak. She stood unsteadily, holding on to the gurney, cold sweat popping out on her face and back. Slipping her laptop backpack on took nearly all of her strength.

Another couple of ambulances had come in bearing airport passengers with minor injuries, but the passengers were very vocal. They wanted care *now*. For the first time in her life, Felicity was happy to hear loudmouths sounding off. They took up all the oxygen and attention in the room. Great. She carefully made her way around the emergency room, surreptitiously holding on to the walls. Nobody paid her the slightest bit of attention.

She eyed the glass doors. The outside portico was well lit but beyond that, snowy darkness. Her attacker could be anywhere, lying in wait just outside the circle of light. But it was a risk either way. If she stayed here he could come back and she couldn't be sure the same trick would work. Soon the influx of agitated passengers would slow to a trickle and they'd pay more attention to her. She'd be formally admitted. It occurred to her only now that however badly she was wounded, she couldn't find treatment here. She didn't have alternative ID. Her attacker had to know her name and checking for a Felicity Ward admitted to the hospital would be child's play.

Another factor. She wasn't going to stay conscious for very much longer.

And yet another factor. She was going to need to convalesce. She longed with an intensity that shook her to the core to be with someone who was a friend, who didn't wish her harm. To be with someone and let her guard down without fear. The wound made her feel violated in her essence. To heal she would need a safe place and there was only one possible safe place.

She couldn't go to the hotel she'd checked into, since she'd checked in under her own name. She couldn't stay out in the open. She needed sanctuary and a friend. Her only friend here was a virtual friend—a woman she'd never met but whose online vibes fairly radiated friendliness and affection. So Lauren was it, had to be it.

Lauren was in a relationship with a security expert,

a former Navy SEAL. Fantastic, because Felicity was about to bring trouble to Lauren's doorstep.

She had no choice.

But first she had to get to Lauren. She knew where Lauren lived. Of course she did, she'd gotten fake ID for Lauren with that address on the ID. Before leaving, she'd done a quick check of Google maps. Only a mile and a half away. On foot it might as well be on the moon. By car, even driving slowly, maybe twenty minutes. Thirty tops, in the snow.

Could she hold out for twenty to thirty minutes? God only knew. And only one way to find out.

Her father had defected to the West within a five-minute time frame. He'd had five minutes to make it work while his Soviet minder—muscles on muscle with a gun, her father had described him—went to the bathroom. In that time, her father and mother had changed the course of their lives and hers, by being brave enough to take a leap.

Well, she had Darin blood flowing in her veins. And though she wasn't going to leap to another country she could show the courage her papa had shown and get the hell out of Dodge. Fast.

First, wheels.

She'd named herself after Felicity Smoak, Arrow's super bright friend. So. What would Felicity Smoak do? Steal a car, of course. *Borrow* a car. The thing was, she wasn't near the hospital parking lot. She had no idea where it was. Maybe at the back of the building and so that too might as well have been on the moon. And there was the added disadvantage that she had no idea how to break into a car and get it started.

As she slowly made her way to the entrance, carefully

watching all the faces around her, she tried to scout outside. The only vehicles were ambulances, nothing else.

They were coming in all the time, medical personnel bearing people in twos and threes. None of them as wounded as she was, thank God.

Felicity was painfully aware that there were security cameras everywhere and even a person less gifted than she was could access the cameras. Actually, these days even a chimpanzee could access security cameras. Even if she managed to shake off her attacker, he could leisurely go over the security cameras of every place she could have gone to, including this hospital, if he felt he might have overlooked something.

Not much she could do about it now. Right now, sheer survival took precedence over wiping her tracks.

Most cameras covered the middle areas of public spaces so she hugged the walls. No sense making it easy on her attacker. She kept her head low, which wasn't hard considering how weak she felt, shuffling like an old lady, barely able to lift her feet. The bill of the baseball cap would hide most of her face.

The huge entrance sliding doors were flanked by smaller doors, for personnel. She took the left-hand one and emerged into the snow. It was dark enough for the bright lights under the portico to be necessary. Felicity shivered. Her body was too weak to compensate for the sudden drop in temperature. It felt like being at the North Pole.

Calling a taxi was out of the question. She could wipe the records of the taxi service but she couldn't wipe the memory of a driver.

God, where was the Tardis when she needed it?

A thousand hours of playing Grand Theft Auto was

her only hope. A feeble one because she'd never boosted a car in real life and she was a lousy driver in sunshine, let alone in snow. But that was her only hope and a narrow one at that, because the chances of her surviving this were small and growing smaller with each passing minute.

The only vehicles under the portico were ambulances. So it was going to be Grand Theft Ambulance.

Oh God. She had no idea how to drive one. Had never even been in one until an hour ago. Anxiety lapped around her like a rising tide of black water.

Remember Dad, she thought. That five-minute window of opportunity with the KGB watching his every move. He'd gotten away just after being awarded the Nobel Prize for Physics. Accepting congratulations, shaking hands with his right hand, his left holding her mother, he'd slipped into a corridor and into the waiting arms of two CIA agents.

He'd been fast and smart, her father. She was going to have to be fast and smart too.

Leaning against the outside wall, just beyond the glare of lights, she waited. The wail of ambulance sirens was starting to subside. Ten minutes ago there'd been an ambulance arriving every minute. Now there were fewer of them.

Hurry, she told herself, *before they stop coming altogether.*

Two ambulances pulled away, going back to the airport and another pulled into the driveway. The driver rushed out to help unload the patient in back and there it was. Her shot.

Moving fast was impossible so Felicity simply set herself in forward motion, not stopping until she was at the driver's side door. She closed her eyes in relief when she saw keys still in the ignition. Silly of the driver, of course, but who would be crazy enough to steal an ambulance parked right outside the hospital?

She didn't have the energy to check if anyone was watching. If they were and they stopped her, that was that. Right now she focused all her energy on doing this. The engine ignited immediately and the controls were understandable. She just had to hope she could drive it in the snow without tipping over or sliding on ice.

Okay.

She pressed the accelerator and moved forward under the portico, to the off-ramp, switching on the windshield wipers after a desperate search. There was a loud male cry—*Hey!*—but she simply pressed harder on the accelerator. The conditions were awful but the ambulance was very stable.

She could do this. She could, she could. Maybe.

Lauren's address was on her computer's display, a teardrop over her house and Felicity a moving dot. Her hands were slick on the wheel. The movements were making her bleed more. She was going to leave blood in the ambulance. *Don't think about that.*

The police weren't going to run a DNA analysis for what would be considered a joyride in an ambulance, were they? She hoped fervently that the attacker didn't have resources behind him that could order a DNA test.

To her knowledge she didn't have her DNA on file but these days, who knew?

Her fingerprints were definitely on file but she was wearing gloves.

Her father had been paranoid with regard to governments and she grew up with conspiracy theories ringing in her head. Her attacker belonging to some shadowy government agency was an idea she had to actively push out of her head because navigating the streets in bad weather while bleeding was using up her entire hard disk.

In normal miles and normal driving time, Lauren's house wasn't that far. Losing blood by the minute, exhausted and terrified, driving in snow, it felt like scaling Mount Everest backward in heels.

Every time she glanced at the GPS dot that was her, it looked as if it was stationary. But slowly, slowly, one turn after the other, she moved forward, ever closer to the Lauren teardrop. Finally, after what felt like weeks, she carefully pulled over four blocks from Lauren's address, on a side street. Driving right up to Lauren's house would be a huge arrow aimed straight at Lauren's heart. She'd have parked farther away if she had been certain she could walk more than four blocks, but four blocks was pushing it.

Felicity killed the engine but stayed in the warm cab, damp hands clenched on the steering wheel. Outside it was cold and dark and slippery and inside it was warm and dry. But she was still bleeding heavily and if she stayed any longer, she wouldn't have the strength to get out.

Opening the door proved to be almost beyond her and for a moment she wondered how close to death she was if opening the door of a vehicle was so very hard. But it was a stiff wind beating against the door that made it hard to open. She finally put her weight against it, nearly falling out when the door finally swung open. By some stroke of luck, or the help of the goddess of nerds, the wind was at her back, blowing in the direction of Lauren.

Go with the flow took on a new meaning.

Felicity carefully exited the ambulance but fell to her knees immediately, staying there for a full minute, head down. She lifted onto her haunches, like a sprinter—only she wasn't ready to sprint. A hand to the ground, crunching snow beneath the palm of her hand, and she slowly stood up, shakily.

The snow was four inches deep and muted all noise. It was quite beautiful, actually, on this quiet little street, dark and silent, snow only visible in the cones of light thrown by the street lamps. She rested a hand on the side of the ambulance and watched the scenery dreamily, until she suddenly focused and realized she'd been about to faint.

She had to get to Lauren's right now, or she'd fall to the ground and stay there.

It occurred to her with a sudden fierce pang of doubt—what if Lauren wasn't home? What happened if she'd gone shopping or to the movies or—God forbid—gone on a little vacation with her lover, this Jacko guy?

Well then, she was dead. And Lauren would find her frozen body on her doorstep.

No use thinking about that now because Felicity had zero options. None whatsoever. Her only option right now was to put one foot in front of the other, eyes slitted against the snow, and hope that she could walk four blocks and climb a couple of steps. And of course hope that Lauren was home.

Because if she wasn't, Felicity was dead.

It was a nightmare trip. Four blocks was nothing, even for a geek couch potato. And yet it was the hardest thing she'd ever done in her life. There were handholds along the way, otherwise she wouldn't have made it. A fence, lampposts, the fenders of cars parked along the street. She would lurch forward, clutch something, then use the handhold to propel herself forward again.

If she collapsed without having made it to Lauren's there was no way Lauren would know that the body found not far from her house was her, Felicity. Lauren would keep trying to contact her and email her and would be sad when her friend never answered, without realizing her friend had died feet away from her.

Lauren couldn't even check up on her because Felicity had never told her where she lived. She'd die anonymously, unclaimed.

It was that, more than anything else, that propelled her forward, one trembling foot in front of the other. An anonymous death, her entire life lost, the same kind of death her parents had had. They'd died as if the entire first half of their lives hadn't existed and she didn't want that. Her death would be even worse—lying unclaimed in a morgue, no one knowing what had happened to her.

God, no.

Time stopped, became an endless now of trudging forward, swiping snow from her face, holding herself upright by sheer willpower. At one point, to her horror, her heart stopped pounding. Became slow, sluggish. Her heart wouldn't hold out much longer.

But by the time her heartbeat changed, Lauren's house came into focus. Felicity had Googled Street View and knew what it looked like. Small, tidy, pretty. Blue trim around the door and windows. She held it in her mind as a goal and then finally, *finally* there it was.

Safety. Or the closest thing to safety she had right now.

And Lauren was home! Light shone through the windows, a soft welcoming glow. A beacon, that would lead her to safety.

Once the image of getting to Lauren, seeing her, finding refuge penetrated her mind, it gave her an extra spurt of energy, pulling in the very last of her reserves. She stumbled up the porch steps, clinging to the railing with both hands. She was so focused she couldn't see much, just what was in front of her. Steps, a small porch, the door. The focus was getting narrower and narrower and she recognized that as a sign that she was about to pass out.

She shuffled across the porch, unable to lift her feet, and pounded weakly on the door. She pounded again and saw a video intercom and shuffled sideways.

Please, *Lauren*, she thought, her heart now painfully slow. She pounded again and looked toward the monitor. She was wet from the snow but she could also feel cold sweat beading her face. She shook with the effort to stay upright.

The loudspeaker crackled and she focused desperately on the monitor. "Lauren?" she asked. Then—*you dummy. She won't recognize you.* She used the handle Lauren had given herself in their private chat room. "Runner?" Her voice came out a weak wheeze. *Oh God, please answer! Please open this door before I collapse.*

"Felicity!" The door opened and there she was, Lauren. Prettier than in the photos Felicity had used for her ID. A little plumper, happy. Lauren held out her hand and Felicity took it, stumbled over the threshold, fell.

Or, didn't fall.

Something very strong and big was there.

Felicity had been so concentrated on Lauren that she hadn't noticed that she was with two men. One dark, one dirty blond. Both big, but the blond was very tall besides being as big as a house. He was the one who'd stopped her fall, who gently laid her on the floor.

He was looking at her intently, opening her coat, frowning when he saw the blood. He lifted her shirt and looked up at Lauren.

"Knife wound and it's bleeding heavily. We need to get her to a hospital. She's lost a lot of blood." He was probing the wound and though the painkillers still masked some of the pain, she gasped.

Something about what he said—

"No!" She tried to shout but it came out a hoarse croak. Felicity clung to the man's thick wrist. He had big, powerful hands attached to big, powerful arms. He felt so warm and strong and alive. Touching him was like getting a little infusion of energy.

What he wanted was so dangerous. She clung to his wrist, leaving blood streaks on his skin. She looked at him, at Lauren, then back at him. Lauren was looking at him too, so he was the decider. She tried to tighten her fingers around his wrist and wondered whether he could even feel her.

"No hospital!" she gasped, the tiny spurt of energy coming straight from her terror at the idea of going back to the hospital and being found by her attacker. "*Please.* He's after me! He was waiting for me at the airport. He'll find me in a hospital. I just escaped from one and he—" She coughed, felt fresh blood flow from the wound. "He was there," she finished weakly.

Lauren knelt down next to her, and took her hand. Lauren's hand felt warm and vital too. Felicity stared up at her, at this friend she'd never seen before. That she was a friend was unmistakable. She looked so concerned, so distraught. Her eyes were filled with kindness and sorrow. "Honey—" She stopped, took a deep breath. "Honey, we need to get you to a doctor."

Felicity knew that but also knew that medical care would leave a trace her attacker could easily follow. The doctor would save her life, only to have her attacker take it later.

Felicity let go of the man and reached for Lauren's warm hand with both of hers. Her hands were slick with sweat and blood but Lauren didn't seem to notice. She curled her fingers around Felicity's hands. Felicity gave Lauren's hand a little shake, looked up into her friend's pretty face and pleaded with everything in her. "Please," she whispered hoarsely. "Please. He'll kill me if he finds me."

The big man who had been examining her wound with careful hands looked at Lauren. Though his hands were huge they were very gentle. "I can take care of her."

His voice was low and so deep it seemed to reverberate in Felicity's belly. He switched his gaze to Felicity, light brown eyes warm in a fierce face. He was enormous, rough-looking, but for all his size he didn't scare her.

"At least I can stop the bleeding. There's a clinic I know where we can do X-rays, reinfuse her. Completely off the grid."

Off the grid. Oh yes. Felicity nodded weakly. "Please," she whispered, looking up at him. It was all she could say now. *Please, please, please.* She shivered, closed her eyes, drifted for a second, then forced herself to open her eyes. She wasn't safe yet.

"Yes. That place. Take me there." Her voice was so weak that Lauren frowned and moved her head closer. The man didn't seem to have any difficulty hearing her.

She focused on his face, on those light brown eyes, her one lifeline. "Keep me off the grid."

He nodded. "You're safe. Don't worry. You're safe with us. I promise." That deep voice sounded so reassuring.

Right words, wrong music.

"Sounds nice," she gasped. "Not true, but…nice."

Lauren's head snapped back in surprise, but the man's expression didn't change. His deep voice was very gentle as he called to the other man in the room, the dark-skinned one, for his medic kit. That man was bare-chested, with a recent surgical scar. A little nursing station had been set up in the living room. Was the man kneeling next to her a doctor? He didn't look like any doctor she'd ever seen but he opened the bag that had been brought to him and pulled out some gauze.

Felicity looked up into Lauren's pretty, worried face and felt it—that connection she'd felt over the computer. That this woman was her friend and that she could trust her.

She tried to smile, though it came out shakily. "Nice to meet you, finally."

Lauren was clutching her hand, almost visibly trying to infuse strength into her. She nodded, eyes wet.

Oh God, don't cry, Felicity thought. Because she'd start bawling too. She didn't want to die, not after having just found a friend. Not just a virtual friend, either. A real friend, in meatspace.

To stave off the tears she sketched another shaky smile. "You know," she said weakly, "I've always wanted to say this." She held out her hand, Princess Leia in the hologram. "Help me, Obi-Wan Kenobi, you're my only hope."

And she blacked out.

TWO

SEAN "METAL" O'BRIEN took over.

Lauren was shocked and his teammate Jacko put his arms around her. Lauren was Jacko's priority but that was okay. Jacko wasn't a trained medic and he was.

The woman had fallen into *his* arms, like a wounded comrade. She was his.

Her eyes fluttered shut, then she forced herself to open them. She didn't want to let go, was afraid to.

She needed care but she needed reassurance more. He peeled back the coat, pulled up the sweater and examined the wound.

Thank God it wasn't as bad as he'd feared. She'd lost a lot of blood. God only knew when she'd been knifed and the wound hadn't been dressed. But though the wound was about an inch deep and was going to require a lot of stitches, it hadn't nicked any arteries or organs.

He stopped for a second, overwhelmed with rage, willing his hands to stillness. The wound itself wasn't that serious—the main danger was blood loss. With a blood transfusion and antibiotics it was just a question of healing time.

He'd seen far, far worse in battle. Teammates who had been blown up, who'd been gut shot. This was nothing like that.

But they had been warriors, trained for battle, ready and willing to inflict worse on the enemy. Not this.

He looked at the slice, gaping slightly open, sullenly bleeding. It was an abomination on the smooth pale skin of this beautiful young woman. She was lovely, delicately built, scared at what had happened to her.

What had happened was some fucker took a knife to her. Sliced her open. Probably willing to do even more to her if she hadn't managed to get away. He didn't know the story but if she managed to get away from a man with a knife she must be smart and resourceful. What the fuck? In the world as it should be, she shouldn't have to worry about men with knives.

Metal was all about making the world a safer place, a place where beautiful young women didn't have to dodge knife-wielding fuckheads.

"Metal?"

Jacko's low voice jerked him back to reality. He wrestled his emotions back into his combat box. No place and no time for emotion when dealing with wounds.

His kit was well organized and he got what he needed without looking.

Felicity's eyes hadn't left his face. He was her lifeline and he wasn't going to let her down.

"Okay, honey," he said. "I'm going to disinfect the wound and bind it up, then we're going to a place where we can reinfuse you and stitch that slice up. Okay?"

She grasped his wrist with both hands. Her hands were ice-cold. He kept a frown off his face as he held her hand, surreptitiously putting a thumb on her pulse. A thready fifty beats per minute. Blood pressure very low. They had to get going.

"No…hospitals," she gasped. "Can't…leave a trace."

"No hospitals," he agreed, pulling on latex gloves. She'd already made that clear and he'd already factored in that whoever had sliced her was still out there, look-ing. The fucker would never get his hands on her again. "No trace. Now hold still just a second, this might sting."

Her face scrunched when he disinfected the wound, but she didn't make a sound. Good girl.

"So, Felicity," he said calmly, "it is Felicity, isn't it? That's what Lauren called you."

Try to keep the patient engaged, try to ask simple yes or no questions.

She nodded.

"That's a pretty name. Felicity. Sort of means hap-piness, doesn't it?"

She nodded again, huge sky blue eyes unblinking.

"Well here's the deal, Felicity. I'm going to apply some coagulating powder on the wound and then bind it up. I understand you don't want to go to a hospital, you're afraid the guy who attacked you might find you. He will not find you. And even if he does, Jacko—that's the mean-looking guy over there—and I have your back. You're safe with us, I promise. But we need to take you somewhere where you can get a blood transfusion be-cause you've lost blood. Do you know your blood type?"

"A positive," she whispered.

"Good girl," he said. "If we know your blood type we don't need to use plasma, we can use blood directly. And you know what? I happen to be A positive too, so if where we're going is low on your blood type I can donate. I'm really healthy, don't worry about anything."

She was watching him so very carefully. Listening hard with every organ she had, it seemed. Not just her ears but through her skin and eyes. She nodded. "Okay," she whispered. "Gotcha. No worries." Then she rolled her eyes and tried to grin at him.

Oh God. Beautiful and brave. With a sense of humor.

He taped gauze over the wound then wrapped it, the best he could do if she didn't want to go to an official hospital. It would hold until they got to where they were going.

"I'm going to carry you to my vehicle, is that okay?"

She nodded, blue eyes big with fear.

Metal slid his arms under her and rose easily. She weighed nothing, certainly less than the heavy rucksack plus heavy medic bag he carried into battle.

"It's going to be okay," he said. "Promise. You're safe now."

"No such thing as safe." She closed her eyes.

Lauren had her coat on. "Where are you taking her?" she asked.

This was tricky. Jacko knew, but nobody else in the company did. Manuel's clinic was a secret. Manuel wasn't going to appreciate having outsiders brought along. However, Felicity would be reassured by Lauren's presence so Lauren was coming.

Metal made his voice hard. He liked Lauren, but this was serious. "We're going to a place you are going to forget about as soon as we leave. Am I clear?"

Jacko narrowed his eyes at the tone Metal took with Lauren, but tough shit. This was important.

Lauren merely nodded. "Yes, of course. If they can help Felicity without notifying the authorities, which is what she's frightened of, then great. But I want to stay with her."

Metal nodded, walking out the door with Felicity in his arms. She was conscious but kept her eyes closed. Her energy was draining minute by minute.

On the ground were traces of blood. He cut a glance at Jacko, who nodded. He'd clean up the trail later.

"We'll go in separate vehicles," he told Jacko, who immediately steered Lauren to his SUV.

Metal put Felicity in the backseat, lying down.

"Okay," he said softly. She'd opened her eyes again and looked at him. It was dark outside, the only light coming from the streetlight and the lamp over Lauren's porch. Felicity's sky-blue eyes reflected the little light there was, making it look like her eyes glowed in the dark. "I'll drive as fast as I can but without any sudden stops or fast curves. I can't put the seat belt on you, but you should hold on to it. Okay?"

She nodded silently. In the dim light he could barely make out her features, the streetlight illuminating only the pale blade of her nose and outlining high cheekbones. The urge to kiss her on the forehead was so great that he scrambled out fast and climbed into the driver's seat.

The weather was really bad but Metal was a good driver. Rain or shine, he could get just about any vehicle smaller than a tank to where he wanted to go. It was tricky driving as fast as he could while making the ride as comfortable for her as possible, but he managed.

Pity she couldn't go to St. Vincent's, which wasn't far. Instead they were going to *La Clinica*.

It was a clinic for illegal aliens who didn't dare go to the hospital for medical care because they had no documentation. No health insurance, either. It was run by Manuel Gomez, a former marine Metal had bonded with on a cross-training exercise in Somalia. Gomez had had an illustrious career in the military and no one had known that he was illegal. His parents had crossed the border, desperate to flee from the first of the cartel drug wars, when Manuel was eight. He'd enlisted with fake documents but he'd been such an outstanding soldier that even if someone suspected, they'd turned a blind eye. He'd trained as a medic and had gone on to medical school afterward. Manuel was one of the best doctors Metal had ever seen.

He'd set up the clinic that ran with volunteer doctors on the basis of donations, which were generous. Many legal immigrants had relatives who were undocumented but needed care. The clinic saved lives daily.

Metal had phoned ahead and Manuel was waiting for them. Metal carried Felicity in, careful not to jostle her. Jacko and Lauren trailed behind.

The clinic was in a warehouse carefully disguised from the outside to look abandoned. Lucky thing Felicity was unconscious as he carried her in because she might have balked. Lauren and Jacko followed him in, Lauren muttering darkly until Jacko shushed her.

They went through two rooms, dusty and dark, with broken machinery and rusted parts scattered over the bare concrete flooring before they came to big double doors. When Jacko reached past him and opened them, Metal heard Lauren gasp.

It was a small, immaculate clinic, capable of dealing with everything from broken bones to minor surgery. Jacko contributed money to the clinic and Metal contributed money and time.

No one asked for documentation or insurance papers.

When Metal got Felicity on a gurney, Manuel wheeled her into a side room and started infusing her. Metal stayed with her while Jacko and Lauren remained in the small entrance that served as a waiting room. There was a row of chairs and they sat, Jacko's arm around a pale Lauren.

Felicity regained consciousness while being infused. After about twenty minutes, Metal gently took Felicity's hand and pinched the nail of her right index finger, hard. The nail bed turned white then immediately turned pink as blood pressure reinfused the nail. Metal looked at Manuel, who nodded.

He'd injected a local anesthetic and had started stitching her up. Metal stayed by his side. They'd worked together often, but here Metal wasn't assisting. He was holding Felicity's hand. She clutched his, silently asking him not to leave her.

No, he wasn't going to leave her. You wouldn't be able to pull him from her side with bolt cutters and a crane.

Manuel had a delicate hand with stitches, which Metal didn't. It was the reason he was happy to have Manuel do the honors. Metal was used to battlefield stitches and nobody gave a shit what kind of scar they'd leave. Manuel's stitches were small, precise, delicate. They'd leave a scar that in time would fade to a thin white line. It would barely mar that smooth, pale, perfect skin. Metal would have left a big Frankensteinian ladder-back scar.

When Manuel finished stitching her up, Metal checked her out. Her hand in his was warmer, not cold and clammy like before. His thumb at her wrist revealed a faster, stronger pulse. Manuel would measure her blood pressure but Metal could measure BP without instrumentation. He pegged it at 120 over 70 and he was never wrong.

Manuel pumped up the cuff and looked at the dial. "120 over 70," he announced. "Pretty good."

Felicity's face had more color in it, lips no longer with a bluish cast. Her eyes were losing that bruised look.

She was on her way to recovery.

Her eyes had never left his as Manuel stitched her up. He started dressing the wound. "So, Miss—"

"Felicity," Metal answered at the same time Felicity did.

Manuel laughed. A patient who didn't want their last name known was nothing new to him. "So, Felicity, then." He had a pleasant voice, with the faintest of Hispanic accent. "I'm leaving you in Metal's care. He's good, he knows what he's doing. I'm going to give you a course of antibiotics and Metal knows how to change your dressing. You're good to go."

"Thank you," she whispered, rolling her head on the gurney to smile faintly at Manuel.

Manuel laughed. "I don't want to say 'anytime' because I sincerely hope never to see you here again. But in any case—you're welcome. And now if you'll excuse me, I have a gunshot wound to see to. Bad guys are busy tonight."

With a cheery wave, he disappeared.

No mention of money had been made but Metal made a note to up his monthly contribution and to donate a few extra hours.

An hour after carrying Felicity in, Metal wheeled her back out again. Lauren jumped up and ran to Felicity's side. Lauren blinked and smiled. "Oh my gosh, you look so much better!" Lauren shuddered. "I've been—we've been so worried!"

"Nah." Jacko placed a heavy arm around around Lauren's shoulders and smiled down at Felicity. "I wasn't."

It was so fucking *weird* to see Jacko smiling. Metal

had been Jacko's teammate for eight years and they'd both worked together at Alpha Security International for the past couple of years and he'd seen Jacko smile more in the past weeks than in the past decade. Smiles looked strange on his face. "I wasn't worried. I knew you were in good hands."

Lauren gave him a sharp look but then smiled back down at Felicity. "So, let's get you back home and—"

"No." Metal and Jacko spoke at the same time. Lauren looked at them, confused.

"Whoever this guy is who is after her, we can't know if he is aware that she was coming to you." Metal gave the logical explanation because he couldn't give the illogical one. Which was that he wasn't letting Felicity out of his sight.

Lauren blinked. "*I* didn't know she was coming to me. How could anyone else possibly know?"

Felicity opened her mouth to talk, but coughed instead. It pulled her stitches and she grimaced.

"Look," Metal said reasonably, though he was perfectly prepared to be unreasonable. Felicity was going home with him. No question. "She's slightly sedated and in no condition to give us a rundown on what people could know about her movements. If she came here for you, there is probably some trace of that somewhere. It's not likely, but you have Jacko to protect you and he will, but he can't protect two people. So we're splitting it up. Not to mention the fact that my house is more secure than yours. Speaking of which, I'd recommend you spend the next few days at Jacko's. At least until we find this asshole."

"Yeah," Jacko growled.

Lauren bit her lip. Everything Metal said was true.

Jacko hadn't had time to make Lauren's house secure, certainly not as secure as his own and Jacko's. The two of them had security built into their DNA and Lauren sure as hell didn't. She was an artist and a good one. But clueless in terms of securing her safety.

He and Jacko weren't clueless. In fact, they were fucking good. Good luck to anyone trying to attack them in their homes. So yeah, Lauren was going to stay with Jacko for a while.

And Felicity was going to stay with him.

Because his home was secure and he was one farther step away from Lauren.

Because he was a trained medic and could take care of her medically.

Because…because.

Metal bent over Felicity so all she'd see was his face. "Felicity?" She licked her lips and nodded. Her beautiful eyes shifted left to right as she watched his eyes. She opened her mouth and closed it. Talking took too much energy. That was okay. She didn't have to talk. She just needed to be informed. "I'm taking you home with me. If the guy after you somehow knew where you were headed, he won't find anyone at Lauren's. But we'll have cameras running so if he stops by we'll catch him on film. Lauren will be staying with Jacko and you'll be staying with me. My home is secure and I can look after you. You'll be just fine. I'll be there if infection sets in or you need anything. Nod if you understand me."

She nodded, eyes huge.

"Nod again if this is okay with you."

She hesitated a second and his heart sank. Because the hard truth was she was coming home with him whether she liked it or not. Someone was after her and was not going to get a second crack at it. After a second or two she nodded her head.

"Good girl. I'm going to carry you to my vehicle. Is that okay?"

That earned him a small smile and a nod and something in his chest gave a hard thump.

She was staying with him.

Yeah.

THREE

Manhattan

BORODIN SIPPED HIS after-dinner Armagnac and thought of lost worlds and worlds to come.

A generation ago, he and a group of other young KGB officers had seen the handwriting on the wall, though none of them in that long-ago summer and fall of 1989 could ever have imagined how great the loss would actually be. No one imagined that the Soviet Union could actually fall.

At the time, all their hopes had been pinned on the great closed city of Chelyabinsk, one of an archipelago of *naukograd*, science cities. The rest of the Soviet Union was going to hell, the situation even worse than the idiots of the Politburo realized, but in the *naukograd*, things held. Orderly and wealthy and elite, great things were coming if only the country could hold out.

The greatest invention, what was going to change the world forever, was being slowly pieced together by a genius-level nuclear physicist named Nikolai Darin in Chelyabinsk, a *naukograd* specializing in nuclear weaponry. Darin was working on man-portable nuclear weapons, called Deti, Little Ones, and they were going to change Russian history. World history.

Borodin had seen the specs of the nuclear weapons. They could fit into a backpack. He had no idea how

Darin could do it, but the end result would be nuclear bombs that were shielded and could be carried in on foot and manually set with a timer. The backpacks were light enough to be easily carried and would pass unnoticed.

As a KGB officer, Borodin had trained with backpacks heavier than the bombs.

The KGB plan had been to deploy six man-portable nuclear weapons in America, one for each of the great cities: New York, Boston, Chicago, Los Angeles, Houston, Miami. All the great military deterrents America could deploy would be useless. They were bombs that had no trajectory, could not be destroyed in midair. The bombs would suddenly, without any warning and with no known source, explode. The President of the United States couldn't counter attack because no one would claim the bombs.

Six cities destroyed, radioactive deserts until the end of time. America plunged into another Great Depression or worse. The Soviet Union finally ready to soar after having lost Afghanistan.

When pressed, Darin could give no deadline for completion of the bombs.

The KGB was putting enormous pressure on Darin's team. The Deti were necessary.

The Soviet Union pulled back from Afghanistan in February, 1989. The Berlin Wall fell in November. In December, Darin was awarded the Nobel Prize for Physics. The evening of the ceremony, he and his wife were killed in a car accident.

Hearing the news, Borodin and three other KGB officers rushed to Chelyabinsk only to find…nothing. The Deti were not there. Darin's colleagues swore that the Deti were years from reality.

Two years after that, the Soviet Union was no more, and the country plunged into chaos. Tanks, weapons, RPGs—gone. Entire missile silos were lost. No one ever mentioned man-portable nukes ever again.

Borodin and his coconspirators, now that there was no Soviet Union to save, scattered to the winds. Like everyone else, Borodin plundered the state that was falling apart before his very eyes, grabbing rights to natural gas fields in Siberia.

He made his peace with being on the losing side of history by becoming a very rich man.

Yet history has a way of bouncing back into the present. Borodin's world turned upside down.

The American government had been peppered with spies and moles put there by the KGB for decades. An entire machine had been built for this—children in remote locations trained from a young age to be infiltrated into America. They attended special English-only schools and grew up watching videotaped American TV programs specially airlifted into the Soviet Union. Access to the finest dentists was provided because the one thing the *Amerikanski* did well was dentistry. The program had been a wild success and spies had been seeded everywhere, a battalion of them. The program was code named Operation Yankee.

But then the Soviet Union fell. Nobody could have predicted that the country they had sworn allegiance to, the country that had given them a lifetime journey to fulfill, would disappear, almost overnight.

The KGB office running the moles melted away. The KGB itself disappeared and reappeared as the FSB with an entirely different staff.

The moles aged, rose up through the ranks, and most

of them had forgotten the motherland. After all they'd been trained to be Americans from the age of ten onward.

Borodin had forgotten all about the program, busy building Intergaz into one of the largest corporations in the world.

And then a report crossed his desk.

A Russian double agent recruited in 1987 into the FBI under the auspices of Operation Yankee. Career FBI, now retired with a very nice pension. In the early years he'd faithfully filed reports but in the end, with no one to read them or even accept them, he'd simply gone native. Had a great career in three major metropolitan areas, won several commendations and had forgotten a lot of his Russian. Yuri Grigori had permanently become Roy Gregory.

During the run-up to his retirement Gregory came across some reports from the Domestic Terrorism desk, Russian subsection, which after 9/11 had become a dusty backwater. Gregory had spent his last years at the FBI overseeing the transferral of paper documents to hard disk.

He'd found what he considered something of minor interest and, as a last volley of his truncated career as a Russian mole, had sent it on to his masters at the FSB.

Knowing that Borodin had always been interested in the object of the report, someone faithful to him in the FSB forwarded it to him.

This changed absolutely everything. Everything he thought he knew had been wrong.

Nikolai Darin was *alive*.

Or rather, he was dead but he'd died in 2009 not 1989.

He hadn't died after receiving the Nobel Prize for Physics, he'd *defected*.

A sharp encrypted email to Roy Gregory to gather more intel had spooked the man and only the promise of a substantial payment ensured his cooperation.

The FBI files were classified, of course. But a lot of time had gone by and Russia wasn't a priority. They were hard to get but not impossible. Certainly not for someone who had a hundred thousand incentives like Gregory did.

Nikolai Darin and his pregnant wife, Irina, defected to the CIA in Sweden right after the Nobel Prize ceremony on December 10, 1989. The CIA faked their death, debriefed them and then passed them on to the FBI, who debriefed them again and then they were finally settled by the U.S. Marshals Service in their new identity.

The files made interesting reading. Borodin could almost feel the frustration the Americans felt with Darin. Because it was clear he was supposed to deliver…something. Something he never did deliver.

Borodin knew exactly what that something was.

Six somethings. Six tiny but powerful nuclear bombs that could destroy a country with no payback.

Darin hid the six bombs and the codes. The Deti were somewhere in America, Borodin was sure of it. Darin and his wife were dead, but there was a daughter.

It took another fucking hundred thousand dollars to get Gregory to dig farther into the files but he finally came up with the current identity of the daughter, who'd changed her name. Her birth certificate said Katrin Valk but she'd changed her name when she turned eighteen. She was now Felicity Ward.

Felicity Ward, mid-twenties and a graduate of MIT, lived in Burlingham, Vermont.

There was a photo taken of her upon graduating the technical university and Borodin, who had eyes to see, could see Mother Russia in every line of her very pretty face. She looked like her mother, who had been a famous beauty.

It was as if the world had been slumbering, just waiting for Borodin to push the levers of the world and move it in a new direction. Suddenly, the pace of events picked up.

Via a roundabout route, Borodin contacted a *vor*, head of one of the great Mafiya clans, who in turn had strategic alliances with the Chechens, who in turn had connections to their terrorist brethren. Borodin was delighted not to have contact himself because he could never hide his distaste for the kind of men who'd delivered the first nearly fatal blow to the Soviet Union. But via the *vor* he was able to send a clear message.

What was the going price for a "small" nuclear weapon, that did not require a missile launch?

Ten million dollars was the price. Each.

Borodin was very rich but sixty million dollars was sixty million dollars. And someone else was willing to set them off. The goatherds hadn't even asked if it would be possible to detonate them remotely which had been a big problem in Borodin's day. How to deliver without sacrificing the deliverer.

Luckily, the Islamists didn't have that problem. They had plenty of *kretin* lining up to sacrifice themselves for the cause, stepping instantly into paradise after blowing themselves up.

Perfect. Absolutely perfect. A whole worldwide movement willing to bring America down. They'd happily take the blame should a devastated America still have some resources left for retaliation. Russia would watch America implode, take revenge on the wrong people with what resources they had left and happily scoop up Europe and bring its traitorous breakaway provinces back into the fold. Russia would become the indispensable country.

And Borodin himself would be sixty million dollars richer.

Doing well by doing good.

Of course, he needed the girl. Darinova.

He checked his Patek Philippe and frowned. Anatoli should have reported in by now. He'd sent one of his ambitious young managers to intercept the girl. Anatoli Lagoshin. He'd volunteered, hoping it would further his career.

So where was he?

In that very instant Borodin's cell phone rang and he smiled. Yes. Yes, perfect. He was moving with the very tides of history. He could feel it in his bones.

He was still smiling as he checked the caller and accepted the call. He wasn't smiling ten seconds later.

"I've lost her," Anatoli said.

"PIZDETS!" FUCK!

Anatoli Lagoshin winced as he heard his boss swear in a low vicious tone. Borodin usually had himself on a tight rein. His cold-bloodedness was famous inside Intergaz. In the five years Anatoli had worked for Borodin as part of Borodin's personal staff, he'd never even heard the oligarch raise his voice.

It was moments like this that Anatoli remembered that Vladimir Borodin had not always been an oligarch. He'd once been a colonel in the KGB.

And he, Anatoli Lagoshin, had failed *that* man. The man who had sent thousands of men and women to their deaths or to the gulag, which was the same thing. The man who had fought in Afghanistan and become famous for his ferocity, earning the nickname of the Butcher of Kabul.

Borodin's voice was glacial. "How did that happen? You knew the plane she was on, you had a photograph. How the fuck could you lose her?"

"She got away and pulled a bomb alert at the airport." Anatoli tried to keep the sullenness out of his voice. Damn it, this is not what he had studied so long and so hard to do. He wasn't a thug. He was a modern business-man with two majors in business administration and accounting, who spoke excellent English, pretty good French and German, and passable Chinese. He wanted with all his heart to be a leader in the *new* Russia, built on business not bones.

"*How* did she pull a bomb alert?" Borodin sounded enraged but also bewildered. In many ways, though a canny businessman, Borodin was a dinosaur. Anatoli was sure he was imagining this Felicity Ward going up to a wall, breaking a glass pane and pulling down a handle.

The man was a dinosaur but a big dangerous one, with claws and teeth. Dinosaurs had ruled the earth for millions of years and it took an asteroid to kill them off.

"She hacked into the airport security system and ini-tiated a bomb alert. Not before I wounded her, though. She got away but she was bleeding."

Silence. Anatoli knew Borodin was scrolling through reactions.

Anatoli had been given strict instructions to capture the woman but also not to harm her in any way. Con-tradictory instructions, of course. And he'd managed to hurt her and let her get away.

Borodin let the hacking issue go. Anatoli knew he didn't really understand that. But he understood the other part of his comment just fine. "Wounded her?" he asked.

"I used a knife, easier to hide." The instant they discovered that the woman they were after had booked a flight to Portland, Oregon, Borodin had directed his pilot to fly directly across the continental United States. Anatoli had landed two hours before Ward's flight, since she'd had two connecting flights.

He'd waited in Borodin's luxurious A318 Elite jet until they checked the flight status of her flight and saw that it had landed. The pilot, who looked like he ate steel for breakfast and shat nails, and who was undoubtedly ex-military, had showed him a secret compartment with enough firepower to start a small war. Anatoli knew how to shoot but wasn't comfortable with firearms. The pilot looked on with contempt as Anatoli chose a ceramic knife, capable of passing a metal detector. Going into an airport, that seemed like a good idea.

The plan had been for Anatoli to grab Ward when she exited and make their way to the private sector of the airport. The airplane was in an isolated position with very few people around. The pilot would fuel up in the meantime and the moment Anatoli got back with Ward in tow, they'd take off.

That had gone to hell. Now, the pilot would wait in the plane in a private hangar for as long as it took for Anatoli to find the woman.

"She was wounded, you moron," Borodin said coldly. "She would seek medical attention."

Anatoli ground his teeth. "Yes. I rented a car with my alternate ID and made the rounds of the hospitals. There are four hospitals in the greater metropolitan area and I did not find her anywhere. Nothing in her record showed that she'd ever even been to Portland, but if she has a private doctor friend, then there is no way I can track her down."

"Is her cell phone still off?"

That he could answer. "Yes."

"What are you doing now, besides sitting around with your thumb up your ass?"

To speak like this, Borodin was beyond furious. Anatoli had no idea why this woman was so important but apparently she was. And if he was to keep his job—and he was beginning to suspect more than his job might be at stake—he was going to have to find this woman soon.

Damn Borodin for putting him in this position! He tried to inject some authority into his voice.

"In the meantime, I need more information. I was sent in blind." Not to mention the fact that no one told him the woman had lightning reflexes. "The more information I have the easier I can track her down. You're the one with the resources, so contact me when you have something I can use."

He closed the connection with a sweaty finger and pulled in his first deep breath in minutes.

The pilot clapped slowly a couple of times. "Found your balls, eh? That's always dangerous if you don't know what you're doing. So either you find this woman and get a promotion or if you don't—" His face was a cruel mask, one corner of his mouth turned up in a cynical smile. "If you don't, well Borodin, as you know, is ex-KGB. They showed their displeasure with a bullet to the back of the neck. And they'd dock the bullet from your last paycheck. Those old guys didn't fuck around."

FOUR

EARLY THE NEXT morning Metal watched as Felicity came up slowly, like scaling a high mountain.

Her hand fluttered in his. Once, twice.

He'd been sitting all night by her bedside, holding her hand. If he lived to be a hundred he would never forget the look on her face as she stumbled into Lauren's house. Lost, in pain, desperate. He didn't want her waking up alone, in a strange house.

The instant that beautiful women fell into his arms, he felt a ferocious protectiveness rise up in him. She was Lauren's friend, which automatically made her okay in his book. But she was also fragile, delicate, scared witless.

Hurt.

Someone had tried to kill her and it burned in him. Someone had taken a knife and had sliced her open.

Metal knew knifework up close. He'd killed with a knife and he knew exactly how to do it. He'd seen teammates cut up and had closed more knife wounds than he could count.

But that was war. Men equipped to fight, trained to fight, meeting on the battlefield. Something as old as time.

But slashing open a beautiful and defenseless woman—that made his blood boil. It violated everything he knew about life. Smart women like Felicity were supposed to be protected. That was why humankind had protectors, like him and his father and his brothers. His dad and four O'Briens were gone, lost in the ashes and dust of the Twin Towers, but by God another O'Brien was left, and he was going to stand guard over this woman.

He'd find out who had hurt her and then he'd take the fight to the enemy.

Whoever was after her wasn't giving up. Felicity had regained consciousness a few times in the night and she'd managed to gasp out some info. Metal could fill in the rest.

Her attacker was waiting for her at the airport. He'd put a knife to her back and wanted to walk her out. That could mean someone from Portland but it could also mean another passenger. There were ways to get knives through security, and a ceramic knife wouldn't even show up. Some ceramic knives were sharper than steel. He and Jacko would look at airport security footage and check passenger lists. Felicity had said she'd gotten a good look at him so if they had footage they'd have him.

The attacker had fucked with the wrong girl. Metal smiled grimly as he held her hand and watched her face. Lauren had said how smart Felicity was and he had to admit, getting away from a knife-wielding attacker must have taken real smarts.

She'd used her brains because God knows she couldn't outfight the man. He'd seen her. She didn't have fighting muscles. She was soft and slender.

That was okay, he had fighting muscles and he'd stand for her.

Her hand stirred in his again.

Metal leaned closer to the bed. He calculated it would

take her another five to ten minutes to wake up fully. Gomez had administered enough ccs of tranquilizer to ensure that she rested without being knocked out. Everything medical that could be done had been done. Now, her body needed rest and nourishment and warmth to do its part. She was warm, he saw to that. He'd put two eiderdown comforters on the bed. As soon as she woke up, he'd feed her. And she'd rest. He'd see to that too.

Her eyes opened and closed.

God. She had the most amazing color eyes he'd ever seen. A deep magnetic blue. He'd once heard Midnight's wife, an interior decorator, refer to that color as robin's egg. All he knew was that he'd never seen eyes that color before.

Actually, he'd never seen a woman that beautiful before.

His company, Alpha Security International, was awash in beautiful women. His two bosses were married to beautiful women. Their friend Bud Morrison of the Portland PD was married to a beautiful woman. Jacko had fallen for a beautiful woman, though he hadn't screwed up the courage to ask Lauren to marry him. Yet.

None of these women were anything like Felicity, who looked like a cross between an angel and a top model, only shorter. The ASI women used elegant clothes and makeup to enhance their beauty. Felicity didn't need that. With no makeup and in a T-shirt of his that hung down to her knees, she was stunning.

Her eyes popped open again, stayed open. Focused on his face.

"Hey." Metal scooted his chair closer to his bed, clasped her hand more tightly.

She frowned, looked around his room, though there

wasn't much to see. Big bed because he was tall, a dresser, bedside table, a chair. Luckily, he was sailor-neat. Her eyes traveled back to him.

Metal smiled at her. "Hey," he said again. "You're awake."

She licked her lips. Her mouth would be dry with the drugs. He had a Thermos of hot tea with honey waiting. But first she had to relax. She probably didn't remember much about last night.

"Where...what..." She could barely form the words.

Well, Metal was good at this. He was good at giving reports, marshaling facts, giving a clear picture. He knew how to put on a warrior's face as he did so.

But he was also good with his nieces and nephews who didn't know him as a Navy SEAL but as the uncle who always brought gifts and played with them. So he made his face bland and nonthreatening.

"You were wounded, Felicity. Do you remember?" She gasped in a breath, nodded, eyes huge. "Someone attacked you at the airport, but you were smart enough to get away. Do you remember that? And then you made it to Lauren's house. Do you remember that too?"

Her mouth opened and she blew out a breath. Nodded.

"Before we go any further, I'll bet you're thirsty, right?"

She nodded, surprised. As if she hadn't realized she was thirsty until the exact moment he mentioned it.

He let go of her hand and reached for the Thermos. He poured almost a full cup into the top, lifted her head with one hand and with the other held the cup to her mouth. He'd made sure it wasn't boiling hot when he put it in the Thermos. It was just hot enough to make her feel better without burning her mouth.

"Drink," he said quietly. "You're going to be hungry soon and I have food for you. But first you need to drink."

It was his command voice in gentle mode. His nieces and nephews responded to it like magic.

Felicity too. He lifted her up and held her rock steady while she sipped. She cupped her hand under his, as if he would spill the tea if she didn't. He let her because her soft touch was amazingly pleasureable but it wasn't necessary. He wasn't going to spill the tea. He was a very good shot and he had steady hands. But beyond that, he wasn't about to allow hot liquid to spill on her. Nothing bad was going to happen to her while she was in his care.

"Sorry about the plastic cup. I think my mugs might be heavy for you to hold. Lauren has these fancy porcelain cups that are light as air that I'm sure you'd like better, but for now this will have to do."

"Lauren," she whispered, licking her lips again. "Where—"

Metal watched, fascinated as she licked her lips. She had the prettiest mouth he'd ever seen. Then he shook himself. *Stop being an asshole.*

Usually it wasn't hard for him to focus. He focused really well. And as a trained medic he'd learned to disassociate the care he was giving from the person. Medics didn't take the Hippocratic oath but they took their skills seriously. He sure did.

So, yeah, mooning about a patient's pretty mouth and beautiful eyes wasn't something he was proud of. But *damn* she was gorgeous.

Focus!

She shifted in the bed. He was holding her up with one hand against her narrow back. He could feel her heart beat fast and light against the palm of his hand. She was scared.

Metal had a deep voice and he'd shouted a lot in the teams. His voice was rough. He didn't know how to modulate it, soften it. He could only speak as quietly as he could.

"Would you like to stay sitting up? Or are your stitches pulling?" God, he hated to think of her in pain, but she probably was. The painkillers would have worn off hours ago. He had meds with him.

"Sit up," she said. "Against pillows."

Okay. He understood that. Lying down or sitting up leaning against his hand would make her feel vulnerable.

She was watching him out of those huge sky-blue eyes, wary. Not frightened. He knew how to make people scared but he was making an effort to be reassuring. So she wasn't scared of him, but she was with a stranger in a strange place and she'd been attacked and wounded. She'd be stupid not to be wary and this was not a stupid woman.

Moving slowly, Metal put pillows against his headboard and very carefully and very gently lifted her until she was sitting up against the pillows.

It was hard to let her go. As he'd lifted her, she'd clutched at his arms with elegant hands. He felt every inch of her that was touching him and even where he wasn't touching her, he felt her body heat. She was light, delicate. Every single inch of her was beautiful. He had to consciously open his hands and step back because he was powerfully drawn to her. Wanted to lay her down and follow her, lie on top of her, feel all of her against him. Hold her head still and kiss that luscious mouth.

He stopped his thoughts right there, appalled at himself, deeply ashamed.

He was a medic. He knew what stitched wounds felt like. They fucking hurt. Knew she'd be feeling weak, turned inward on herself, the very opposite of sex. What the fuck was the matter with him?

He cleared his throat. "Do you want something to eat?"

She shook her head, eyes glued to his face.

"You should try to eat something," he said gently. "You need to get your strength back. You lost almost a liter and a half of blood. We reinfused you, but still. Your body's been through trauma." Metal smiled. "I'm not a bad cook. I could make you some nice scrambled eggs."

Her long pale throat bobbed up and down in a convulsive swallow. Okay. Not scrambled eggs.

"Or toast. I have some excellent whole wheat bread I made myself. I could toast a slice. Do you think you could keep that down?"

Eyes enormous, she nodded.

"Okay, good." He shook two pills out in his hand and picked up the glass of water he'd put on the bedside table. "Take these."

She was still, no expression on her face.

He didn't sigh. Kept his face bland. "They're painkillers. You have twenty stitches and you have bruises on your back and arms. You must be in pain. These are ibuprofen. You won't be groggy and you won't be out of it—it will just ease the pain. Trust me, please."

"You're a friend of Lauren's," she said, and he understood what she was saying.

He dipped his head. "I am. And a friend and colleague of her friend Jacko. And we are all on your side. Absolutely."

She looked around at the unfamiliar surroundings then back at him. "Where am I?"

"224 Jackson. My place. You are completely safe. If someone somehow knows there's a connection between you and Lauren, they sure won't know about me. And my place is secure. Jacko and I work in security and we have military backgrounds so we know what we're doing."

She was watching him carefully. "Lauren said that Jacko is a former SEAL. Are you?"

He nodded. She seemed to relax just a little. Damn straight. You're in trouble? Then you want a SEAL at your back. No better friend, no worse enemy.

"But you seem to know a lot about medicine."

He dipped his head again. "I was a medic."

She frowned, blond eyebrows pulling together. "Medic. Okay."

God knows what she was thinking. He wasn't a doctor. But a battlefield medic deals with more emergency trauma than any hospital ER doctor. He'd pit his trauma skills against any doctor. He couldn't treat diabetes or high blood pressure but you got shot? He was your guy.

"Medic. The Navy trained me to deal with emergency wounds and that's what you had. I didn't stitch you up, though. I didn't want to leave an ugly scar."

Not on that pale, perfect skin.

"Who—who stitched me up?" She touched her side under the clean T-shirt he'd put on her. It fit like a huge nightgown. "I remember we went to this…place. With a nice doctor. You called him…Manuel?"

Sharp lady. He didn't think she'd absorbed much. She'd been wounded and in pain. But she had.

The clinic was a secret that wasn't his to share. "Someone else who knew what he was doing. But we made sure no one else could know that you were there. Look, I'm going to go get you something to eat and drink because that's part of the healing process. And afterward I'll answer all your questions, okay?"

She nodded.

He took one last look at her, sitting up in his bed, dressed in his T-shirt. Looking lost and vulnerable and so incredibly beautiful he had to turn on his heel and go to the kitchen fast before he did or said something he'd regret.

Metal was fast in most things. He was so big people naturally assumed he was slow but he wasn't. In just a few minutes, he had a freshly brewed cup of tea and two toasted slices of his five-grain bread on a tray together with some butter and honey.

She hadn't moved. She watched him carefully as he put the tray on her lap. As he bent over her he could smell Betadine and faintly, under that, lavender. Looking down, he saw high cheekbones and long light brown eyelashes tipped with gold and a straight, perfect nose. He saw the most delicate skin he'd ever seen, ivory and smooth as satin. Two delicate collarbones rose above the collar of his T-shirt, which gaped open enough to see the swell of two small, rounded breasts.

A pulse of blood shot through his groin and he stood up, fast, ashamed.

Metal had had problems with women all his life. He knew what he looked like. For some reason, Mother Nature had given him the looks of a thug. Any normal woman in an urban environment crossed the street to avoid him.

It was a source of sorrow to him because he liked women, a lot. He liked the sound of their voices and the way they smelled and the way they thought. But not too many women were willing to break through the barrier of his rough looks to find out what he was really like.

Suzanne and Allegra, his boss's wives, they'd made the effort. And Claire Morrison, Bud's wife. They treated him normally, smiling and teasing him. He loved it. A lot of women were instinctively scared of him and he hated that.

To compensate he made sure his body language was unthreatening around the ladies. SEAL training had taught him how to intimidate, how to threaten without words. He was good at that. But he also worked at looking harmless, though it was hard when he was taller and bigger than most people.

One thing he never did was be overtly sexual with women unless they were in a bedroom and it had been established that they were going to get it on. Certainly not with a woman he didn't know.

Having his dick stir in his pants was the last thing he needed and was guaranteed to make Felicity scared. She was alone in the house with him, she was wounded, she was vulnerable and he'd rather slice his own throat than be considered a menace.

So he shut his dick down, fast. Shutting it down was harder than it should have been, because he controlled his dick, it didn't control him but, *man*, the lady was so frigging beautiful, everywhere.

He snagged a chair and sat by the bed watching her eat, trying not to notice how sexy those lips looked when she put a piece of toast into her mouth, how delicate those long slender fingers looked holding the cup of tea. How his T-shirt hung off her neck, exposing pale smooth shoulders.

She was here, under his protection, and she was scared. He had no intention of making her even more frightened.

So he did the very best thing he could. He sat completely still and didn't talk.

Stillness was a gift and he had it. Stillness was a subconscious signal to her. Violent or untrustworthy men couldn't stay still.

Finally she finished the tea and the two slices of bread. She had more color back in her face, which pleased him.

They stared at each other. She swallowed heavily again. Not nausea, fear. Fear of betrayal. But she was going to have to trust him, no way around it. She trusted Lauren who trusted Jacko who trusted him.

A chain of trust. That was the way it worked. Otherwise you couldn't navigate the world.

She opened her mouth, closed it. Sighed. "Did I lose my laptop?"

Well, that surprised him. Of all the things to ask about when you were wounded by a stranger and woke up in the home of another stranger, a computer wouldn't be the first thing that sprang to mind.

He nodded. "It's safe and it's here." He didn't smile. "We had to pry your fingers from the strap. You want it?"

"Yes, please." Her voice was polite, but shook.

Metal had it back to her in a second. He placed the case gently in her lap. She didn't open it immediately, just rested her hand on the tough canvas case. "There was a key in my pocket. Did you find it?"

"Yeah, Jacko's got the key. It's the key to a vehicle. Where's it parked?"

Earlier, after midnight, when Metal had taken Felicity back to his place, Jacko had driven around Lauren's house, pressing the fob but didn't find the vehicle.

"I parked—I parked as far away as I could, in case *he* found it and somehow traced it to Lauren. I left it on Waller."

Christ, that was a brisk ten-minute walk in the sunshine. She'd done it wounded, in a snowstorm. She really did want to protect Lauren. She could easily have not made it, would have fallen and died in the snow, to protect Lauren.

Metal had real respect for courage. This was right up there with anything any SEAL had ever done for his teammates.

She looked down at her hands then back up to him. "It's the key to an ambulance. I stole it."

Fuck. One shock after another.

"You…stole it?"

She nodded. "From the hospital. When they took me there, I thought I was safe. When he slashed me at the airport, I got away, hid in the bathroom, hacked into the airport security system and pulled a bomb alert."

Metal's jaw dropped. "I heard about that. About a false bomb alert at the airport. That was *you?*"

"Yeah." She found his hand, curled her fingers around his. "I didn't know what else to do. I was terrified. I managed to get away from him after he cut me. I, um, I stole a baby blanket to staunch the bleeding but I was losing blood and I felt faint and I knew he would eventually find me. I looked around for guards or a cop but couldn't find one. So I made it to the bathroom, went into a stall, hacked into the airport's system and called in a bomb alert."

"Fuck," Metal breathed. Damned if that wasn't the smartest thing he'd ever heard of. Then he realized what he'd said. "Sorry."

Jesus. That was quick thinking. And really fast hacking. It would have taken him a full day to get into the security system of a major airport. If he even could. He was okay with computers but not more than that. "That was…amazing. What did you do then?"

"I, um, hacked into the emergency service of the airport and told the ambulances to come to the arrivals area. The guy was at the center exit, looking for me as the passengers were panicking and trying to push their way through. The first ambulance that came, I showed him the wound and they loaded me onto a gurney and went to Portland Memorial. I had to abandon my carry-on. God knows where it is now, but I keep my essentials in my computer backpack. ID, money, credit cards, cell. I was in shock at the hospital. I didn't know whether to call Lauren or not. I pulled my backpack up to get to my cell when—when I saw him."

Metal nodded. "You insisted that we shouldn't take you to a hospital. Now I see why. You thought he might be there. So, Sherlock, or maybe Houdini. How did you escape the second time?"

She flushed slightly, a small smile on her lips. The flush was like watching a flower bloom, like watching dawn in the mountains. He wasn't a fanciful man at all but those were the only things he could compare it to.

"I thought I was safe at the hospital. But he arrived and I—" She hesitated, shuddered. "I pulled the sheet over my head and pretended to be dead. After he left, I stole an ambulance."

This time his jaw didn't drop because he got it that she was supersmart and resourceful, but still, he was surprised. "You pretended you were dead and then took an ambulance?"

"It was close by the exit and the guy left the key in." She looked at him out of sky-blue eyes. "I'm really sorry," she whispered. "But I didn't have a choice."

Metal picked up her hand and leaned forward. This beat anything they'd been taught in SERE school. Survival, Evasion, Resistance and Escape. She'd done it all, superbly well, with no training.

"And you left it on Waller?"

"Yes. I would have left it farther away but I didn't think I'd make it."

"No," Metal said soberly. "You wouldn't have. You'd have fallen in the snow and died of hypothermia."

"That's, um, that's what I thought."

"You did what you had to do to survive. Nothing wrong with that. Nothing at all." He pulled out his cell, dialed Jacko without taking his eyes off her. "Yo. Felicity escaped her attacker from the hospital. She… requisitioned an ambulance. They're probably looking for it. Park it near the hospital. And wipe it down. It's on Waller. Yeah, I know exactly how far that is from Lauren's. She parked far away to keep trouble from her friend. And she walked four blocks in the snow, wounded. I swear she was a SEAL in a former life."

A blush appeared over her cheeks and her lips turned up. Damn, she was beautiful when she smiled. Hell, even when she didn't smile.

"Uh-huh." He held the phone out to her. "Lauren's hopping up and down. Want to talk to her?"

"Oh yes, please!" She held out her hand and he placed the cell in it.

He could hear an agitated female voice but he couldn't make out what Lauren was saying, though he could imagine it.

"Yes," Felicity said. "No. Just a little weak." She met his eyes. "Um, yeah, Metal has taken very good care of me. Yes, a little. Oh God, yes. Can't wait!"

She handed him back the cell. "Lauren and Jacko are coming over. Is that okay?"

"Sure. But he'll take care of the ambulance first."

Felicity smiled briefly back, then chewed her lip. "Am I going to be in trouble for stealing it? And—God! For sounding that bomb alert? I'm sure that's a federal offense."

"Don't even think of that." He'd make goddamned sure of it. She'd been fighting for her life. He had friends in Portland PD. No one was going to touch her, guaranteed. "Not a problem. The problem now is to figure out who's after you. We can start when you feel better."

"No," she said, beautiful face suddenly stony. "We start now. That attack was out of the blue and it could happen again at any moment." The effect of being safe, of the tea and bread, and of talking to Lauren, was wearing off. She'd lost color in her face, her eyes drooped. She was exhausted and scared but she wanted to attack her problem anyway.

Damn. Just like a SEAL, only gorgeous and female.

She had a very pretty, slighty pointed chin and he was absolutely certain that chin spelled stubbornness.

But she was also kindhearted. So he took the whole thing on himself.

"Listen," he said, scooting closer. "We're definitely going after the guy, but I'd feel much better if Jacko was here. Do you mind waiting for him to arrive so we're all on the same page?"

Metal could tackle this himself, but he'd just given her an out. She needed more rest.

"Okay." She stifled a big yawn behind a small fist. "Sure."

"In the meantime maybe you should rest."

She wasn't saying anything but she was in pain. His admiration went up another notch. Suck it up. *Embrace* the suck. SEAL life mottos.

"Thank you," she whispered and he nodded. He didn't want thanks, he wanted the fucker who'd slashed her. Badly. Her eyes searched his. "Why are you doing this for me? I can understand Lauren and maybe Jacko because he's with her. But why are you helping me?"

Metal took a minute. He wasn't good with words. Put a rifle in his hand, give him a lung-shot teammate and he knew exactly what to do. But this? It was hard to put into words because he surprised himself with the depth of his feelings.

Since she'd stumbled into Lauren's house, white-faced and bleeding, he knew he had to take care of her. No other options. But he couldn't say that. It would scare the shit out of her and confuse her. So he said part of the truth.

"Okay, here's the deal." He took her hand in his again, scooted his chair closer. "I hate this. I cannot tell you how much I hate this. I don't know what this fu—guy wanted—"

"You can say fucker," she said quietly, a faint smile on her face.

"I say it a lot," Metal warned.

Her smile grew wider. "That's okay."

He gave a brisk nod. "So, whatever this fucker wanted, he was more than willing to hurt you to get it. I know you're really smart. Lauren says so and you thought your way out of a very dangerous situation like you'd been trained for it. But though you're smart, you're not physically strong and violence isn't your thing. And I hate that this fucker thought he was going to win and I hate even more the fact that he's out there looking for you. This is exactly what's wrong with the world. The strong using their strength to hurt. If there's anything in my life I want, it's to stop that. And this guy is going to get stopped."

It was probably the longest speech he'd made in years and he hadn't even touched on the heart of it.

Metal was born strong. He was always the biggest in his class and his father and brothers taught him self-defense from when he was a toddler. He'd never been bullied but he'd stopped a lot of bullying.

That's what the O'Briens were all about. Generations of them—siblings, father, grandfather and great-grandfather just off the boat from Ireland. Generations of big, strapping O'Briens, all firefighters and cops. Guys who protected, guys who made a difference, guys who *helped*.

Guys who were there on that terrible day in September in New York, all rushing *into* the burning buildings and never coming back out. Father and four brothers, all gone in the space of a couple of hours. His mother died a week later of a broken heart. After burying his entire family, eighteen-year-old Metal, who'd been thinking of breaking with the firefighter-cop tradition and going to med school, enrolled in the Navy, intent on becoming a SEAL. And he'd done it.

He wasn't a SEAL anymore. He had almost more metal in his body than bone. But by God he still had his SEAL heart and his SEAL skills and no one was getting near Felicity again.

Unless it was him.

That spurted up out of nowhere and he repressed it, hard.

"We're going to stop him."

She listened to him so carefully, taking in his words through her ears but also her eyes and maybe even through the hand he was holding.

Her eyes were amazing but more than their beauty, they were alive. It was as if she operated at a higher level than other people, vibrated to a faster vibe, like a hummingbird.

"This feels familiar." She clenched her fingers around his. "You held my hand all night, didn't you?"

Metal blinked. "Yeah." Was she angry? "I'm sorry, I—"

"Thanks," she said quietly. "It helped."

He nodded. No way he was going to say that it helped him more than it helped her. He knew intellectually that she wasn't in danger of dying. She'd suffered blood loss but had been transfused. Other than that, once the gash was stitched up and she was taking antibiotics, she was fine.

But Metal had had men, good men, die in his arms, even while he was working frantically to save them. He never let down his vigilance. If she had had any problems during the night, he was right there. And holding her hand, feeling it warm up in his, reassured him on the deepest level there was.

"What's your name?" Her head cocked to one side, eyes half-closed. "You saved my life, you held my hand, I'm in your bed and I don't know your name."

She was toppling. He answered as he eased her back down with a hand cupping the back of her head.

"Sean Aiden O'Brien. But most people call me Metal. And yours?"

"Metal," she murmured sleepily. "Nice to meet you. I'm Felicity. Felicity Ward. That's my name—for now."

A minute later she was fast asleep again.

FIVE

Washington, DC

BORODIN HAD NEW intel that brought him to Washington.

Roy Gregory, in exchange for another infusion of cash, had dug farther into the files and uncovered the interesting information that Felicity Ward had a mentor inside the FBI. He'd originally handled the Darin family before handing them over to the U.S. Marshals Service and had kept in touch with the family over the years. Al Goodkind, now retired, living in Alexandria, Virginia. A product of the Cold War, he even spoke some Russian. Or at least he had a minor in Russian Studies and a major in Law from Georgetown University.

Gregory discovered that it was Goodkind who had put Felicity Ward's name forward as a freelance consultant.

Other information—Goodkind lived in a residential area of Alexandria, in a house with a large lawn. Neighbors at least a hundred meters away. He was a widower, no children, lived alone. He was a former FBI agent, it was true, and could be presumed to be armed. But he was also seventy-five years old. Gregory included the latest medical report from his FBI-appointed doctor and Goodkind wasn't in good health. He had high blood pressure, incipient diabetes and had had prostrate cancer seven years ago.

He wasn't going to live much longer anyway.

It was time to pay Goodkind a call.

If Lagoshin was fucking this up, Borodin would have to unfuck it. Find Felicity Ward via a lateral route. Via her affection for Al Goodkind.

Borodin himself could take care of Goodkind. He was still strong enough to take on a sick old man. But that was one of the many advantages of being rich—never having to get your hands dirty. Borodin had his two pilots with him and they could grab the old man. His pilots were all ex-military and knew their way around weapons and hand-to-hand combat. On trips, his pilots often doubled as bodyguards. Borodin trusted them. His current pilots, Yevgeny Milekhin and Lev Zolin, had saved his life in Uzbekistan on an inspection of a gas pipeline.

Borodin checked out of the hotel. His time in New York was over.

Zolin picked him up in a rented town car and drove him out to the private aviation sector of JFK. Zolin and Milekhin had been sleeping in the airplane, which was perfectly comfortable. They'd certainly slept in worse places. Having the pilots in the plane insured that they would be ready for takeoff at any moment.

By the time Borodin arrived at the plane, a flight plan to Washington, DC had been filed, the plane was fully fueled and they took off fifteen minutes after he boarded. The plane was registered to a shell company headquartered in Aruba and could never be traced back to Intergaz.

They were ghosts.

That's what money did. Made you invisible, nearly untouchable.

Another town car met them at Ronald Reagan National Airport, rented by one William Novella, whose cloned credit card Borodin had bought on the black market. He had about a hundred of them with him. In the parking lot, Zolin switched plates with another car. The car would take Borodin into Alexandria. Zolin drove and Milekhin waited with the plane.

The weather was overcast and cold. The forecast was for snow. Apparently it was snowing in Portland, their next stop. Borodin laughed when he watched the weather reports from anchors breathlessly announcing "heavy snowfalls" and subzero temperatures.

What would these weaklings do in Siberia, where a snowstorm could dump 160 centimeters in twenty-four hours, where temperatures in winter dropped to minus twenty-five degrees Celsius, where kids played "snow bomb"—throwing a bottle of boiling water in the air and watching it freeze before it hit the ground?

He and his men could move around just fine in the cold.

Finding Al Goodkind's house with GPS was easy. By the time they made it to his neighborhood light was draining from the sky. It was a quiet neighborhood, very few people were about. Alexandria was where apparatchiks went to die. Men and women who had spent a lifetime in service to their government. You'd think a lifetime in government would be enough to induce paranoia, but no. The homes were separated by large open lawns and there were no fences.

In Moscow, former KGB functionaries—those that lived long enough to retire—resided in gated communities with twelve-foot walls and barbed wire because they'd made enemies. No one was foolish enough to live like these people.

They passed by Goodkind's home four times, twice

from the east and twice from the west. They daren't risk any more pass-bys. The house was dark.

"What do we do?" Zolin asked.

This was their only lead. "We wait," Borodin said.

Portland

FELICITY WOKE UP when the front doorbell rang. She heard Metal's deep bass and then Lauren's quiet voice.

Sun was streaming in and it gave her cognitive dissonance until she glanced at her *Doctor Who* watch. The only way what she read there made any sense was if she'd slept almost sixteen hours. She'd been sleeping for almost two days straight.

"In here," she called out, wincing. But, surprise. Her side hurt much less than it had before. She found she could even sit up in bed without Metal's help.

Metal, such an odd name.

Well, she should talk.

She'd named herself after a comic book character, Felicity Smoak. Was he called Metal because of all those muscles? They were as hard as steel. When he'd carried her, when he'd helped her sit up in bed, whenever he'd touched her, she'd felt those steely muscles. He'd been enormously delicate but the man was built. Amazing muscles. Hard, warm.

He'd held her hand all night. For two nights in a row.

She was certain that it was that hand that was helping her heal so quickly. Even asleep she'd somehow felt the strength and warmth, a constant infusion of power, like Peter Parker having been bit by a genetically modified spider, only without the bite.

This time forty-eight hours ago she'd been flying over

the Rockies, happy to be meeting an old friend who was actually a new friend.

And there she was, that old and new friend, standing on the threshold of the bedroom.

"Felicity?" Lauren held the doorjamb with one hand and the handle of a carry-on case with the other. The night before last, Felicity had barely glimpsed her. She'd been so weak and in such pain she mainly remembered Metal's broad face above hers, reassuring, his deep voice almost lulling her to sleep.

She knew what Lauren looked like. She'd arranged her fake ID, after all, and she'd needed photos to do that. She'd been the one to change Anne Lowell into Lauren Dare. Even in the photos Lauren had been pretty but she was stunning in person. Better than in her ID photos, where she'd looked drawn and pale, faint lines bracketing her mouth. Well, being hunted down by a drugged-up psychopath would do that to you. Being on the run was not exactly like going to the spa.

Right now, though, Lauren looked pink and happy. Smiling. Most of the reason she looked happy loomed behind her. Jacko Morton, her new love. At first glance he didn't look like the kind of guy to make a lady happy. Not tall—Metal towered over him—but very broad in the chest and shoulders, and he looked like trouble.

Snow still pinged against the windowpanes of Metal's bedroom windows. Despite the weather, Jacko wore only a T-shirt under his jacket, which he'd already taken off. Felicity could see barbed wire tats and some kind of tribal tat spilling out from under the sleeves. He looked like he could and would chew you up for breakfast and spit out the bones.

Until he looked at Lauren, that was, and his face changed.

It was amazing to watch. A big bruiser's brutal face sort of melting when he looked at Lauren, then morphing right back into toughness when he looked away.

"Ma'am," he said in a basso profundo voice, nodding at her.

She nodded back. "Jacko." She felt as though she was in a Western, only she didn't have a six-gallon hat with a brim to touch. She smiled at Lauren. "We can't keep meeting like this."

Lauren gave a choked laugh and launched herself across the room. Felicity opened her arms, saying at the last minute, "Careful of the war wound."

But Lauren was already wrapping her up in a warm, careful hug. She buried her face in Felicity's neck, tears wetting her skin. "We stopped by yesterday but you were sleeping. You looked okay and didn't have a fever so we let you rest. I'm so glad you're healing. I was so scared for you," she whispered.

Felicity's throat tightened as she gave herself up to Lauren's gentle, perfumed embrace. She tried to think who in her life would cry for her but gave up the attempt immediately. Her oldest friend was Al Goodkind, a retired FBI agent, and though he undoubtedly cared for her he wouldn't cry. Nothing could make the tough old coot cry except maybe if something happened to his beloved granddaughter. And even then…

So feeling the tears Lauren shed for her gave her a warm tingly feeling, like a promise made and kept. "I'm okay," she whispered. She looked over Lauren's shoulder to where Metal stood, huge and still, light brown eyes intent as he watched them. She spoke to Lauren but watched Metal. "He took real good care of me."

Something flared in Metal's eyes. Something hot.

And then crazily, something flared in her. Something hot.

It was such an unusual feeling that at first she wondered whether she had a fever, a temporary one. Like a two-second fever. But it wasn't that. It was looking into Metal's eyes and seeing…power. Pure male power and male interest…directed at her.

He'd been so kind, like a doctor would have been. Impersonal, efficient, dedicated. But this was something else and it popped something to life inside her.

"Whoa." Lauren opened her arms and stood up, wiped her eyes, looking for traces of mascara on her fingertips. "You scared me. Us." She looked over her shoulder. "And I'm really glad Metal took good care of you, because if he hadn't I'd have beaten him up."

It was ridiculous. Lauren was half Metal's size, slender and delicate. Metal was huge. But he didn't smirk, didn't smile at the notion.

"And I'd have let you beat me up if something had happened to her. But as you can see, she's fine. As a matter of fact—" He looked to Jacko, back to Lauren and then to her. But when he looked at her, his face changed. Subtle but definitely there. With the punch of heat. Echoed in her. "She needs to eat if she wants to regain her strength. I cooked some stuff so if you guys want to stay…"

"And we can talk about all of this," Jacko growled, waving a hand at her. He sounded pissed. Was he—was he *angry* at her? Well, of course. She'd brought trouble to Lauren's door. Whoever was after her could maybe

track Lauren down, hurt her. Oh God, just the thought
of it made her feel awful. She cringed.

"I'm so sorry, Jacko," she said miserably. "So sorry
that this happened. As soon as I get back on my feet, I
promise to leave. I had absolutely no idea that—"

Her words were muffled by Lauren's hand covering
her mouth. She looked angry, exasperated. "Good lord!
Don't even talk like that. That's not what he meant, isn't
that right, Jacko?"

"God, no," he rumbled. That hard, expressionless face
was scrunched into a scowl. "Sorry. I'm mad, but not at
you. I'm mad at the fuck—" He shut up suddenly when
Lauren shot him a look. "I'm mad at the shithe—" He
bit his lips. "At the man after you. We're going to figure this out and get him off your back. In the meantime,
Metal and I talked about this. We both think it would be
a good idea for you to stay here. You tight with that?"

Metal watched her, this huge wall of muscle between
her and trouble.

"Oh yes," she breathed and then blushed. Because it
came out sounding all wrong. She sounded like Mari-
lyn Monroe singing "Happy Birthday" to the president.
She'd seen it on YouTube a billion times. All breathy and
sexy. Felicity didn't do breathy and sexy. She was married to her computer. It must be the fact that she felt so
weak that it came out that way.

"Okay. So that's taken care of." Lauren straightened
and walked back to Jacko, who put a heavy arm round
her shoulders. "Did I hear you mention food, Metal? Did
you mean it or was that an empty promise?"

"Meant every word." He lifted his shoulder from the
doorjamb, came to the bedside and offered Felicity a
huge hand. "Do you want to see if you can walk?"

She nodded. Metal pulled back the covers, put a big hand to her back. "Take it easy," he said. "Just say the word and I'll carry you to the kitchen."

Oh man. Being carried in those huge arms. He spoke as she swung her legs to the side of the bed and stood up. The image it conjured made her knees go weak, just for a second. Before she had time to stiffen her knees, he swung her up as if she was a child and carried her out of the room.

She had a vague memory of being carried by him, but it had been like being in a car. A big, warm, sentient car, with no emotions attached. But now…oh man, now it felt like romance and power and sex all mixed together.

Felicity had never been carried that she could remember. As a child, as soon as she could walk, she wasn't carried anymore. Her parents had been loving but distant. She could count the number of hugs on one hand. And of course, as an adult woman, no man had ever carried her. She frequented fellow geeks, whose thighs were smaller than Metal's biceps.

Above all, they didn't have his alpha macho vibe. He wasn't in-your-face macho but it was there, as much a part of him as his nose or ears.

If you had a guy who could carry you, why weren't women carried around *all the time?* Because, man, this was *ace.* Simply because of their position, her cheek was closely aligned with his. He carried her really smoothly, like carrying a bag of peanuts, but every once in a while her cheek brushed his. It was slightly bristly and utterly delicious, as was his smell. It wouldn't be polite, but what she really wanted was to bury her nose where his strong neck met those amazing shoulders and take a big sniff, like a dog. Mint, soap, leather—an amazingly heady mix. If she'd taken biochem instead of computer science she'd try to duplicate it in the lab. Of course the smell had to be paired with muscles, so maybe that wouldn't work commercially.

His hold was utterly steady, no sense of strain whatsoever. It felt as though he could carry her for miles without being winded. His arms tilted her slightly facing him so she had most of her front side plastered against all those amazing muscles.

It turned out that the most comfortable way to be carried was to put your arms around the man's neck and, oh God, that was amazing too. His neck muscles and shoulder muscles simply hummed with power that was transmitted to her through the skin of her arms. Like touching a power plant, only warm.

He strode across the living room and she looked around curiously. So far she'd seen the bedroom and the en suite bathroom. It was remarkably pleasant, which was a surprise. He was so rough and tough, such a guy, she imagined he'd have one of those guy pads like her geek pals in college. Empty except for monitors everywhere and the hum of electronics with that ozone smell when too much electrical equipment is concentrated in too small a space.

And, well, the smell of geek too, which was often very pungent. Add in a house that was cleaned up once a year and you had a very noncommercially viable smell.

This place smelled clean and fresh. It looked clean and fresh. Very masculine, no frills, but comfortable, functional, everything in earth tones. No flowers, no plants but bare branches in a tall bucket and a huge glass container with a sand sculpture inside.

A TV that was smaller than ginormous, which was a surprise.

Then they were in the kitchen and that, too, was a surprise. There were plants here—all cooking herbs, not her forte. She recognized basil, rosemary and a plant of chili peppers. Mainly because she recognized the shape and smell of the plants. There were lots of others too, but she had no clue what they were. Usually she'd just look it up. She had a special app where she'd photograph something and compare it to Google images and presto! There the name was. For the first time in forever she didn't have the internet at her fingertips but she wasn't missing it. Not just yet.

A big pinewood table, pine cabinets and granite countertops. Appliances, but not many. A big wood block with a billion knives, all of them no doubt razor sharp.

That was it.

The kitchen looked out over a small, neat backyard with no flowers but a small wall of trimmed hedges.

Orderly and comfortable.

Lauren and Jacko had gone ahead and were setting the table. Metal hooked a chair with a big boot and set her down gently. When he stood, he rested a big hand on her shoulder, squeezing gently.

You okay?

It was as if he spoke the words aloud.

"I'm fine," Felicity said, turning her head to look up at him. "Thanks."

He nodded and started taking things out of a huge refrigerator. Felicity caught glimpses inside and was instantly ashamed of her own fridge, with curling slices of take-out pizza and a few pieces of rotting fruit. She was always so busy working. These past few months, she'd eaten takeout more days than not.

Metal's fridge was full of fresh food, bowls covered in plastic wrap, milk and fruit juice and only a few bottles of beer, the vegetable bin full of produce. Her vegetable bin was full of servers and two boxes of flash drives that she wanted to keep cool.

To her knowledge, she hadn't had a bowl of leftovers covered in cling film, like normal people did in, like, forever.

While Jacko finished setting the table, Lauren sat down and covered Felicity's hand with hers. "So how are you feeling, really?" A small pucker of concern between her brows.

She wanted the truth so Felicity didn't bother baring her teeth and gritting *fine fine*, which she would have with anyone else. Though they didn't know each other, they *knew* each other, they'd been through hard times together. Lauren wasn't asking out of politeness, she was asking out of concern.

"I feel a little weak and very tired," she answered, squeezing Lauren's hand. "But I feel much better than I did two nights ago, and I feel better now than I did an hour ago, so the trend is good. Like I said, Metal's taking very good care of me."

Lauren smiled faintly. She looked around at Jacko getting stuff from the cupboards and Metal at the stove, and lowered her voice. "I'll be honest. I wasn't too happy when Metal took over, so Jacko told me a few stories. And…well, Metal's incredible. Do you know why they call him Metal?"

"His taste in music?"

"Uh-uh." Lauren smiled. "That would be Jacko's taste

before my friend Allegra introduced him to music that doesn't make your ears bleed. I have no idea what Metal's taste in music is. No, they call him Metal because in whole sections of his body he's more titanium than bone. During an ambush in Afghanistan he was blown up by a mine and he *crawled* with his medic kit to where two teammates were bleeding out. He had a shattered hip and a broken femur and he crawled thirty yards under intense fire and he saved their lives. Got a big medal for it too. The kind they don't give out often. That was his last mission, but all during his service he kept people alive under battlefield conditions with people shooting at him. He's brought back guys from the brink of death while under fire, and though you certainly weren't on the brink—" Lauren closed her eyes and shuddered, "¾it looked really bad."

"Because I'd lost a lot of blood. Yeah."

Lauren nodded, swallowed again. "I was so scared. But Metal and Jacko were amazing. All that blood didn't faze them at all. Metal moved fast and of course he knew exactly what he was doing. And, Jacko assures me you are safe in every way here, with him. Otherwise I wouldn't leave you here."

"I know."

"Jacko says—"

"Food. Jacko says food. Right now." Jacko kissed Lauren's cheek as he sat down. Metal put a large steaming pot on a trivet and slid a big platter of that whole wheat bread and some cheeses on the table. Whatever was in the pot, it smelled delicious.

Felicity watched him moving easily in his kitchen. She didn't know much about medicine but he must have done incredibly intense physical therapy to recover from the wounds Lauren had described.

He was incredibly brave.

And he *cooked*.

Metal ladled some soup into her bowl and she leaned forward and sniffed. Mushroom soup. Heavenly. Her nose loved it but…her stomach simply closed up. She was hungry. She could feel that, feel hunger behind the rising nausea. Her stomach was knotted up in cramps. It was horrible, to want to eat but not be able to eat.

She was breathing deeply, trying to keep the nausea down, trying to hide the fact that she was nauseous. It didn't work. Everyone suddenly stopped eating and looked at her.

She picked up her spoon with a trembling hand, started to take it to her mouth when a hard hand took the spoon from her, placed it back in the soup.

Metal curved his shoulders inward as he turned to her and she realized he was creating a little wall of privacy for them. He held her hand with one of his, the other was against her back, smack between her shoulder blades, right where the muscles were frozen and tense. He started rubbing lightly with that huge hand, so large it covered a good portion of her back along the spine.

He bent his mouth to her ear. "It's okay. You're still a little shocked and we gave you a massive infusion of antibiotics, which messes with your stomach. Kills the intestinal flora and can cause stomachache and cramping. The pain is like having an ulcer but you don't have an ulcer. It's just a reaction to the antibiotics. Once you get some warm food in your stomach you'll be fine. Just take a few spoonfuls."

Felicity turned her head and he was so close. So close

she could see gold flecks in his light brown eyes, could see the white stripes of crow's-feet in his tanned face. See the light gold stubble starting to show on his cheeks.

He was watching her carefully. "Take a little food for me. I promise you'll feel better."

He was mesmerizing. Felicity had no idea how he could fascinate her so much. It was a plain face—broad cheekbones, flat features, a broken nose, nothing special. Not handsome in any way. But there it was—she couldn't tear her eyes away from him.

He nodded at the soup and she dipped her spoon in and swallowed a spoonful. It was delicious and it went down. She ate because she knew she needed food but also because he had a natural authority to him, a doctor's authority though he wasn't a doctor.

"Better?" His eyes watched her so intently she wouldn't be surprised if he said he could follow the soup down to her stomach and observe what happened to it there.

She nodded. Her stomach still hurt, but now that she knew why it didn't scare her. She was rarely sick and never had stomachaches. For a panicky moment she'd wondered if the attack had affected her internal organs.

"Good girl." That hard harsh face slipped into a smile and her stomach swooped. It wasn't the antibiotics that made it swoop, though. No. It was him. "More."

It was a voice made to command. She dipped her spoon again and swallowed. "Another." By the third spoonful of soup the ache had lessened and her hunger roared into life. It was only when he was satisfied that she was eating that Metal turned and dug in himself.

"Great stuff," Jacko said, eating fast but neatly. "I

don't want to know what it is because it looks like crap. Literally."

"Moron," Metal said affectionately. "Cream of mushroom soup and it does *not* look like crap."

"Does too," Jacko insisted. "Looks like what came out when I got bin Laden's revenge in the 'Stan and—" He stopped when Lauren drove an elbow into his side. "Sorry." He looked at Felicity sheepishly.

She didn't care what it looked like. More to the point, her stomach didn't care either. She was famished and it was absolutely delicious. She held out her bowl. "More please."

"Attagirl," Metal said. He ladled another bowlful. "Here you go, honey."

At the term, Felicity turned bright *bright* red. She had very fair skin and it telegraphed every single emotion she felt.

There was a reason she avoided people.

But crazily, no one commented on her sudden and totally embarassing stoplight-red face. Jacko and Metal were discussing something that had to do with vectors and lines of sight and Lauren was handing her a chunk of a yellowish cheese and another slice of bread. "Try this, it's a local cheese. Tillamook, delicious."

It was. The men were drinking a local beer but Metal had made tea for her and Lauren. The combination of hot soup, bread and cheese, and tea made her feel warm and sated.

"So, Felicity." Jacko planted his elbows on the table, shoving away the bowl and plate, and clasped his big hands, looking down at them for a moment then lifting his head to stare at her. "How did you come to show up on Lauren's doorstep sliced and bleeding?"

Lauren gasped and Metal growled. There was no other term for it. Instinctively, Felicity laid her hand on his forearm. "That's okay. He has a right to ask."

Metal glanced at her without moving his head. His jaw muscles tightened so much she wondered if he'd crack a tooth.

Jacko made a fist and banged it lightly on the table. "Damn right I do. I like you, Felicity, and I know Lauren cares for you and that goes a long way with me. But there's no denying that you brought trouble to Lauren's door. Metal and I are on it and we can keep you safe, but we need to know what we're up against. And I need you to know that my first priority is Lauren's safety."

Lauren was practically quivering with outrage, but Felicity shook her head.

"I'm really glad Lauren has you on her side," Felicity answered and she meant every word. It was a dangerous world out there and Lauren had had some dangerous men after her. Jacko had saved her life and clearly was in that life to stay. Lucky Lauren. "And I would love to answer you, but truly, I have no idea who that man was and why he was after me. I'd feel better if I did, believe me."

"I do believe you. And I also know that Lauren is alive thanks to you, thanks to your help." He unclasped his hands and pointed a thick finger at her. "I know you provided her with the fake ID that helped her disappear. So could it be someone you provided a new identity for who wants to eliminate you?"

Jacko had every right to interrogate her, to dig in to why someone was after her. Felicity didn't begrudge him in any way. He was doing it because he wanted to keep Lauren safe. But the warmth that had been created by the food and eating in company was starting to dissipate.

She felt a chill run through her and jumped when Metal took her hand, holding it openly. His hand was so strong and so very warm, it chased away the sudden chill.

"We need to do this, but take your time," Metal rumbled. "No one is rushing you."

She shrugged. "It feels so unreal. If I didn't have a bandage and pain I'd think I dreamed it. No one knew I was coming to Portland, not even Lauren. It was sort of a last-minute decision. I'm self-employed and can work on the road. I don't report in to anyone. And I lead a fairly secluded life anyway."

"Why didn't you let me know you were arriving?" Lauren asked. "I would have come to the airport to pick you up."

Jacko's dark eyes widened and Felicity could see the whites of his eyes. He was imagining Lauren with her when the man attacked her.

Felicity was really grateful she hadn't called Lauren ahead of time. Lauren could have been there at the airport. If something had happened to her she'd never have forgiven herself. "I—I wasn't sure of my welcome. I was thinking I'd stay in a hotel, call you up, say I was in Portland for business, could we meet. I thought—"

"Did you book?" Metal asked.

"I'm sorry?"

"Did you book a room?"

Felicity gasped. Oh my God, she had! It had totally slipped her mind. "I did."

"Which hotel?" Metal asked.

"The Regency." She'd picked it and booked it on the internet.

Metal had been checking something on his cell. He got up from the table, punched in a number and walked into the living room. All Felicity heard was the deep rumble of his voice without making out the words.

She missed his body heat, missed having him sitting beside her. Which was weird because she always ate alone. Sitting beside someone at the table was an exception, not the rule, so why was she missing him?

He walked back into the kitchen and sat down. He moved quickly and very quietly for such a large man, with an easy athletic grace. He was huge with muscle and she assumed men as muscle-bound as he was would be a little stiff, but no. He was graceful even packing all those muscles.

Metal nodded at Jacko but addressed her. "You were booked into room 724. I spoke with the head of security at the Regency and he looked at the tapes of the seventh floor. I had him run through the tapes. At 9:15 p.m. the night you arrived, someone jammed the security cameras on the entire floor for fifteen minutes, which is more or less the time it would take to get into your room and see that it was unoccupied. How long did you book for?"

"Three days," Felicity answered. Figuring if Lauren was happy to see her, they could hang out for a few days and if not, she could visit Portland. It was her first visit to the West Coast.

"Don't cancel," he warned.

"No, of course not. Let him wonder where I am."

Metal nodded, looked at Jacko again. Some unspoken signal passed between them, which was odd. Felicity thought only women could do that. But what did she know? She rarely communicated with anyone.

"The head of security is sending me footage from the lobby security cameras half an hour before and after the blackout to see if you can recognize the guy. He probably took the stairs up but he had to cross the lobby. The back entrance was locked all day. And later today we'll be talking with a friend from Portland PD, purely informally. He's a homicide cop and this isn't homicide but I know you want to keep a very low profile. This is a way to get some law enforcement on our side without stirring up the waters. And when we catch the sick fuck he won't know what hit him. Throw him in a cage."

"Perfect," Felicity breathed. "Thank you so much."

She was smart and fast but was completely out of her depth here. She'd barely begun to think it through and he was already on the attack.

He covered her hand with his. And there it was again—some kind of electrical circuit that warmed her up and made her a different kind of hot at the same time. Like throwing a switch.

"We've got you, honey. You're safe now and we're going to get this guy. You have Jacko and me and we work for a company that has a lot of resources. And Bud, our cop friend, is a really smart guy too. We're going to figure out who this fuck is, why he attacked you, and we're going to stop him. I promise." Those light brown eyes were intent as he watched her eyes. "You're safe."

To her horror, tears welled in her eyes. *Whoa.* Felicity didn't do tears, ever. She never cried, never got emotional and here she was—a big ball of emotions she couldn't begin to analyze filling her chest, moving up her throat, coming out her eyes in the shape of water.

Safe must be her trigger word.

"Safe doesn't exist," she said sharply, instinctively. "There's no such thing as safe."

Both Jacko and Metal narrowed their eyes. What was

up with that? Of all people, two former soldiers should know that safety is an illusion.

There was utter silence, which she was thankful for. She couldn't argue while all these sharp emotions were rolling around in her chest and her eyes burned. Her voice would crack and maybe other things would crack and come spilling out.

Finally, Lauren broke the silence, leaning forward, tucking a curl of dark hair behind her ear. She glanced quickly at both Jacko and Metal as if seeking their permission. "We'll keep you safe, Felicity. Jacko and Metal are really good at that. It's what they do."

"You were kidnapped and Jacko was shot. How safe were you then?" Her head was bent and she spoke to the table.

Something perverse in Felicity made her say the words, just pushed them out of her mouth. She regretted them the instant she said them. These three people were doing their very best for her, though they'd never met her before. And she'd only known Lauren online. She'd stumbled, wounded, into Lauren's house and they'd done nothing but look after her and care for her.

She lifted her head, forced herself to meet their eyes, one at a time. Lauren. Jacko. Metal. "I'm so sorry," she said miserably. "That was uncalled for—"

"But true." Metal sighed. "No offense taken. We thought the danger was over and it wasn't. We don't make mistakes like that twice, though, believe me. So no one is going to be catching us unawares until this whole thing is resolved. You have my word."

Oh, Metal, Felicity thought sadly. *Some things are never resolved, not even over a lifetime.*

Her father's issues had never been resolved and he'd

been frightened, looking over his shoulder, for as long as she could remember.

Of course her father had been a physicist, not a warrior. But still.

"Let's go over the known facts," Metal said. "What's our basic intel?"

She nearly smiled to hear him speak soldier-speak. Al, an FBI agent his entire life, would have called it intelligence.

"I understand from Lauren that you help people disappear." Metal directed his even gaze at her.

"No," she said. "It's more complicated than that, and that's not my main job. My main job is as an IT consultant. This is more of a…a sideline. I create background identities and social media profiles for the…the government on a freelance basis. But I do that rarely. Mainly, as I said, I work in computer security."

Metal leaned forward a little. "So you don't think the most likely explanation is that someone you gave a new identity to wants to erase his tracks and eliminate the person who knows his new identity? You don't think it's connected to someone you've helped?"

If only it was so easy. Felicity shook her head. "No, for three reasons. First, I don't actually create the heavy-duty documents, particularly passports. I created an Ohio driver's license for Lauren, but that's because she was my friend. She had a very nasty man after her. I looked at his computer files and he was crazy and bad, a nasty combo. Like Deathstroke. You've got Deathstroke after you, you need help."

Metal smiled. "Unless you've got Arrow on your side. Then you're okay."

Felicity smiled for the first time in what felt like

forever. "Unless you've got Arrow on your side," she agreed. "But Lauren didn't have Arrow. She does have Jacko now and, no offense, Jacko, and I mean this in the best possible way, you look like a real badass. Not many people would want to cross swords with you. But when Lauren and I first connected she was alone with bad guys on her trail. Which is why I agreed to provide actual documents. Usually I provide background ID and social media backstopping for the FBI."

Both Metal and Jacko reacted as if they'd been touched by a cattle prod. "The *FBI?*" Metal asked.

"You didn't tell me that," Lauren complained.

"No." Felicity sighed. "I keep it to myself. But I figure I can tell you two without compromising national security." She peered at the two men. "What clearances did you have? SAP? I imagine that by definition SEALs have been subjected to SSBIs, am I right?"

Single Scope Background Investigations were thorough and they wouldn't have achieved elite Special Forces status without passing them with flying colors.

"Yeah." Metal sounded like he had a constriction in his throat. "You?"

"SCI." Which was a higher clearance. "I wouldn't be talking about this if I believed that my work for the FBI was in any way involved. So like I said, what I did as a freelancer was provide background for new identities the FBI, and also the U.S. Marshals Service, wanted created. They'd take care of documentation but I would backstop the identity. I create Facebook and Twitter accounts that go back a few years, I create Amazon accounts with a specific intellectual profile, buyer accounts at major retailers, I could fill their laptops with so much detritus that nobody would question the ID. But I was given the photos of the persons whose identity needed filling out and I can assure you that I have never backstopped anyone who looked like my attacker."

Jacko pursed his lips, eyes narrowed. "Plastic surgery? Surgeons can turn men into women and vice versa. No problem with changing the shape of a nose or cheekbones."

Felicity shook her head. "It's not like I do thousands and so a face or two could conceivably escape my notice. I provide backgrounds for about three or four people a year. It's very labor-intensive and time-consuming work and I'm only called in when it's really important that the cover story be good. I work with these people, getting to know their likes and dislikes, so I don't give a tone-deaf person a passion for classical music or make a couch potato a hiker. They would blow their cover immediately. I would remember the guy who attacked me, even if he had undergone plastic surgery. He was definitely not one of my clients."

"And people like me? Your extracurricular activities?" Lauren asked. "You took me off the grid." She grabbed Felicity's hand. "And saved my life."

Felicity curled her hand around Lauren's. "I only help women outside government work. You were my third. I think the FBI and Marshals Service would really frown on me doing this on the side. I don't think my helping three women has anything to do with this."

Lauren shook her head sharply. "If Jorge had found out somehow that you'd helped me get away, he'd come after you to get my new identity, to find out where I was. Do you think these other two women—do you think they talked and unwittingly betrayed you? That the men they were running away from found out about you and thought you might be the key to finding who they were chasing?"

"It's not that." She didn't want Lauren to think she wasn't taking this idea seriously. But…no. "Lauren," she said gently. "We emailed each other for, what? A year and half?"

Lauren nodded.

"So, where do I live?"

Lauren's mouth shut with a snap.

Felicity nodded. They'd communicated often, sometimes sharing intimate details, but Felicty was always very careful never to give away identifying data. It was a lesson she'd learned almost before she could talk. "You don't know. You don't know if I live on the East Coast or West Coast, in a city or a town. You don't even know what I do for a living."

"I suspected you worked for the NSA or CIA," Lauren said with a half smile. "Considering the things you knew."

Close. But no cigar.

"Are you going to tell us what you really know? What's going on?" Jacko asked, his voice harsh. Lauren slide her gaze to him without turning her head, lips pinched with annoyance.

Oh God, no. Jacko was protecting Lauren, trying to figure out what kind of danger Felicity represented. Lauren shouldn't be mad at him for that. Having someone watch out for you was…magic. Felicity would give anything to have someone always there, always watching her back.

Metal put a big hand on her shoulder. "Don't give us any classified intel you're not comfortable sharing. But the more we know about your life, the better we can try to figure out who's after you."

She took in a big breath and turned to him. Watched his face carefully. Though he had thuggish features, thick and rough, and a crooked nose that had been broken several times, she saw intelligence in his eyes. And kindness. And he was demonstrably tough, if he'd been a SEAL. She was safe in these hands. Both Metal and Jacko had been elite warriors, entrusted with ensuring the safety of the country. They'd demonstrated trustworthiness a million times over in their careers. Jacko had saved Lauren's life and was clearly devoted to her. Metal had saved her life, too, and was sitting next to her just waiting to hear how he could help.

And apparently they'd enlisted the security company they worked for in the quest to help her, not to mention a Portland homicide detective.

These were serious good guys who were offering serious backing.

All she had to do was trust them. Easy enough, no? The freaking US government trusted them.

Her throat seized up.

Not trusting *anyone* was practically the family motto. You'd think the Darins had been vampires in hiding, keeping far from the human race. From her earliest memories on, Felicity had been taught not to trust anyone. It hadn't been subtle either. Once when she had invited home a friend she'd made in first grade, her mother had the friend out the door in five minutes and had been shaking when she told Felicity never to do that again. Trembling with fear, terrorized.

She'd never invited anyone home, ever again.

There was no place in her head for trust, except for

Al. And Lauren. And, well, looked as if Metal and Jacko were now inside the circle. And Metal's company…

Apparently there was now a dizzying number of people she trusted. Had to trust. There was no choice. She was in trouble and couldn't get out of it herself. She'd always been self-reliant, never needing anyone, but right now, she could barely stand. Getting out of bed and eating a meal had taxed her resources.

If everyone abandoned her right now, she was as vulnerable as she'd been at the airport. More.

Felicity looked around the table, at these three people. Lauren was almost quivering with eagerness to help. Metal and Jacko were more low-key but they gave off very strong male *we're gonna do this come hell or high water* vibes.

Lauren cared for her. Jacko was in because she was Lauren's friend and it looked like he'd do anything for her. And it looked like Metal was in because…because.

She was walking through Mordor trying desperately to avoid coming into the cone of light of the Eye of Sauron.

Frodo didn't do it alone. He couldn't.

And yet…Felicity had never asked for help, not once in her life and it scared the hell out of her. How did you do that? What could she legitimately ask of them and what was overstepping the line?

This was so *hard*.

She bent forward, biting her lips to prevent a low keening sound coming from her, like a wounded animal.

Lauren tilted her head, watching her reaction. "It's hard, isn't it?"

Felicity nodded. Hard didn't even come close to describing what she felt. She'd been wrapped in secrecy and distrust from her childhood on.

Jacko opened his mouth and Lauren covered his huge dark hand with her own and he stilled immediately. "Metal?" she said softly.

He leaned forward, forearms on knees, casual, but focused intently on her face. "Sounds like you're having trouble opening up."

She nodded again.

"We have that problem sometimes, particularly just back from a mission. We're trained, and trained hard—with harsh punishment as reinforcers—to keep confidential intel confidential. Sometimes the stupidest thing—saying what the weather was like on a deployment—could be a leak that the enemy could use. There's no way really for us to know what could be dangerous intel or not so, so basically we just shut up. Married guys who can't tell their wives anything at all about the last three months of their lives, and I mean nothing. Black hole. And it bleeds over into the rest of your life. Censoring yourself every time your open your mouth is hard, it's easier just to shut up. But then you find you're not saying anything to anyone but your teammates, and that's not good. Not healthy."

Even less healthy when you don't even have teammates.

Well, looked like she had a team now. A temporary one. Her first unless you counted Al. And Al was more a mentor than a teammate or a friend. He'd been as old as dirt for as long as she could remember.

"Take your time, but you're going to have to talk to us," Metal said, his voice low and calm.

It was time. Was it time? Yes.

"Okay. Okay. This isn't easy." Her fists were bunched in her lap and Metal's big hand covered them both. His grip was warm and hard and secure.

Body is mind and mind is body, she reminded herself. So she unclenched her fists, straightened her back, made sure her central chakra was open, breathed deeply.

"First of all, I live in Vermont." When she'd passed through Vermont years ago, right after her parents died, she'd immediately felt at home, felt it call to her. It was only after a few years when she saw a photograph of where her father had worked that she realized it was exactly the same climate, landscape. Her DNA had led her there. "I work on my own as an IT security consultant. I have a high level of clearance but I don't work on highly classified stuff because I don't work for the government as an employee. Never wanted to. I don't like the idea of going into an office. Like I said, through an FBI contact I help provide background on new identities. The FBI IT people don't have the right touch, they're not…loose enough, I guess, to put themselves in other people's shoes. Outside of that I mainly work corporate cybersecurity and we're not talking defense contractors, we're talking restaurant chains and tractor manufacturers. They were two incredibly boring but very lucrative accounts and they've eaten up most of the past year."

Metal watched her. It was as though he was listening to her through his ears but also through his skin and bones. He flicked a glance at Jacko then back to her.

"We'll go through those clients with a fine-tooth comb. And pretty soon we'll be getting the hotel footage. But in the meantime, there's something else."

She looked at him mutely, a pressure starting up in her chest.

"When I was trying to keep you awake before we got to the clinic I did what we do in the field. Ask simple questions so the patient focuses on something, but something easy. The easiest question in the world is 'what's your name?' No way to flub that one."

Oh God, she knew what was coming next.

"But you flubbed it." Metal's face was grim. "When I tapped your cheek to keep you conscious, and asked your name, you know what you answered?"

She swallowed, shook her head no, though she had a good idea what she'd answered. She'd been weak, wounded, exhausted. He'd taken her unawares.

"When I asked what your name was you said, '*Felicity Ward—for now.*' And last night you said your name was Felicity Ward. For now. So I guess the first thing we need to know going in is what your real name is. And why you seem to have several."

She couldn't talk.

"Felicity? There's more, isn't there?"

She nodded.

Metal's voice was very gentle but very firm. "The only way we can help you, the only way we can protect you, is to know the truth. Do you see that?"

She nodded again.

"Are you ready to tell us the truth?"

She sat very still. She couldn't move, couldn't talk, could barely breathe. This day was a long time coming, but it was here. A lifetime of hiding couldn't stop this day from coming. Was she ready to tell the truth?

She looked at the three of them, watching her patiently. Metal holding her hand.

Was she ready?

She'd been holding her breath and found she had to

gulp in air. Her gasp sounded very loud in the silent room.

Was she ready?

Yes, she was.

She nodded.

SIX

Alexandria, Virginia

GOODKIND FINALLY CAME HOME. Borodin had been prepared to wait a long time since that *kretin* Lagoshin
was making no progress in Portland. For the moment
Al Goodkind was their only lead. In the end, though, he
only had to wait twenty-four hours. He had only Zolin
with him. Milekhin was in the plane.

An elderly gentleman with stooped shoulders arrived
in a taxi and entered the front door with a key, carrying a small traveling case. Even without the identifying photo which matched the old man's face, Borodin
knew it was him.

A light in the back of the house came on.

Zolin, who knew what he was doing, detected video
cameras at the front, under the porch roof, and said that
they were ancient. Zolin slipped out after punching the
button on a device that blanketed cell reception within
a hundred-meter radius.

He was carrying a combat knife, a Taser, a Beretta
92F in a shoulder holster and a preloaded syringe of
etorphine. He also had strict instructions not to use the
Beretta. Borodin wanted information without having to
tend to a gunshot wound. Not to mention the fact that
blood would ruin the beautiful interior of his Airbus.

Borodin knew how to extract information. Goodkind

was former FBI and presumably tough but no one held out forever. They had a six-hour flight ahead of them. That should be more than enough time.

All he needed was contact information regarding Felicity Ward's friends in Portland. The woman had to have friends to have disappeared so completely. A wound required medical care, stitches, antibiotics, a place to recover. Where could she have gone to ground? Goodkind would know. And if he didn't, Goodkind would be forced to contact Ward with a bloody face and swollen eyes and Borodin would pry her out of her lair.

So much was at stake that Borodin felt an itching under the skin. It had been years since he'd felt anxiety and it wasn't pleasant.

Since he'd become rich, small troubles had simply melted away and big troubles—well, he had people for that. He wasn't used to being uncertain about an outcome. His outcomes had all been good these past twenty-five years.

And yet everything about this Deti business—starting from having to find Darin's daughter—was unnerving.

A hard knock at the window made him start.

Borodin *hated* being taken by surprise. Had Zolin seem him jump? He should know better than to startle him like that. It was true that the cell phone towers were temporarily out so Zolin couldn't call ahead on his cell, but still.

And then Borodin peered closer. Zolin looked stressed, pale even in the darkness lit only by the streetlights. He had an unconscious Goodkind over one shoulder. Zolin was very strong but had difficulty shoving the man into the backseat of the town car and moved stiffly.

He limped as he walked to the driver's side of the car.

"What happened?" Borodin asked.

Zolin blew out an angry breath as he checked the rearview mirror and pulled out. "Fucker was armed and *waiting* for me. There must be sensors to the side of the house I couldn't see. Winged me. Had to wrestle him to the ground. We're going to keep him handcuffed all the way to Portland."

Shameful, to let an old man best him. "Are you okay to drive?" Borodin asked, voice cold.

"Yeah."

He winced as he drove.

"Where'd he get you?"

"Outer thigh. Took a chunk out of it. Didn't hit anything vital."

"You're bleeding," Borodin accused. Thank God Zolin's DNA wouldn't be on record here. But if the American authorities somehow caught him and traced him back to the abduction of a former FBI agent...

Zolin glanced down. "Yeah." His voice was dismissive. Well, hell. Zolin hadn't thought it through. Bloodstains were bloodstains. Borodin was going to have to hire cutouts to eliminate the town car, break it down into pieces and spread them over a wide tract of terrain. He hated this, fixing problems on the fly. In a foreign country.

The rental agency would put a black mark against the name of one William Novella who hadn't returned a vehicle. So that identity was compromised.

"Will you be able to pilot the plane?"

Zolin must have sensed something in his tone because he glanced over to Borodin. "Don't worry about it. I'll patch it up and inject with a painkiller. And I'll be copilot. But you're going to have to watch this guy. He's tricky."

Borodin simply turned his head to look at Zolin. Zolin flicked a glance at him, then gripped the wheel harder and concentrated on the road.

Message received.

They rolled up to the hangar in the general aviation sector of the airport. No one stopped them, no one questioned them, no one paid them any attention at all.

Amazing. Simply amazing. It was as if America had built up a series of private airports all over the country for the rich to move around in, encased in their own private bubble.

When the town car rolled to a stop, Borodin got out and stood watching while Zolin wrestled with the still unconscious body, face an expressionless mask. But he was very pale and the side of his trousers was black with blood.

Milekhin appeared at the top of the stairs and casually descended. Without saying anything, it was Milekhin who carried the body up the airplane steps. Zolin headed up, trying not to limp, like an alpha wolf that doesn't dare show weakness.

Borodin was last up. By the time he stepped into the luxurious cabin, Goodkind was duct-taped to one of the seats, head lolling on his shoulder.

Borodin had a preloaded syringe of norepinephrine that would wake Goodkind right up. In six hours, a lot of information could be gained, particularly in an enclosed space ten thousand meters above the earth where no one could hear him scream.

Though Borodin sincerely hoped not to have to use the instruments in one of the briefcases. Maybe he'd gotten soft in his years as a businessman, decades after the hard things he'd done in Afghanistan, but he'd prefer not to shed blood if possible. He'd rough Goodkind up a little, test his mettle. Then decide how to proceed.

He didn't care either way what happened to Goodkind. All he wanted was Darin's daughter. All he wanted were the Deti.

Zolin had patched himself up and was in the cockpit. Borodin had a platter of cheese and fruit and a nice Sauternes, and then with a sigh, somewhere over the flat plains of the middle of the country, brought out the syringe of norepinephrine, the natural hormone of vigilant concentration, a stress hormone. Goodkind would wake up with a pounding heart, hypervigilant, with an increased blood flow to muscles and brain.

In excellent condition, in other words, to answer questions.

Borodin injected the syringe in Goodkind's thigh, sitting across from him in one of the hypercomfortable leather seats, separated by a small table. The ideal layout for two businesspeople getting business done.

Which was exactly as Borodin considered it. He and Goodkind were going to have a trade-off. Goodkind had something he wanted—the location of Darin's daughter. And Borodin held something of value to Goodkind—his life.

Borodin sat patiently while Goodkind rose back up into consciousness, step-by-step. He saw the actual moment when Goodkind became aware, but still pretended to be unconscious. Someone less observant than Borodin would have missed it.

"Welcome back to the world, Special Agent Goodkind," he said calmly.

Goodkind's head lifted and he looked directly into Borodin's eyes. As his medical records indicated, he wasn't in good shape. He was very pale and from the skin hanging from his jawline he'd lost a lot of weight recently. But his light gray eyes blazed and his lips pressed together in a thin line.

The message couldn't have been clearer. *Not talking.*

All right. The dance now began.

"Now, you might be wondering what you are doing in a plane. You might even be wondering where we are going. And you might be curious as to whether you are going to survive this. Well, let me ease your mind. You are flying to Portland, Oregon with us because we are looking for a young woman I'm told you consider your ward. Which is interesting because that is her name. Felicity Ward. Except it is not. Felicity Ward is actually Nikolai Darin's daughter."

Goodkind's eyes fluttered and his mouth grew tighter.

"Ah, I see these names mean something to you, as they should. Nikolai Darin defected to the West in 1989 with his wife, Irina. And they had a daughter, whose name eventually ended up as Felicity Ward, which is a ridiculous name for a Russian woman. But—ridiculous name or not, we'd like to talk to this young woman because she might know the whereabouts of something that belonged to the Soviet Union and now belongs to the Russian Federation."

Sudden understanding. Goodkind probably thought that he presented a blank facade but he didn't. He was fairly easy to read.

"And now, Special Agent Goodkind, we come to the last point I made. Whether you are going to survive this trip. The answer is yes. Of course you will survive this, as long as you give us information that leads to our apprenhending Felicity Ward."

"Go to hell," Goodkind growled.

"No doubt I will." Borodin yawned. He was quite tired. "But not just yet. And certainly not for this. I fought in Afghanistan. I will certainly not go to hell for torturing and killing one American."

When Borodin used the words *torture* and *kill*, Goodkind's expression didn't change. *Pizdets*. A brave man. Brave men were terrible to deal with. Recalcitrant and unyielding.

"However, beyond that, I have no desire to deal with the consequences of, let's say, commandeering a US federal agent. So once I have the information I need and we have parted ways, you will be free to go."

Goodkind gave a feral smile. "Riiiight." Drawing the word out.

"Alas, certain nuances of the English language elude me, but I take it that is sarcasm. Yes?"

"Yes."

"And yet I have every intention of letting you go, albeit as you would say, a little worse for wear. So. You give me information on Nikolai Darin's daughter, and when the time is right I release you and no mention of this is ever made by you to anyone."

Goodkind glared. But he was impotent.

"So, when was the last time you saw or heard from Darinova?"

Those thin lips turned upward. "You can call her that, but she is as American as I am."

"Indeed. So where is this paragon of Americanness?"

Goodkind smiled fully. "Bite me."

Borodin sighed. "Another idiom. Probably not a flattering one."

Borodin smiled into Goodkind's eyes.

"So, Special Agent," he said. "It looks like we are going to have a nice, long talk."

THREE PAIRS OF eyes were staring at her. Blue, dark brown, light brown.

It was time. She'd been keeping secrets all her life. There'd been secrets in her life since before she was born, even. She'd had to switch identities in the womb. All those secrets, all those years. They felt like boulders weighing her down. Sometimes Felicity felt as though she was at the bottom of a deep well and only knew the world through the opening way up high, unreachable, untouchable.

Lately, she'd felt as if she was choking, only it wasn't physiological, it was psychological. The choking sensation came upon her more and more often, as if something heavy was on her chest, pressing in. It was her isolation and loneliness, of course. She was a homebody by nature but it was turning into agoraphobia. Talking to people was becoming harder and harder, while at the same time she craved human contact, like a prisoner craves sunlight.

She had three people here who wanted to communicate with her. Well, maybe not Jacko. At times he seemed on the verge of hostility, but that was because he suspected her of endangering Lauren. It didn't make her angry, it endeared him to her. In her world, affection, loyalty, devotion, love were rare things. Lauren was lucky.

None of the three showed any signs of impatience as

she worked through this in her head. Felicity was really good at working through problems in her head. She liked it and she trusted herself. But this time it wasn't just her head that was involved, it was her heart. And she had a lot less experience trusting her heart.

But you had to start somewhere and these three people quivering to help her seemed to be a good place.

Or not.

How to know?

The man after her might not have anything to do with her past and her family's past. But if her father was involved, there was no one she could turn to. The Marshals had officially given her one last identity and turned her loose. She no longer had a case officer. The only person in that world that knew of her past couldn't help. Al Goodkind was old and not well. He'd retired to his country house in Virginia and tended roses and drank bourbon.

Maybe she had her new team right in front of her. And maybe not.

This was horrible. She was tearing herself apart. This had to stop, right now.

"Metal," she said, turning to him, putting a hand on his powerful forearm. Warmth, strength. Electricity. His light brown eyes seemed to glow.

"Yeah."

"Can you bring me my computer backpack?"

"Sure." In a few seconds he was back, placing her backpack on her lap.

Felicity sat still for a moment, fingers stroking the straps. The backpack was gray but she could see where her blood had stained it. She should wash it.

Stalling. She was stalling.

With a sigh, Felicity unzipped the top, took out her specially designed laptop, then dug down deep, ripping open a hidden pocket covered with a flap that had a Velcro closure. The pocket was lined with Kevlar and didn't show anything on airport-quality metal detectors. It would show up on the FBI and NSA and CIA metal detectors, but for flying she was safe.

She scrabbled with her fingers for a moment. Ah, there it was.

Right after her parents died, she'd kept it close in a small pouch under her clothes. Her last connection with her parents. But she didn't wear it anymore. She just always kept it with her. If she lost it, she'd lose a part of herself.

Her father had said to keep it with her, always.

The pouch was made of very soft suede. She pulled it out and placed it on the table between her two outstretched hands, palms down. All three of them looked at the pouch, at her, back to the pouch.

She blew out a breath. Point of no return. Her mother had had a saying when taking a decision. Either it will turn out really really well or really really bad.

Time to find out.

Knowing all eyes were on her, knowing those eyes were friendly, she opened the string closure and gently tipped the contents of the pouch on the table.

A large gold medallion.

She nodded at Metal, waved a finger at it. "Go ahead."

He picked it up gently in his big hand, examined it. A pure gold medallion, measuring almost three inches across. It nearly covered the palm of her hand but looked tiny in Metal's huge one. On one side a bearded man in profile. On the other, a goddess emerging from the clouds. Around the rim the words *Inventas vitam juvat excoluisse per artes.* They improved life on earth by their art.

Felicity recognized the exact moment when Metal understood what he was looking at. His expression didn't change, but his features tightened.

"This is a Nobel Prize medallion," Metal said.

She nodded. "For physics. The 1989 Nobel Prize for Physics was awarded to Nikolai Darin. My father. At the time, a citizen of the Soviet Union."

"A Nobel. He must have been really smart," Metal said, and she nodded. Yes. Her father had been a sad man for as long as she could remember but he had been very, very smart.

"Your dad was a defector?" Jacko asked. The way he said it made her bristle a little.

"Yes." She gave him a hard look. "He defected from the Soviet Union, a dictatorship at the time. Actually, it still is, though it's called Russia now."

Metal frowned slightly. "I remember reading about it. Didn't he die right after? I remember thinking what a bummer to die just after receiving the Nobel."

"No," she said. "He defected. He had the KGB following his every footstep but he managed to contact the CIA head of station in Stockholm and they got him out. The CIA faked his death and they escaped, my father and my mother. At the time, though she didn't know it, my mother was pregnant with me."

Silence.

"Wow," Lauren finally said softly.

"Are your parents still alive?" Jacko asked, eyes narrowed. "Is this about them?" Lauren jabbed him in the side with an elbow, but he just looked at her then back at Felicity. "Are you caught up in some Cold War thing?"

"I don't know," Felicity answered truthfully. "I've thought about it, but I don't see how. The Russians at the time were satisfied that my parents died. Then they—" Her voice caught. She waited a minute to steady it. "They really did die in a car accident but years later, in 2009. Whoa." She wiped the moisture from her eyes. "Sorry."

"You're entitled." Metal's deep voice was very gentle. "That's quite a story. I imagine after they defected they were relocated by the Marshals Service, given new identities."

She nodded. "Aleksandr and Anna Valk. My parents' English was never really good, certainly they couldn't pass as native speakers. So they were relocated as Estonians. This was the period in which the former peoples of the Soviet Empire were starting to rebel. Estonia, Latvia, Lithuania. Ukraine. There were lots of dissidents emigrating from the countries of the former Empire. My father worked as an engineer at a factory near Chicago but he disappeared for weeks at a time."

"Being debriefed, probably," Metal said.

"I suppose so. We never really talked about it. My… entire childhood, we never talked about big things. We never talked about the past and certainly not about the future. My mother spoke only Russian to me and I learned to read Russian before I learned to read English. I was twelve when they told me the truth. Soviet Russia was only a vague concept to me, pure history. It imploded when I was two. I guess they figured I was old enough to keep secrets. There were these huge black holes in our lives. Like an astrophysicist I had to try to figure out things from the size and shape of the black holes. My parents told me very little, except for the story of their escape the night my father received the Nobel."

"What kind of physicist was he?" Jacko asked.

"Nuclear," she answered and a deep silence filled the room. Metal and Jacko exchanged glances.

"Well, that's…interesting," Metal said finally. "So we have nuclear weapons here in the mix."

"This was over twenty-five years ago. A generation ago. I don't know what bearing it could have on what's happening now."

"Tell me about the names," Lauren said suddenly. "How you have so many names."

"Actually," Metal said, "I'd rather talk about nukes."

"Yeah," Jacko growled.

"We're hardwired to respond to nuclear threats," Metal added apologetically.

"Names first," Lauren said, her tone so decisive the guys looked at each other and shrugged. "How you ended up having lots of names."

"Okay. Names." Felicity blew out a breath. "The name on my birth certificate was Katrin. Katrin Valk. Estonian for Katherine. I think someone simply went to an encyclopedia and looked up Estonian names. My parents had no say in naming me. They were simply presented with it. My mother hated it. But then she hated more or less everything about her new life. We were in a small town about fifty miles from Chicago and the Marshals Service discouraged trips. So my mother, who was a biochemist and a highly cultivated woman, was forced to stay in a small town and she wasn't allowed to work. They said it was bad enough my father insisted on having a job. My mother never called me Katrin, not once. She called me Alina, after her sister. I was in first grade when I discovered I was actually named Katrin because when the teacher did roll call I didn't answer to Katrin. And my English was very shaky. It was…a lesson."

God. Coming home in tears because she'd fought the teacher on the issue of her name and she'd done it in a language she didn't speak well. And in the end she was wrong. She'd felt frustrated and ashamed and angry.

Her father had listened to her telling the story, gulping with sobs, and retired to his study. Her mother was just angry and told her that she had to use Katrin in school. But never in the home.

"So," she said with a sigh. "That was Katrin. When I was twelve something happened. I never understood exactly what and of course no one talked to me. With hindsight I realize that someone in the Marshals Service or the FBI—because they followed my father's case closely too—thought that someone had been leaking information. That there was a mole in the system. We were uprooted in the middle of the night, transferred to a small town in Iowa and given new names. So I became Emma. Emma Lukas. We became Lithuanian. My mother hated Iowa too."

Lauren was listening wide-eyed. "How many more to go?"

"Names?"

Lauren nodded. "My mom had a friend who had eight names, seven marriages. Are you going to break that record without the fun of marriage and divorce?"

"Nope. Just one more name."

"Piker." Lauren smiled and Felicity smiled back. "So we're now at Emma Lukas."

Felicity nodded. "Emma didn't last long. After my parents died, the Marshals contacted me. I was an adult and no longer under their protection in any way. But this old marshal, together with another old FBI agent, got together to give me a going-away gift. A new identity, birth certificate, passport, the works. And this time I got to choose my name. First name. They'd already chosen the last name. Ward."

"So you chose Felicity."

She nodded. "I was ready to apply to MIT. I'd been using Felicity as my internet handle for a few years. I probably shouldn't have chosen Felicity as my name but I love Felicity Smoak and I wanted a name that meant something to me. So they created Felicity Ward from the ground up. I had a straight A average except for a journalism class my sophomore year. I was acting out and got a C. They wiped the C out and gave me a perfect score."

"Whoa," Lauren said. "That's quite a story."

"Okay. That's it with the names," Metal said. "Now the nukes."

"I can't imagine that we're talking any kind of nuclear threat." Felicity was sad and tired. The sky outside the window was turning dark but there was still enough light to see the snow falling.

All of this needed to come out, but it was so wrenching. "My father was a scientist. I don't know much about what he did back in Russia but he was a good man. I think he worked in the field of energy, nuclear reactors. But I'm not certain. He never ever talked about his work, certainly not his work in Soviet Russia. He worked in a city called Chelyabinsk."

Metal came to attention like a dog coming to a point. "Chelyabinsk. A *naukograd*. A science city. Cities that were closed off to the outside world because they worked on top secret stuff. They worked on all kinds of weapons in those cities, bioweapons, chemical weapons, nukes."

"They also did basic research," Felicity said stiffly. "That was what my father got the Nobel for—uncovering the structure of neutrinos in magnetic fields."

"So why did he defect?" Jacko asked. His tone was aggressive and though Felicity couldn't blame him, she felt worn-out. Yes, her father had defected, had betrayed his country. But the country had been a dictatorship and in any case, the country he betrayed was no more, hadn't been a country for a generation.

These were battles that had been fought before she was born. The Cold War, the hostility between the United States and the Soviet Union, had cost her family dearly. Her father had uprooted himself and her mother from what her mother said had been a comfortable existence in search of some ideal he never found. Her mother had spent the rest of her life embittered at the move, unable to settle in the United States, living through a daughter she steeped in Russian culture and literature as compensation.

Felicity had been a battleground from the moment she'd been born. A child of divided loyalties, of a decision whose effects were felt a generation later, still painful like a sword to the heart. The only answer was—had always been—to lie low, curve in on herself like a small animal in a forest of predators.

She was so freaking *tired*. Tired of the drama of her parents' defection, tired of switching identities every few years, tired of dark secrets she couldn't understand—and now never would—swirling around her head. Those dark secrets had affected every second of her childhood and now were spilling over into her adult life, like a curse she couldn't shake. She'd spend the rest of her life in its shadow, keeping secrets that weren't hers.

Her eyes closed under the weight of them.

Metal rapped his knuckles on the table, hard, and she started.

"Okay," he said standing up. "I'm the medic here and my patient has had enough. She's been cut, she's bled, she's had stitches. We'll go over this when she's rested, and we'll consult with Bud. Bud's our Portland PD guy. Good guy, really smart." This to her.

"No," she said. "I'm fine." But she didn't sound convincing, even to her own ears.

Jacko was up, cupping Lauren's elbow. Lauren walked around the table, bent to hug her. "I brought you some clothes in the carry-on, and some other stuff. You should have everything you need. It's going to be okay," she whispered. "Metal and Jacko are good at this stuff. So's the company they work for. And Bud Morrison will definitely help. You've got some amazing people on your side. You're safe."

Everyone kept *saying* that. Felicity didn't want to rain on anyone's parade but she couldn't see how anyone could say she was safe. Except for right this instant, of course. She was safe *right now*.

She'd seen her attacker and though he'd been young and fit, he wasn't anything like Metal, who all but had *don't mess with me* tattooed on his forehead and whose muscles had muscles. As a former SEAL, he'd know weaponry and martial arts and stuff. God knows she'd played Call of Duty enough. He knew what he was doing. If he'd been the one who wanted to kidnap her no way would she have escaped. It just wouldn't have been possible.

Right now, right this minute, even weak as she was, with Metal in the room and Jacko, too, she was as safe as safe could be. It would take an earthquake to hurt her and she had no doubt that Metal would throw himself over her to protect her.

So maybe that should be enough. She was safe. For now. Maybe that's all it ever would be. Safe. For now.

"Thanks." Felicity hugged Lauren back, savoring her soft warmth. Absorbing through her skin the affection Lauren felt for her. They'd only just met in meatspace but she was as sure as she could be that they were friends. Like Beast Boy and Cyborg.

Lauren held her by the shoulders, a frown on her pretty face. "You look really tired, honey. We shouldn't have kept you up talking for so long."

"Well." Felicity shrugged. "Considering we were talking about how to find the guy who attacked me and how to stop him, I think it was a conversation worth having. And I'm fine. A little tired, as you say, but fine. I got really good medical care." The corner of Metal's mouth lifted.

Lauren's frown deepened. "Listen. I'm really sorry but—" She glanced at Jacko. "I have an out-of-town appointment tomorrow morning I can't put off. This media mogul who is building a brand-new house…mansion…*palace* actually. He wants me to take sketches of the house in various stages of construction and then I'll make a series of watercolors. I had a sketching session scheduled for tomorrow morning. The place is on the south slope of Mount Hood. It's near Timberline Lodge, and Jacko and I made reservations to spend the night. We'll be back tomorrow afternoon. I can cancel if you want—"

"Oh God, no!" The words escaped her mouth without even thinking them. Lauren had been on the run for two years. She'd nearly been killed a couple of weeks ago and Jacko had been shot. They needed—they deserved—a little getaway. "I couldn't bear the thought of you canceling your stay. Metal is taking very good care of me and besides, I think I'm going to sleep for, like, two solid days."

"After she's rested, she's going to have to look at a lot of footage and nobody else can do it for her." Metal's deep voice chimed in. "Airport, hotel. If she finds the guy in the footage it'll go to facial recognition databases. That's all stuff she has to do and the computer systems have to do. Come over when you get back from Timberline." He glanced at her, his gaze like a sudden wash of heat, then focused again on Lauren. "She'll feel better by the time you guys get back. Promise."

Lauren nodded. "Yeah, okay." She rubbed her cheek against Felicity's. "You'll be fine here," she whispered.

Felicity squeezed her hand. She would. She felt utterly safe with Metal. Though she felt something else too, something so new and scary she wasn't sure she welcomed it.

Patting Lauren's hand, she smiled up at her. "I'll be fine. I told you. Right now I feel like sleeping for a week."

Metal's voice was hard. "Felicity is going to sleep and eat and do nothing else for the foreseeable future. Except check footage when we get it."

"Sounds like a plan," she sighed. Some switch somewhere had flipped and she was exhausted. The restorative effects of sleep and good food had worn off. She had to fight to keep from laying her head down on the table and falling asleep again.

"Okay." Jacko clapped his hands and stood, taking Lauren's elbow in what looked like an affectionate but unbreakable grip. He looked down at her and Felicity could so easily see what he was feeling. He probably imagined himself a tough guy who didn't show emotions but she had grown up with Russians who had a thousand emotions a day. He wasn't hard to read at all. He liked her but he loved Lauren. So to the extent that Lauren cared for her, he was okay with everything. But he was not okay with anything violent touching Lauren.

Man, Felicity was down with that. She didn't want anything to touch Lauren either. Lauren had had enough violence for ten lifetimes.

Metal and Jacko had had violence in their lives, too, but every line of their bodies showed that they were perfectly equipped to deal with it.

"Take care," Lauren said. Jacko held her coat up for her, and then they left.

It was late afternoon and the weather was scary bad. The sky was already dark, swollen with bruised-looking clouds. When Lauren opened the door to leave, Felicity saw huge icy snowflakes blowing diagonally and a gust of cold air blew in. There were several inches of snow on the ground.

That was fine. Snow was in her DNA. God knew how many Darin ancestors had lived through seven-month winters. Snowstorms didn't scare her. When the weather reports indicated snow and cold coming to Vermont, she just planned to spend even more days in the house than normal.

Thinking about it now, though, she realized that she

never acknowledged the sadness that had laced through her at the thought of spending days and days on her own without hearing a human voice that didn't come through a screen.

Now? Now she had Metal who was going to look after her. She could be weak and it wouldn't matter.

"To bed with you." It was as if he was reading her mind. "Lauren brought you some stuff from her house. A winter coat and yoga pants and sweaters and socks and underwear and stuff. You're a little taller than she is but you both have more or less the same build. So you'll have some stuff to put on when you wake up."

He looked her up and down thoroughly. Usually Felicity didn't like scrutiny. For as long as she could remember, her family had avoided any kind of attention. But this didn't feel like scrutiny, it felt like…appreciation. Male appreciation.

And it felt delicious.

She shivered and that gleam in his eye was instantly replaced by concern. "You're cold. I'll turn the heat up. In the meantime let's get you back to bed with some hot tea."

Without even questioning it, Metal bent and picked her up, as if she had lost the use of her legs. Maybe she had. Between feeling weak because she'd been stabbed and feeling weak every time Metal got close, she didn't trust herself to walk back into the bedroom.

There was no thought involved, she simply reached up and wound her arms around his neck as he picked her up and carried her through the living room to the bedroom. Time slowed to a crawl.

She was aware of every single thing, with a shocking intensity. Mostly she lived inside her own head. She could finish a meal and not realize what she'd just eaten, at any given moment she wouldn't remember how she was dressed. She could spend entire days without noticing the time going by.

Now everything was hyperintense, each object glowing, a heaviness to the air, every second imprinted in her brain.

Just as when he carried her into the kitchen, Felicity was aware of the play of Metal's muscles against her arms and her side as he walked easily into the bedroom. Everything was saturated with color, deeper and richer. With her nose so close to his neck, she could smell him. Nothing overt like a cologne, more like soap and man and something delicious that was probably sex. She nearly sighed at the thought.

Though she was weak and wounded, though she'd only just met him, Felicity recognized—more from reading novels than actual personal experience—that she was wildly attracted to this man. It didn't have any known rational reason behind it, it just was. He wasn't in any way good-looking. His features were rough, his nose was crooked, his skin was weather-beaten, which made him look a little older than he probably was.

Her hormones didn't care.

Because the entire outer package was pure sex. He hadn't even really done anything, either, other than a few looks that could be interpreted as male interest.

She knew she wasn't ugly and she'd had more than her share of male interest. It was rarely reciprocated. Mainly she dated nerds and had gone to bed with a few in entirely unmemorable encounters lasting, on average, about five minutes, start to end. As a matter of fact, overt male stares made her uncomfortable and was one of the reasons she mainly just stayed home.

But, wow. This time she *was* interested. Her entire body had turned into an erogenous zone so that yes, her womb and her breasts felt warm and heavy—right out of the romance novel playbook—but she also tingled in the most unlikely places. The insides of her arms, for example. Where they touched Metal's shoulder muscles. Boy, were they turned on. The backs of her knees held in the crook of his elbows, they were sitting up and taking notice too.

Her nose twitched with the desire to rub against the skin of his neck and just inhale.

Being sliced open had messed with her. Her attacker had somehow sliced her heart open, too, because feelings and sensations she'd never had before were pouring in.

This was crazy, to feel so intensely for a man she knew nothing about except for the fact that he was the friend of her friend's friend. And was brave. And amazingly sexy.

Crazy.

They reached the bedroom and Metal put her down on her feet, keeping one big arm around her. The only light inside the bedroom was a dim lamp on the Shaker dresser. Metal was visible more in outline than anything else, tall, broad-shouldered, his face in shadow.

Oh God, in letting her slide down she'd brushed against the slabs of his chest and abs and…a definite bulge. He was paying no attention to his own body as he pulled down the covers and eased her under them, pulling the covers back up over her.

He ran the back of a long finger down her face. "I'm

going to make you some tea and after that I want you to rest."

Felicity nodded, unsure how to respond.

She had no experience being looked after. Zero. Her mother had been an interesting and intellectually gifted woman with no motherly instincts at all. Felicity couldn't remember the last time someone had looked after her, fussed over her. The last time someone had said "you should rest." There were no responses in her tool kit other than staying very still. Feeling his finger against her skin, watching him watching her.

Ice suddenly beat against the windowpane and she gave a little start. She usually disappeared when working at the computer, and she wasn't used to being so focused on someone else that she forgot the outside world

Metal's face didn't give her any clue as to what he was thinking. Was she this chore he'd been landed with? *Here, take care of Lauren's friend because you know medicine and can change dressings and besides, where else can she go?*

Did he mind having her invade his space, take up his time?

God. Did he have a girlfriend he was going to have to explain things to? *Hey, honey, listen. Sorry, there's this girl in my bed. No, it's not what you think. She landed on Lauren's doorstep wounded with someone after her. Well, what could I do? You tell me.*

All those thoughts were buzzing around in her head like angry bees. Metal leaned down and kissed her cheek. All the buzzing stilled and a lazy warmth spread through her, completely void of thought.

It was pure instinct. If she'd thought it through she

would never have done it, never. She didn't overthink it the way she did everything. She didn't think at all.

His cheek was warm, with a tiny bite of bristliness that was exciting. With his face in darkness, backlit by the lamp, she could see faint blond stubble on his cheeks as he came closer to her. She just closed her eyes and moved instinctively.

Her hand lifted, curled around his strong neck as she felt his warm lips against her cheek. She sighed and her fingers tightened.

Metal had planted a hand on either side of her so she was caged in by him, but she didn't feel trapped. Oh no. When Metal pulled back, narrow-eyed, frowning, she tightened her fingers again. *Come to me.* She might as well have spoken the words out loud.

Because though his face tightened and he wasn't smiling, something else was going on. The skin above his cheekbones was flushed, his nostrils widened as if he had to take in more air than usual. The skin around his eyes crinkled.

She'd led what most people would consider a reclusive life but even she could recognize male arousal. She was looking right at it. She'd read about it in books of course, but this was the real deal and didn't need labeling. And this wasn't nerdy arousal, either, where the guy's voice rose an octave and his hands shook.

No, this was a man's man and he wanted her.

"Felicity?" His voice was guttural, rough. Not tender. She responded to his voice and his look with a flood of heat running through her body.

She turned her head just as he turned his and oh. *Oh.* One of his hands lifted from the mattress and cupped the back of her head. His mouth settled on hers, warm, chin slightly bristly, electric. Just as she got used to the feeling of his mouth on hers, he opened his mouth and slanted his head and kissed her deeply. Her hands shot to his wrist to hold on as he explored her mouth. Every time his tongue met hers heat shot through her and her womb contracted. She felt moisture pooling in her sex, the very first time that had happened to her. Ever.

She gasped in his mouth and he lifted his head.

He wasn't smiling. His face was tight with tension as he stared at her, light brown eyes glowing with heat and light.

Felicity's heart was pounding so hard she was sure he could see it if he lowered his gaze. Instead his golden eyes held hers. "You okay?"

Was she okay? It was really hard to tell. Her stitches hurt a little. Her breasts felt supersensitive, a little bomb had gone off between her legs. Her lips felt swollen. All in all…

"Hmm. Yeah."

And then he smiled and oh God, he shouldn't do that. Not when her emotions were all over the place—it wasn't fair. Because though the smile didn't make him handsome it sure made him sexy in a "Me Tarzan, you Jane" sort of way.

His hand followed her head down to the pillow and then he touched the tip of a finger to the tip of her nose. "Tea," he announced.

What? Oh yeah. She nodded. "Tea. Definitely."

SEVEN

In the air, en route to Portland

THE PLANE WAS very luxurious, so it beat the interrogations of his past. Borodin had interrogated men in caves and dank prisons that smelled of fear and sweat and blood. An Airbus had those beat, hands down. It was warm and comfortable and they had food and excellent wine on hand.

Not for Goodkind, of course. Goodkind slipped in and out of consciousness even after Borodin had given him an injection of adrenaline. He'd passed out for the fifth time. And he hadn't talked yet.

Borodin slapped Goodkind across the face, hard, taking pleasure in Goodkind's appearance. In service, Goodkind would have had the arrogance of being a public servant in one of the US government's elite services. A successful member of the most powerful government in the history of the world. There was an built-in status to that, the kind of pride that was both earned and conferred.

This man was defeated, no longer looking like he belonged to his country's *nomenklatura*. His face was sagging from pain, stress, fatigue.

Borodin needed to keep him alive until he found Darin's daughter, so of all the many and varied tricks he'd learned in the KGB—tricks that would make the most hardened prisoners, men who'd survived the gulag, talk—he used only the mildest. Intimidation, sleep, and food and water deprivation. And not too much of that, either, because he didn't want Goodkind to die on him before his usefulness was over.

Once Felicity Ward—Darinova—was in their hands and Borodin had what he needed, Goodkind could be dispatched quickly with a bullet to the back of the head.

Borodin did not have the pain sickness some of the agents in the KGB had had. True, they had all been adept at extracting information. Many an Afghan insurgent had talked after gut-wrenching torture sessions and though many said torture didn't work, in Borodin's experience it actually did. Everyone broke eventually under toture.

The torturers included.

Because whatever it was that was in them that could inflict pain for hours, for days and do it over and over again was like a loose cog in a machine that eventually broke the machine itself.

Borodin wasn't like that. He wanted to extract the information from the FBI agent like you extract oil from the ground, then eliminate him neatly, cleanly.

Goodkind's swollen eyes opened briefly and he gave a brief laugh. "She escaped your guy, huh? She's really smart. Too smart for you."

His face was messed up. At the start, Borodin had been certain that low-level rough tactics would work. After all, this was a retired man, basically a bureaucrat all his life. He was flabby, as many Americans were. The good life took its toll. Borodin had slapped him around a little, dispassionately, to shake some information loose and found to his surprise that the old man was made of steel under the flab.

"We'll see how smart she is," Borodin told Goodkind. "Portland is a small city. My man is good. He'll find her. You can be sure of that."

They'd had this discussion before. Goodkind shrugged.

Borodin crossed his legs and swung one foot. A very well-shod foot. He'd had them made in Florence in a small shop just off the Ponte Vecchio. Beautiful and stylish. The West did have its uses. He would never have found a cobbler like Renzi anywhere in Russia. He extracted sharp shears from the briefcase at his feet, showed them to Goodkind.

"Theoretically speaking, if I were to cut off a few fingers, would you tell me who Darinova was meeting in Portland?"

"Sorry." Goodkind bared his teeth again. "I'd like to think that I could resist the pain, and maybe I could, who knows? But the truth is that I have no idea who she could be meeting. I had no idea she was going to Portland. I had no idea she was even traveling. Felicity rarely travels. She mostly stays in her house. I honestly know very little about her life. So if you cut my fingers off—" he gave an apologetic smile, "—it would be wasted effort."

"Pity." Borodin was annoyed. "Her house was singularly void of any information at all. It was also void of most objects people might consider necessary to a home. She has the basics—bed, couch, kitchen, desk. Very few clothes for such a beautiful young girl. Mainly electronics and a collection of computers and tablets. One computer appeared to be missing. If she made reservations online it was on the computer she traveled with." Good-kind made a grimace. "What?"

Goodkind was actually smiling. "Even if you had her computer right here, trust me when I say it wouldn't tell you anything she didn't want you to know."

Borodin drummed his hand on the table. Stalemate.

His cell buzzed with an incoming message. He read it and tried to keep his face impassive. But this was a potential breakthrough.

He looked up from his cell into Goodkind's bloodied but unbroken face. "So, Mr. Goodkind. I understand you have a granddaughter you are very fond of. Kay. Dr. Kay Hudson. And I know where she lives."

He smiled as the blood drained from Goodkind's face. Everyone has a weak spot and Borodin had just found Goodkind's.

METAL WALKED STIFFLY into the kitchen. Man that was close. Looking down into that incredibly pretty face, sky-blue eyes fixed on his, lips swollen and wet—fuck, walking away had been *hard*.

About as hard as his dick.

He'd never been so happy to have a woman staring at his face. Usually that was a deal-breaker for sex. His face wasn't what got chicks into his bed. They usually looked at his body and often their gaze just went straight to his junk. Some women knew he'd been a SEAL and wanted a piece of that. That was sex he didn't want to have, because they either wanted to fuck a killer or wanted to see if he got violent.

A couple of chicks who *wanted* to be hurt left him feeling sick and sad. He made sure of what he was getting into nowadays and if there was even a whiff of that, of a woman wanting to be hurt, he was out faster'n shit through a goose, as a teammate from Alabama used to say.

One kiss. Almost chaste except for a little tongue and boom! Hard as a rock. So he'd been really glad she seemed to be fascinated by his face because if her gaze went lower he'd have been busted.

Jesus.

She was fucking *wounded*. Had fucking *stitches*. What was *wrong* with him? He was a freaking medic. Medics took healing people really seriously. He sure as hell did. The world was broken and anything he could do to put a little of it back together again, well—he was there.

This was the very first time he'd wanted to fuck someone he'd patched up. It was a weird feeling, except, well look at her. He peeked over his shoulder for a second from the living room and their eyes met and he felt a punch to his chest.

God, she was so fucking beautiful. And so freaking smart too. Genius-level, Lauren had said. Father a Nobel winner. Way, *way* out of his league.

His dick had no business getting involved, it should just shut up and stay down. The bad thing was he'd have to be a dead man not to react to beauty and brains. She was incredibly desireable, the most beautiful woman he'd ever seen

And yet, beautiful and smart as she was, she was also intensely vulnerable. There'd been something so lost and lonely about her as she told her story, her family's story. She'd been like a displaced person all her life, growing up clandestinely learning Russian.

His Irish forebears had done that, generations ago, in

the *scoil ghairid*, the hedge schools. They'd taught their kids Gaelic, though it was against the law. At least they'd all been together. It had just been Felicity and her mom, a woman homesick for her country and a confused young girl, being taught to keep herself secret and separate.

It didn't take a degree in psychology to realize how isolated Felicity must have been growing up, with one name after another, not daring to tell anyone who she really was.

She'd grown up in the shadows and he'd grown up in the light.

That twisted his heart. Cracked it open, actually.

Metal thought he'd left his heart behind in Afghanistan but apparently he hadn't because he could feel it beating hard and fast in his chest. And he was a man whose heart rate didn't go up when intubating a fallen teammate with bullets flying.

Sometimes, in combat, he'd see things with a medical eye. He'd see a guy zigging instead of zagging and think—a bullet's going to catch him. He'd see a teammate react too slowly or react with anger instead of keeping a cool head and he knew that teammate was a goner. If not today, then tomorrow.

So that's how he recognized that he was heading straight for heartbreak, and there was nothing he could do about it.

He made her tea, walked into the bedroom and stopped.

She was lying in his bed, sound asleep, hair a golden halo around her face, one slender graceful hand lying on the bedspread. Well, she needed sleep more than she needed a cup of tea. He went back into the kitchen and poured the hot tea into a one-cup Thermos and set it on the bedside table, then frowned.

She was making small noises. No, he thought as he bent further, she was trying to suppress the noise, as if stifling cries in her sleep. It was painful to hear, both terror and repression at the same time. Reliving her attack in a nightmare. Her eyes were scrolling back and forth under her eyelids, as if she was frantically looking around, trying to find her attacker.

The sick *fuck*. Metal didn't do anger. He'd gone through four fucking years of war without feeling anything but cold righteous duty. But right now? Right now a surge of rage burst to life inside him. He wished he had the fucker in front of him right now because he'd gouge his eyes out, tear his dick off, crush his balls with his hands and then slit his throat. The feelings were savage, unfamiliar.

He watched her, terrified in her sleep. Beads of sweat formed along her temples. Her feet suddenly scissored under the covers; she was running away. Her throat clicked, mouth tightly shut against screams, coming out as whimpers.

God, those whimpers were breaking his heart. He didn't want to wake her up but he couldn't stand to hear them any longer. He touched her shoulder and she quietened instantly. Her face smoothed out, her legs stopped moving restlessly. She reached out in her sleep and her hand curled around his and he could see her move back down into a restorative sleep.

Because he held her hand.

Ah, honey, he thought. He hooked a chair with his foot and sat down, without breaking her hold on him. Man, if holding his hand brought her peace and a feeling of safety, he'd sit here for the next ten years.

He'd sat in the chair by her bed the past two nights, just in case she had a bad reaction to the antibiotics or woke up in pain. And he was perfectly prepared to sit in this chair by her side all this night too. He'd dozed in the chair off and on but he could go without much sleep. All SEALs could, they'd been trained hard to do it.

And right now, he'd do anything, give anything to keep that peaceful expression on her beautiful face. Sitting in a chair was nothing.

So he held her hand and watched over her.

FELICITY WOKE UP SLOWLY, like floating, easy and soft and gentle. She was holding something warm and hard and the warmth from her hand spread through her whole body.

Just before waking up she'd been dreaming about something but she couldn't remember what. A good dream, though. She rarely had those, most of her dreams were dark. In most dreams she was lost and afraid and alone. More times than she could count she would wake up with a start at three o'clock in the morning, sweating and cold and afraid. There was always plenty of milk in the fridge because a bad dream called for a cup of hot milk and honey. But not this dream. It was about emotions more than events, and the emotions were connected to a warm safe place, some kind of haven.

She never had dreams like this so she kept her eyes closed, savoring everything. Her bed felt slightly different but comfortable nonetheless. The comforter felt heavier than usual. She was a little sore along her side, but there was no pain. It was all good. The dream slowly morphed into reality, but she wanted to cling to the dream as long as she could. Finally she opened her eyes and stared at the ceiling, blinking, unsettled. Her ceiling was pale yellow. This ceiling was gray.

But the floaty feeling persisted.

Her hand was held in a firm, warm clasp. She lowered her eyes, looked at her hand, followed up a very large muscled arm to enormously broad shoulders and bright light brown eyes.

Sean. Metal.

The man she'd kissed last night. Not just kissed but *kissed*. The kind of kiss that was a prelude to sex. Sex had definitely been in the air. He'd been aroused and, well, so had she. Her body held memories of that arousal. It had felt as if Metal had thrown some kind of switch and her body had been replaced by someone else's. The feelings had been so strange and new. However strange and new, though, they had been totally unmistakeable. A billion years of evolution had suddenly pushed past her IT-obssessed brain and taken over her body.

What she had felt had been pure sex.

Again, she blushed a bright red, all the blood in her body rising to her face. It was a curse and had been all her life. Her emotions could be read on her skin by just about anybody who wasn't into computers. One of the many reasons she avoided normal people.

"Morning." His deep voice was a soft rumble. As if not wanting to startle her. He was watching her face carefully and if he noticed she was flushed a bright red he didn't say anything. His own face had been flushed last night but it definitely hadn't been from embarrassment.

"Morning." She looked back down at her hand in his.

Her hand had been in his for a long time. Her skin told her that. "Did you sleep at all or did you sit here holding my hand all night?"

He didn't answer which was an answer in itself. She sighed. "You didn't have to—"

"Are you hungry?" he interrupted her.

She was about to answer no when all of a sudden a huge appetite roared into being in her. Extraordinary. She wasn't a big eater, she stayed home all day and she snacked on fruit or yogurt, so hunger was never an issue. Right now it felt as though a hungry lion woke up in her and she was ravenous.

"Actually, I am." Even she could hear the amazement in her voice.

Metal nodded. "Good. That's a really good sign of healing. I'll change your dressing later but first how about breakfast?"

The sky outside the window was dark and bruised-looking. "What time is it?"

"Around nine."

"Wow! All I seem to do is sleep!"

"Yup. And you look it. You look really rested. But I'll bet right now you need to use the bathroom."

As he said the words, she felt an enormous urge to pee. "Yeah."

"Let me help you and you can look at yourself in the mirror. Color has returned to your face, it's amazing. So here's how it's going to work. I'll help you to the bathroom and back and bring you some breakfast, which I think you should have in bed since it's only us. I mean, what's the point of being sick if you can't have breakfast in bed, right? And then afterward, we'll change the dressing and I can help you wash."

Help her wash? She'd have to be, um, naked for that to happen, wouldn't she? Ordinarily she'd shy away from that thought but instead she had an image of her naked and Metal's huge hands on her, smoothing a sponge over her. Her entire body blossomed into heat.

She huffed out a breath in reply, totally unable to form words.

"Good." He gently pulled back the blankets and lifted her out and up, setting her on her feet. "Can you stand? Do you want me to carry you?"

Wow. Being carried again. It had been amazing, *of course* she wanted him to carry her. But she found she could stand on her feet. Honesty and pleasure vied for a brief violent moment inside her and with a sigh of regret, honesty won.

"I can stand, thanks."

It was really true. Standing, walking would have been beyond her twenty-four hours earlier but now she stood without swaying. She felt a little weak but nothing like before. She felt herself again. And though she wasn't going to be carried to the bathroom—her new favorite mode of transportation—he kept a big arm around her back as she walked and that was second best after being carried. She walked normally but slowly, without shuffling, but she also had that strong arm right there, waiting to catch her if she had any problems at all.

It made her confident that she wouldn't, couldn't fall.

He stopped at the bathroom door. Raised his eyebrows.

"I can do this part myself," she said and placed a palm against his chest. Underneath her hand was a slab of muscle, hard and dense. Surprisingly, he placed a large hand over hers, as if to keep her hand where it was.

As if her hand really wanted to be somewhere else insteading of touching the most exciting male chest she'd ever seen.

"Call me if you need me." The tone wasn't a request, it was an order. "I'll be right outside."

She nodded, dropped her hand, went into the bathroom and used the toilet. Washing her hands in the sink, she looked at herself carefully in the mirror. She looked...normal. Her stay-at-home face, sure. No makeup, no lipstick. But her skin color was good and her eyes looked bright, the whites clear.

The T-shirt had to go, though. She'd been wearing it for two days. Though it was kind of cool that she was wearing Metal's T-shirt. To her knowledge she'd never worn anyone else's clothing. It was an odd sensation, wearing someone else's garment so close to her skin. It was blindingly white, very soft, washed many times and huge on her. It could have been a summer nightgown except it gaped so large at the throat.

Lauren had brought her some clothes. She'd have packed a nightgown, as well.

On the sink was a brand-new sealed toothbrush and a travel-sized tube of toothpaste. Smiling, she picked it up and brushed her teeth.

She looked at herself again in the mirror and found that she looked almost exactly as she looked every morning. Better, even. Most mornings she hadn't slept for sixteen hours. The only difference was the slight bulge on her right side which were the bandages. Which Metal would soon change.

There would be healthy flesh beneath the bandages, she could feel it. Stretching, she felt the pull of the stitches but no pain at all. All in all, considering she'd been slashed three days ago, she was in pretty good shape. Some hot food in her stomach and she'd be in great shape.

True to his word, Metal was waiting for her right outside the bathroom. He smiled when he saw her, though he checked her out head to toe. He stuck his elbow out. "Ma'am? May I have the pleasure?"

Oh yeah. "Why yes, sir, indeed, sir. Most chivalrous of you." Two could play at that game.

He walked her back to the bed and she got in. A wooden board rested against the mattress. He pulled her up against the headboard as if she were a doll, settled the pillows at her back and pulled up the board. Flipping open two legs he placed it across her lap.

"A bed tray!" Felicity looked him up and down. Healthy as a horse, strong and fit. The strongest and fittest man she'd ever seen, in fact. "Have you been sick?"

He shook his head. "No, ma'am. Wounded, yes, but never sick."

"Do you have a bed tray because you recovered from your wounds here? It seems a strange thing for someone who looks as healthy as you to have."

"Nah. Made it for you. Look." He directed her eyes and fingers to the undersides of the edges where neat small brass brackets held the bed tray legs open, allowing them to be folded back to the bottom of the tray when not in use. "Took a wooden tray and adapted it so you can eat in bed. Like I said, what's the use of being knifed if you don't get to eat in bed?"

She studied the hinges. They were absolutely perfect. There was nothing to tell that this wasn't a commercial bed tray, that he had adapted it. The workmanship was exquisite. He'd done that for her. She had no idea when.

Maybe while she had been asleep, only she seemed to have a sensory memory of him holding her hand all night. At some point, though, he'd taken the time and trouble to fashion the bed tray for her.

"Thanks." She looked up at him, fingering the brass hinges. "That was incredibly thoughtful of you."

He waved that away. "If you're ready, then we can have breakfast together in here."

"Oh!" Her stomach rumbled audibly and he smiled, patting the air as if saying *patience*.

"Hold that thought. Breakfast. Coming right up."

It was an amazing breakfast. Oatmeal with honey and raisins, hot scones, slices of baked ham, more of that whole wheat bread and a cheese platter. And a bottomless Thermos of hot tea.

Metal put the plate and bowl and a huge mug of tea on her bed tray and used the bedside table as his own tray. He piled his plate with about three times the food she had.

"You first." He was holding a spoonful of oatmeal in front of her. As soon as she opened her mouth he tipped the contents in. A friendly gesture but his face wasn't looking friendly. He looked absolutely completely focused on her.

It was unsettling and sexy as hell to have this man so totally concentrated on her. It was partly the medic in him. He was studying her to see how she was.

And she was fine, just fine.

But there was also pure male interest. The way he looked at her, watched the food disappear into her mouth, observing every movement of her lips. She watched his mouth too.

At one point, they both lifted their gazes at exactly the

same moment. With any other man she'd have laughed but she didn't feel like laughing. They were watching each other so intently the moment felt solemn.

She dropped her gaze back to her food.

"Are you the cook or do you have a sister or significant other who brings you things?" she asked, then realized what that sounded like. It sounded like she was asking him if he was taken. Which wasn't what she meant, of course. Much.

Metal looked her full in the face, expression sober. Felicity was blushing again, cursing herself. She was blurting things out because she was so weak and had no filter between brain and mouth. Her real curse was that she was unused to interacting with people. She was particularly unused to interacting with huge macho guys she happened to find very interesting and amazingly sexy. If she survived this, she was going to make a point of spending time with men who weren't geeks. Practice up.

His face was completely without expression. Not blank so much as unreadable. "That was a question," he said.

Felicity nodded. No use pretending.

"The answer is no. No mother, no sister, no significant other. No unsignificant other, either. No one. You?"

The question stumped her for a second and she knew her face was showing the real kind of blank, as in uncomprehending. Then of course she understood that he was asking the same question back. Was she in a relationship?

Well…no. She seemed to have this relationship force field around her. Men simply bounced off it. And of course she spent most of her time in the house.

No one had ever even asked her if she was with someone. Not even her few geeky boyfriends. They lunged at her when they got their courage together and it had much more to do with them getting in touch with their own gonads than with her.

"No," she answered. "No one. Just like you."

"Why?"

She blinked. "I'm sorry?"

Metal narrowed his eyes and looked her over, making no move to hide what he was doing. "You're beautiful and smart and have all your limbs and teeth from what I can tell. Why on earth aren't you with someone? What's wrong with the guys where you live? They blind or have some kind of illness or something?"

"I…don't get out much. Hardly ever, as a matter of fact. This trip to Portland was my first trip out of town in almost a year. I work on my computer and nowadays it's easy just to order everything online…" Her voice trailed off as he moved closer.

Metal reached across her to lift the tray away, then planted a big hand against her left hip, another against her right hip, leaning forward until his nose practically touched hers. His movements were slow, deliberate and he gave her plenty of time to object if she wanted to. Which was crazy, of course. Why would she want to object?

His face came closer, closer, closer until it was so close it was out of focus and she closed her eyes. Felt the molecules of air shift as he moved his head toward hers then he put his mouth on hers and thought stopped.

She was pure sensation, feeling not thinking. Her brain just switched off, like in sleep only better. Because she was aware of the sensations.

His lips were soft but his stubble was rough against

her skin. He somehow moved above her, in a dominant position and that excited her so much it scared her. He lifted his mouth for a second, so close she could feel his breath—actually she felt as if she was breathing through him. When he spoke, his lips were against hers, voice so deep it seemed to reverberate throughout her chest.

"I'm glad you aren't with anybody. Because you are now."

EIGHT

A BEAUTY LIKE FELICITY, free. Man. Opportunities like this just didn't come his way that often. In battle Metal had two jobs to do—kill and save his guys' lives. So every ounce of opportunity that came his way, he took it, even a split-second opening.

For a second, when she told him she was free— against all odds, against the way the world should be organized because someone like her should be snapped up immediately—she moved toward him. Her mouth opened slightly as she watched him, her hand unfurled, her shoulders relaxed.

She had no idea what she was saying with her body language, but he did.

They were subtle signs but Metal was used to reading subtle signs. He'd once caught a tiny twitch just as a teammate was being zipped up in a body bag. The teammate had been alive, just barely, and Metal had saved his life. He got Christmas cards from the guy, now retired, living with his wife and his dog.

That was all in the land of death Metal had left behind. *This*—this was the land of life, oh God yes. Felicity was life itself.

Moving in on her, moving to kiss her, felt like plugging in to something vast. Like plugging in to the world itself.

He was moving real slow, she could stop him at

any time. But she wasn't stopping him. Nope. When his mouth settled back on hers, she opened up for him, pressing against him, her tongue stroking his.

At the touch of her tongue his dick surged in his pants, from zero to hero in about two seconds. Full-blown erection, too, not some half-assed thing from looking at a pretty woman.

Nope, below the waist he was up and ready for action. He wanted to woo her, court her. He wasn't good at it but he'd seen movies. Except usually the wooing required wit and charm, things he lacked. And on top of that, she had stitches. They were clean and they wouldn't hurt but fucking in the missionary position was out of the question. So those were two good reasons not to jump her, lift up his T-shirt on her, shove his jeans down and slide right in, which was precisely what he wanted to do.

Lucky thing they were taught discipline in the Teams.

He pulled away a little, looking down at her. Fuck, she was beautiful. The Russians were known for their beautiful women. But she was 100 percent nerd, and she couldn't see her own attraction.

He saw it, oh yeah.

Metal watched as Felicity's eyes fluttered open and he smiled at her. It was a real smile. He didn't smile often, mainly he just bared his teeth, so he knew the difference. She was a little mussed, a little confused, completely desirable.

"Hey," he whispered.

"Hey," she answered.

"You know I'm a medic, yeah?"

She nodded, watching his eyes carefully.

"So there's this whole new field of diagnostics to find

out if you're okay. It works really well on women. When being examined by a man."

Now she was smiling, already figuring out where he was going with this. Smart lady. "I haven't heard of that, but it sounds interesting."

Interesting, oh yeah. He nuzzled the soft skin behind her ear, licked it, felt her shudder. He would have smiled back at her but suddenly he didn't feel like smiling. He felt like biting, like crawling on top of her and holding her arms up over her head with one hand and sliding the other up under that huge T-shirt, cupping a soft breast. He felt like sliding her legs apart with his and rubbing his erection against her. He felt like—

Stop that, he told himself. His hard-on was already painful, no use frustrating himself. Concentrate on the here and now, not on what he wanted to do but wouldn't and couldn't.

And anyway the here and now was really great.

"Yeah." He sniffed her, trying not to sound like a dog. But fuck, she smelled good. She smelled of his plain soap but also of something else right underneath. Something fresh and enticing. Her own scent and the hint of female arousal under it. Mmm.

Mouth and nose on one side of her neck, hand cupping the other side, he could feel and see her arousal. Nothing like his, of course. His dick was sending out signals that were probably interfering with cell phone reception. He could feel his heartbeat in his dick. But she was with him, she wanted this. There was no mistaking it and if he didn't feel she was turned on he'd get up off her and move far away. Maybe tie himself to something like those Greeks did when they sailed past the sirens.

She was tilting her head slightly into his hand, giving his nose and mouth more access.

"So how does it work?" she asked, voice a little breathless.

"Hmm?" He was drunk on her skin. Every time she blushed, she gave off a little burst of heat and a little puff of her scent. She blushed often, that pale ivory skin going a delightful pink. He couldn't remember the last time he'd seen a woman blush. When she blushed she went from very pretty to stunning. "What works?"

He could feel her cheeks move as she smiled. "This new therapy of yours. How does it work?"

"Touch." The hand cupping her neck moved down, shifted the gaping neck of his T-shirt to one side uncovering delicate collarbones. "Dermotherapy. Just invented it. Healing by touching the skin." His hand shifted again and the T-shirt fell off one shoulder. Looking down at that pale perfect skin, he saw the beginning of the swell of her breast.

Her eyes were half-closed. "Dermotherapy, huh?"

"That's right." Metal curved his hand over one smooth shoulder. It was like touching warm satin, only better. "I'm going to trademark it. Make a million dollars."

"Not in Russia you won't. Do you know what *dermo* means in Russian?"

Metal pulled back and shook his head, keeping his eyes on hers. Such a brilliant blue, like pieces of the summer sky. "No idea."

Felicity huffed out a laugh. "It means shit. So that won't go over so well, will it? Shit therapy."

"Nope. Not good. Public relations nightmare. Okay, let's rename it kiss therapy." He planted little kisses all along her long, pale neck, along her delicate jawline, back down along her shoulder. He bit her, just a little, right where the neck met the shoulder and felt her jolt. "How do you say *kiss* in Russian?

"Potseluy."

Weird word. He gave an internal shrug. Now he could say it in Russian. He'd say it in Martian if that would help. "*Potseluy* me."

She laughed, touched his neck, then opened her hands like a little blossom, stroking him. She leaned forward and put her mouth on his.

Jesus. Sensory overload. Touching her, her mouth open under his, tongue stroking his…it was more exciting than fucking other women. Under his fingers on her neck he could feel the blood pumping hard through her veins. His was too. He was already so excited he couldn't breathe. Good thing fucking was off the table because he'd have a freaking stroke. Die right here, in his bed, at the ripe old age of thirty-three, brain simply blasted from lust.

Metal couldn't reach her breast from the T-shirt's collar. But! He was a good strategist and forward thinker. His hand bunched the bottom of the T-shirt and slowly pulled it over her head. She lifted her arms for him, which was good. Showed she was in the game. He wanted her so badly he wondered whether he was generating thought waves that could be messing with her head.

He wasn't. Or maybe he was but she wasn't picking up on them. She was okay with being naked for him.

Naked. God.

Metal nearly forgot to breathe as he lifted his head and looked down at her. The rest of her was just as beautiful as her face. Pale and smooth and absolutely perfect.

As if someone had reached into his head and pulled out his ideal woman.

Even the long strip of gauze along her side didn't detract from her beauty. It simply reminded him that she was vulnerable. It was a hard world and wasn't too forgiving to the soft and gentle, however smart they were. Well, whatever happened between them, no one would ever hurt her again.

There were images of naked women more or less everywhere these days. Pneumatic, pumped, sometimes even rubbery-looking. Silicone and plastic and spray tans.

Felicity looked like a woman, slender, delicate, utterly real. Her heart was pounding and he could see and count the beats of her heart in her left breast. Automatically, without thinking, he counted them. Eighty beats per minute. She was excited.

Her breasts were small and incredibly perfect with pale pink nipples and yes, thank you God, the nipples were hard. Growing harder and pinker by the second as he stared avidly. He wasn't necessarily a breast guy. He particularly hated implants because he knew he was feeling sacs of saline solution under his hands. As a combat medic, he'd held plenty of sacs of saline solution and they reminded him of death not life.

But these breasts—ah, these were a miracle of nature. Soft and round and complete turn-ons.

It wasn't easy because her breasts were eye magnets, but he lifted his gaze to her face. Which was eye candy too. "You like touch therapy?"

She nodded, smiled. "Kiss therapy too."

His dick gave a kick in his pants. That's what it felt like, anyway. A surge of blood so intense his dick jerked.

He leaned forward then stopped when she put a hand on his chest.

They both looked down. Her hand was slim and lovely but not strong. If he wanted to move forward her hand sure as shit was not going to stop him. But that hand stopped him as suddenly as a grenade. He wasn't moving if she didn't want him to.

"You too," she whispered.

Yeah? He had no idea what she wanted. "Me too, what?" Whatever it was she wanted, he was going to give it to her.

Felicity curled her fingers around the bottom of his own T-shirt and pulled up. "Take this off."

Shit, *yeah*. The shirt was off and flung to the corner of the room in an instant and Metal moved forward to kiss her. God, the feel of her naked breasts against his chest was just heaven. He was careful not to put weight on her, especially not on the wound. But he could rub against her, feel all that heat and softness right against his skin.

Felicity was naked under the covers that bunched around her waist. He was really glad he still had his jeans on because shit, he wouldn't be able to resist climbing on her top of her otherwise. Her pale, slender, naked torso stopped where his blue comforter started and that was good.

Think of her as a mermaid. Sexless from the waist down. Hard to do when what he could see was so sexy she glowed.

Except, of course, for the bandaged side, which kept him just this side of red-hot. Because he knew that his weight would be heavy for her, certainly uncomfortable, maybe even painful and he didn't want the tiniest shred of pain with them in this bed.

It had been bad enough two nights ago when she had fallen through Lauren's door. This beautiful young woman some fuckhead had *slashed*.

Now that he knew her, now that he'd kissed her, now that he felt a tug as strong as the tides toward her, he wanted to kiss her, pamper her and he could do that.

He just couldn't fuck her.

Not yet, anyway.

Metal pulled a little away, reached out with his forefinger and traced a straight line down the center of her body, from her chin to her belly button. Tracing a line over that soft pale skin that felt like a little slice of paradise.

His gaze followed his finger down, then he placed his palm over the center of her chest, right between her soft breasts. He met her eyes. "You're so beautiful." The words were the right ones, exactly what a guy should say to a beautiful woman. But he got the rhythm and the tone wrong. His voice was rough, hoarse. Instead of a compliment it sounded like a painful confession.

She blushed. Without his T-shirt on her, he saw that her blush extended all the way down to her breasts. The tops of them turned rosy too. Her breasts were already perfect but they became even more of an eye magnet now that they were pink.

His mouth watered. He wanted to kiss her breasts, lick and tug her nipples until they turned even harder. He felt as if he could taste her already.

But something in her expression…

"I can't be the first guy to tell you you're beautiful." He refused to believe that. Men were assholes but any man with gonads would be attracted to Felicity. He bent to give her a quick kiss. "Felicity?"

"No, of course not." She blushed even more fiercely. "It's just that—"

"What?"

"Um, I guess the guys I've...dated, they aren't big on compliments. And I think they were more impressed with my IT skills and video game scores than with my looks."

Metal put on his poker face. "I'm impressed by your IT skills and game scores too. Does that give me points?"

She laughed. "Totally."

"So can I do this?" He bent down, licked her right nipple and saw her shudder. In a good way. He lifted his head and stared down at her. "You okay with that?"

"Oh yeah." She was bright pink, flushed and flustered and absolutely irresistible. He'd lied. He was impressed that she was so smart and he was sure she was good at video games but right now? Right now none of that made any difference to him. What was turning him on was the way she looked at him, huge blue eyes fixed on him. How she reacted to his every touch, how she moved into his touch. "Again," she said breathlessly.

Hell yeah.

Metal bent again and this time he took her nipple fully in his mouth, holding her sides between his hands. Like holding an ice cream cone that was salty-sweet. He pulled with his mouth and she reacted strongly. She shuddered and he saw goose bumps rise along her forearms.

Good. He wasn't alone in this. Because he was about as turned on as he'd ever been in his life. As a matter of fact he needed a new word for what what he felt. Turned on sounded bland. You got turned on by a song or a new gun. This was unexplored territory and it needed a new word. He'd think of one later. Right now he had trouble remembering his own name.

He bent to kiss her again, short nips, lifting and re-adjusting his mouth over hers. He was almost scared of a proper kiss—long, with lots of tongue. Entering her mouth with his with tongue was scarily close to entering her with his dick and that wasn't something he could do. Yet.

The thought of that, the thought of finally entering her whenever it could happen, caused him to jerk a little. She pulled back in surprise.

He was trying to think of something that would explain why he jerked without making him sound like a moron but *sorry about that, I flashed on fucking you and my system went haywire* didn't cut it.

Then he couldn't think of anything at all because she did what he'd done. She placed her palm flat on his chest. They both looked down. Her hand was slender, long-fingered like the hand of a musician's. Ivory skin against his tanned chest. The contrast between her hand and his chest was amazingly erotic.

Metal usually thought that erotic things had to be connected to fucking. Man, he was so wrong. Just looking at her was erotic. Yeah, she was naked, but he'd wanted her just as fiercely when she'd been covered up by his T-shirt. Everything about her was erotic and turned him on enormously. Her coloring—sunny-blond hair, sky-blue eyes, ivory skin. Her shape—slender but totally female, a tiny waist between breasts that were perfect for his hands and hips made to be gripped.

She was so enticing. Not jumping her right now, not sliding into her, was costing him years off his life.

Felicity patted him then her fingers curled into his

muscle. She had short fingernails but even if she had those claws some women had she wouldn't hurt him.

"You feel wonderful," she said. Her gaze switched from his chest to his eyes and back. When she moved her eyes it was like lightning flashing. He was mesmerized.

Her lashes were light brown tipped with gold and he couldn't tear his gaze away from her as she looked up and back down again, the thick gold-tipped lashes like little fans. Her eyebrows, too, were fascinating, gold and ash-brown hairs, the gold glinting in the dim light. And her hair. Purely her own color too. There were a thousand colors in there, though mainly gold. Tiny almost invisible pale gold hairs fluffed around her face. If any hairdresser could replicate that color, he'd be rich.

"What?" she said, as he continued scrutinizing her.

"You're so beautiful you melt my eyeballs. Everything about you is so perfect."

She shook her head, smiling. "I've got defects."

"Name one."

"A mole right above my left buttock."

A mole right above her left buttock. He closed his eyes, imagining it. Oh God. His dick wanted to punch its way out of his jeans.

"Let me see," he said urgently. "I want to see it."

She smiled slowly. "You want to see it? My mole?"

He huffed out a breath that she would have to take on faith was "Yeah".

"All right," she said quietly, that half smile on her face driving him crazy.

Slowly, she pushed down the bedclothes and turned over.

Metal felt his eyes widen, his jaw drop. How could she be as beautiful on side B as she was on side A? Yet she was. That long elegant back narrowing to a small waist, dimples just above her ass which was pale and round and perfect. Like a peeled apple.

He wanted to bite it.

Sure enough, right above the left buttock, next to the adorable dimple, was a small mole. He bent down slowly and kissed it, one hand smoothing over her right buttock.

"Not a defect," he said, voice rough. "More like a decoration. You're going to have to do better than that."

He lifted his head and she turned back over, searching his face with a slight smile.

"Okay. I can't cook," she warned. "I mainly eat takeout and frozen pizza."

"That's fine. I cook." Metal was touching her breasts, rubbing his thumb over the smooth satiny skin. He didn't give a fuck about takeout and frozen pizza.

She was doing the same to him, feeling his pecs. When she scraped a fingernail over a nipple it shot straight to his dick. He made a strangled sound deep in his throat.

"You feel so very good," she sighed. "Just amazing."

He saw her mouth move but couldn't make out the words because his head was about to explode. "What?"

Her eyes were half-closed. The skin was so fine he could see tiny blue veins in her eyelids. "You. Feel. Good."

"God. Can barely understand English." Now the words penetrated. "See what you reduce me to?"

She blinked blankly, not having made the connection of him unable to understand words and her own allure. He placed his hand over hers and man, double whammy. Her palm over his chest, his palm over her hand.

He really was going to stroke out when they had sex if this tiny amount of stimulation got him going like this.

Gently, he eased her down in the bed until she was lying flat on her back. Her breasts were so soft. The last woman he'd had sex with had had breasts that looked like basketballs perched on her chest when she was lying on her back. That was when he'd sworn off implants.

Had been sometime ago too.

Months, in fact, come to think of it. Was that why he was so worked up? Because it was a long time since the last time he'd had sex?

Nah.

He hadn't been having sex because he'd sort of lost interest in it. He was interested now. Oh man, was he interested. A bomb could go off in the next room and he'd still be staring at Felicity's breasts.

He bent his head and kissed her there, where his hand had been. He nibbled his way around her left breast, relishing the hard beat of her heart under his lips.

She was alive and well and that was a miracle. She could have died the other day. The fucker could have slashed an artery and she would have bled out there alone on the airport concourse and he would never have known her. Never held this miracle woman in his arms.

"Metal?" She'd clued into his sudden change, probably to the air molecules shifting around him. Because all of a sudden he needed to claim her, claim this woman he'd almost lost before knowing her.

He looked up at her slightly breathless tone. Did he hear a touch of fear?

No way. No way was he going to hurt her.

"Not going to hurt you," he said in a guttural tone. "But I gotta do this."

As a declaration of intent it wasn't much but somehow it reassured her. Her head had lifted a little from the pillow to look at him, but now she plopped her head back.

He consciously made his hands gentle. When the image of a dead Felicity lying in a pool of her own blood coursed through him he'd stopped himself just in time from gripping her hard.

His hands were strong and if he gripped her hard he'd hurt her. Nope. Not going to happen. So he opened his hands and used only his outstretched palms to touch her, running them over her breasts, down her narrow torso, down over her smooth flat belly.

Down.

Before he had to ask, her legs slid apart. Oh yeah. Smart Felicity.

Metal watched his hand as it smoothed his way down her body. Had he ever seen a woman more gorgeous than this?

Back in the Sandbox, porn magazines had been everywhere. Sex and alcohol had always been stress relievers for soldiers. Alcohol was out because it was a dry country. They doled out maybe one miserable bottle of beer a day, if that. The supplies were kept under lock and key.

Sex—well there were women on base though not out on missions. But the women on base were mostly officers and untouchable. And, well, for him at least, a fellow soldier just didn't inspire sex. Loyalty and respect yes, but sex? After about a month the women were just as sexless as the men. Covered in dust and sand, eating bad food, shitting infrequently because they were so gummed up from the crap food and smelling kinda ripe because the showers were clogged up and disgusting, even for the guys.

No one ever showered barefoot because you could pick up nasty fungi and yeah, everyone stank.

So no sex and the guys just looked at porn magazines. God knows what the women did. But for a couple of years, the barracks were awash in pictures of naked women with tiny hips, humongous boobs, pouty lips and empty eyes. Caricatures of women. He wouldn't have been surprised if they were CGI.

Jesus, this woman was so different she could have been another species.

Soft yet strong. Escaping a killer twice while wounded—well not many soldiers could have managed that. Razor sharp. Amazingly beautiful, and the real deal too.

Amazing.

Between her legs was an ash-brown cloud tipped with gold and farther down gleaming pink lips. She was so beautiful here too.

Carefully watching her eyes, he slid his fingers over her, sliding in gently. Full lips blew out a breath and her eyes narrowed so that only a slit of bright blue showed. She felt like wet silk. He penetrated her with his finger, watching her carefully. He didn't have to look at her to see how aroused she was, he could feel it against his hand. She was hot, wet, her body weeping for him.

His was weeping for her too. If his dick hadn't been encased in briefs and jeans it would have been wet with precome. His balls were tight and his entire groin hurt. That was okay. He could deal with pain. SEALs lived with pain. They marched to the cadence of "pain is weakness leaving the body."

Luckily, Felicity wasn't in any pain. No, she looked relaxed, pleasured.

He slid his finger out, then in again, exactly what he'd like to be doing with his cock. She sighed and he nearly sighed too. God, just this was better than sex with any other woman.

"Like that?" he asked hoarsely.

"Hmm."

"Say it." His voice was sharper than he intended. But he really needed her to say it out loud.

She should have slapped him down but she didn't. Her lips curved in a dreamy smile and she watched out of those brilliant semi-closed eyes. "I like that, Metal. A lot."

"Say my name."

"Metal."

"My real name." Jesus, why was he behaving like such an asshole?

"Okay. Sean, then. I like what you're doing to me, Sean." No censure in her voice. And it slammed him upside the head that she understood, on a deep level, what he wanted. Metal was his military nickname and he was fine with it. Most of the people he dealt with on a daily basis were friends from his soldiering days anyway.

He was Metal. Metal was a soldier. But Sean—Sean was a man. Sean O'Brien of a family beyond his military family. He wanted to be Sean for her. Something more than a soldier.

And who better to recognize that he was two people than someone who'd been someone else all her life?

She did understand. She was smiling at him, caressing his skull trim.

"Sean," she murmured.

Oh God. His heart gave a huge kick in his chest. Even with her eyes half-closed, Felicity saw him better than anyone else ever had. She saw straight into him. And from the dreamy smile on her face she liked what she saw.

Against all the odds.

"I was going to go down on you but I really need to kiss your mouth instead," he said roughly.

She blushed and it was such a beautiful thing to watch.

"Oh, um. Okay."

Metal shifted so that his head was even with hers and kissed her, while keeping his fingers inside her, staking his claim.

The kiss was deep and he didn't lift his head. They breathed through each other. His tongue stroked hers while his fingers stroked between her legs, in rhythm with his tongue. She was wet and warm in both places and felt like heaven.

Carefully, he rolled a little on top of her. Just enough so that his mouth was right above hers as they kissed endlessly. His finger stroked in and out. He reached deep inside her and felt her gasp in his mouth.

"Like that?" he whispered without leaving her mouth.

"Oh yeah." He could feel the exhalation of breath as she said the words.

His finger reached deeper into her softness. "And that?"

She made a noise deep in her throat. But he knew she liked it because she contracted around his finger and her hips lifted slightly. He stroked her inside, deep and slow. Her arms twined around his neck bringing him even closer to her.

Her thighs started trembling as he increased the rhythm of his strokes and her mouth went slack. The kiss deepened. He pressed her harder into the pillow as he stroked her faster and faster. Their mouths and his finger in her sex were making little noises in the quiet room. It was like a little symphony. Then her gasps were added and then another deep noise. It took him a second to realize it was him, growling in his throat as he felt her sex contract once, twice. When he bit her lips she exploded, hips rising and falling, clenching hard around his hand and oh God, he'd never felt anything as wonderful as that.

He held her tightly, kissing her through her orgasm until she subsided, a light sheen of sweat over her flushed body. The hold around his neck relaxed and her arms fell bonelessly to her sides. He lifted his head to look down at her, that beautiful face pure sex. Beard rash, mouth swollen and wet, a slight smile on her face.

She lifted a hand as if it weighed a ton and caressed his face. He was slightly bristly and needed a shave. He was going into the bathroom to jerk off and wash off but first he had to kiss her. Because it was impossible not to.

Her eyes half-opened, like lifting a lid hiding the summer sky. The smile widened. "Wow."

"I'll say."

At any other time he'd be doing internal capers and smiling smugly because he'd gotten the woman off. But this felt different. Real and serious. Felicity's face was so soft as she looked at him. That expression of intelligent wariness had disappeared. He'd heard her story and understood how she'd lived a life undercover, which meant hiding emotions from the world.

Metal had never been sent in undercover. He was too

big and fair for one thing. But it was also recognized that he didn't have the mind-set for it. He was a warrior and he went into battle in uniform. He never had to pretend to be what he was not.

Felicity, her whole childhood, never had that luxury. He recognized now how she hid behind a facade because that facade was…down. She was open to him. And he was open to her.

They were touching only via her hand on his face and it was as if his molecules were melding with hers. It was such an intense feeling it was almost unsettling. He opened his mouth, closed it, then thought *what the hell.* "At the risk of sounding stupid, I never felt anything like that before."

That was exactly the kind of statement dumb guys made just before opening themselves up to being slashed open by a sharp tongue.

She shook her head. "Me either. That was amazing."

Metal nodded. "And it wasn't even sex."

She made a choked sound, like a laugh and a cough at the same time. "Well, it sure felt like sex. For me, at least. You didn't, em…"

"I didn't get off, no. But it was still amazing." His eyes circled her face. "We'll be having the real thing. Soon."

Another choked sound. "Yeah."

"You still have stitches and bandages."

"What stitches? What bandages?"

This time he made the choked laugh sound. He touched the tip of his forefinger to her nose. "Okay. So I'm going to the bathroom for a shower and a shave." And to jerk off. "And then I'll help you wash. No shower for you yet, but soon. And then we go into ASI."

"ASI?"

"My company. Jacko's company. We've put in a request to have the airport footage and it might be arriving soon."

She used her elbows and sat up against the pillows. "You put in a request?" she echoed blankly. "For the footage?"

"Yeah. We'll see if we can get a visual on the guy and then—"

Felicity shook her head, amused. "You didn't need to put in a request. I could get that footage for you in three minutes, Sean. Tops. I didn't do it sooner because I didn't think about it. I felt really awful and weak and I wasn't thinking straight. But now I feel much better and I can get the footage from the airport from here. By the time you get out of the shower, in fact."

Metal didn't even try to argue with her. He knew his hackers and the distinction between legally and illegally obtaining data wasn't one they easily grasped. He used the only argument he could. "We're going to involve the Portland PD and if we catch the fucker there's going to be a trial and he's going to be put behind bars for a long long time. To do that we need to observe legal niceties otherwise any evidence will be thrown out long before we get to trial. So thanks for the thought but we'll do this the official way."

"Okay. But I'll get that footage for you anyway so that we can start work on it. And then when the 'official' footage comes we'll be ahead of the game. Hospital footage too."

Metal nodded. He had no trouble whatsoever with getting the jump on the authorities. If they caught the guy they'd just catch him again on the footage provided by the airport. Which was still pissed at the fake bomb alert. He knew John had to tiptoe around that one. If the airport authorities figured out that Felicity was the one to pull the alarm she'd be in trouble. Even if she'd saved her own life.

Metal was not about to let that happen.

He bent down to kiss her and went to the bathroom for a shower and a shave and a little relief.

He tried really really hard not to hobble his way there because he had a true blue steeler, and it fricking hurt. For a second, just a second there, he'd been about to come in his pants, feeling her wet heat contract around his hand. Ah, God. Hand in her, tongue in her, he'd felt every second of her climax, felt the long rise and sharp fall. Something else he'd felt—her surprise. As if it was all new to her. Unexpected.

He wasn't new to getting his rocks off but this was all unexpected for him, too, even if the getting-his-rocks-off part hadn't happened. Didn't matter.

She was wrong, he thought, as he shucked his clothes and dropped them to the bathroom tiles. He hadn't come, but it had definitely been sex. He'd been with her every step of the way except for the very end when he pulled himself back from the brink because he didn't want to come in his pants. Not cool.

Although everything else about it had been cool. Her tongue tangled with his, mouths eating at each other. Her hands clinging to his shoulders, keeping him close as if there was somewhere else he wanted to be, which was crazy. Her legs and sex completely open to him. He'd felt the trembling in her thighs just before she started coming…

He stepped into the shower and turned the water on.

Cold. He didn't need hot water. His body was generating all the heat he needed. He looked down at himself, stiff as a club, huge and almost inflamed-looking. Tip shiny with precome. He moved under the water and the cold stream did little to cool him down. It was suprising steam didn't come off him.

He couldn't stop the images in his head, that gold-and-ivory goddess in his bed, gasping into his mouth, pulling hard against his finger, so hard her hips lifted against his hand.

She hadn't been able to stay still—writhing against him, lifting one leg to wrap around his hips, making herself even more open to him.

She'd been so hot and wet, arms tightening around him, mouth open under his. Every part of her warm and welcoming and so incredibly desireable.

Metal was as tall as the showerhead. He stepped right under the icy spray, bowing his head so he could fit, looking straight down at himself.

His hand wrapped around his dick. Usually the touch of his hand alone gave him a little relief because Pavlovian little devil that it was, his dick recognized that as a prelude to getting off. It didn't work this time because his dick also recognized that this was going to be a piss-poor substitute for what it really wanted.

What it really really wanted was to slide into Felicity's slick and welcoming sex, slide in really deep and really hard.

Everything he knew about women told him she would welcome him and not pushing in and fucking her was the bravest thing he'd ever done. His medals for operating under fire? Not fucking her had been just as hard.

But he'd been really worked up and he might have

been rough and hurt her and that image—of Felicity crying out in pain and not pleasure—stopped him dead.

It hadn't been easy controlling himself, though.

He gave an experimental slide down his dick and then back up. It wasn't Felicity but it was better than nothing. He couldn't go back out with his dick waving in her face, so it was going to have to be now and it was going to have to be with his hand.

Another experimental slide, then another. If he closed his eyes he could almost imagine he was in her. He'd go in slow at first. She'd been wet but small, and he didn't want to hurt her. So he'd slide in slowly…his fist followed his thoughts. Down, up, down.

He'd fit. He'd make sure of that. Moving in and out of her, he'd kiss her, kiss her neck, maybe take just a little nip. She'd jolted when he'd done that.

Oh yeah.

His hips were following his hand as he remembered how she'd jolted, then shook, then trembled and then came.

Man, that had been ace, feeling her come around his hand.

The same hand that was pumping his dick, faster and faster now until he got harder and bigger and then started coming, in long pulls that made his knees weak.

He shot his other hand out against the tiles to keep himself upright because the memory of Felicity coming, and his own climax, made his knees weak.

It finally ended and he sighed, letting the water cascade over him until finally it registered as cold. He looked down at himself. Even after coming he was still half-erect. But his dick would have to take a hike. And maybe it wasn't possible to not be half-erect when Felicity was in the next room.

He'd gotten off, that would have to be enough. He couldn't stay here forever under the cold shower while Felicity needed him. Nope.

He shut the water off, dried and got dressed, already looking forward to seeing her again.

METAL—SEAN—CAME out from the bathroom bare-chested, shaved, in clean jeans and smelling of soap. Had he shampooed? He had a skull trim and Felicity had no idea how those worked. Certainly he didn't need to blow-dry his hair.

He smiled at her and walked across the room, keeping his eyes on her the whole time, and oh my. She'd been lying in a puddle of pleasure, completely wiped out. But the sight of all that beefcake—tons of ripped muscles moving in perfect harmony as an alpha male moved straight to what it wanted—woke her tired body up and infused it with newfound energy.

Because what this alpha male wanted was her.

Where two seconds before she'd been a formless mass of sweat-soaked bliss all her muscles tightened as he strode toward her. Her most reliable ally, her brain, had gone AWOL and all that was left was hormones and erogenous zones. Breasts, sex, mouth, belly…every inch of her that he'd kissed and touched roared to life.

He couldn't possibly think she was ready for a second round, did he? Because she wasn't. Absolutely not. Well *maybe*, she thought as she watched all those muscles moving. If he asked nicely.

He stopped by the bedside and looked down at her.

She must be quite a sight. Hair spread out all over the pillow, lips swollen. Completely naked.

He held out an enormous hand. "Come on, honey. You'll feel better after washing and putting on clean clothes."

She blinked. "Feel *better*? This is one of the top ten moments of my life."

He didn't smile often but when he did it was spectacular.

He lifted her out of the bed and she stood awkwardly, very aware of her nudity. Covering her breasts and sex with an arm and a hand would be really stupid after what they had shared but she had to practically order her arms to stay down. She wasn't used to nudity in front of other people. Her few sexual encounters had been firmly under the covers and she'd gotten dressed the instant she was out of the bed. This embarrassment was really dumb and she had to get over it.

She stared at the ground and there were his bare feet. His feet were absolutely *fascinating*. Very long but narrow and with high arches. Tendons and raised veins running over the top of the feet, a few blond hairs on the straight toes. They could have been the feet of a Greek marble statue only flesh-toned.

Sex had broken what little filter she had between brain and mouth. Head still down, she opened her mouth and "You have beautiful feet" came out.

And she blushed.

His head was down too. "You have beautiful feet too. Prettier than mine, that's for sure." He stepped forward and placed his big feet outside her much smaller feet. She had on pale pink toe polish. It was an interesting contrast.

"I have prettier nail polish too," she mused.

He lifted his big foot, examined it. "Yep."

They both laughed, lifted their heads. Their eyes met and her awkwardness was gone, just like that.

He tugged at her hand. "Let's get you washed and dressed."

Before, it had sounded so outlandish. She'd been washing and dressing herself forever. She didn't need help. Helping her get washed and dressed made her sound like a child. And even as a child she'd been self-sufficient for as long as she could remember. Her mother had never helped her get dressed and ready for school, she'd always done it herself.

But Metal made it not awkward and infantalizing. And to her surprise, she did need help. She could probably have done it all herself but it would have taken forever and it would have been painful. With Metal's help, it went smoothly and painlessly.

She stood like a doll as he smoothed a washcloth over her. When the washcloth cleaned her between her legs, a wave of heat pulsed through her, so strong she forgot to be embarrassed.

But beyond that, it was a gesture of caring. He'd fed her, loved her senseless and now was washing her. It was almost more intimate than the non-sex sex they'd had on the bed. Strangers can have sex without feelings. But you can't gently wash someone without emotions being there. Sex was one thing. This level of caring was another.

She bent her head down curiously to watch as he gently peeled away the bandage. What had been a terrible slash was now a thin line with tiny black stitches. "Doesn't look so bad," she said.

Metal was very carefully washing it with an antiseptic

solution and applying an antibiotic cream. "No, you're healing really well."

She met his eyes. "I had really good care."

He nodded. "That you did."

"About the clinic," she said and Metal tensed. "I don't remember the whole thing very clearly but I got the impression that it was an…unorthodox clinic. Am I right?"

"Hmm," he said, body language wary.

"Well, I'm all for unorthodox particularly when it's in a good cause. Do you think that later I could make a donation? I accepted a contract from a company that's keeping the Midwest fat. Do you think your doctor friend would mind if I donated the proceeds of that contract to the clinic? I'd be grateful and it would make me feel a whole lot better."

Sean relaxed. He applied fresh sterile gauze and was taping the edges. This strip of gauze was much smaller and she didn't feel like The Mummy so much anymore.

"I think he'd really appreciate that. As a matter of fact—"

His cell, which he kept with him at all times and was on the bathroom counter, played the refrain of "Don't Stop Believing." "That's HQ. Probably calling us in."

Yes. Good timing too. Felicity felt worlds away from the wounded woman who'd stumbled into Lauren's home, bleeding and exhausted. The wound was healing quickly. It didn't hurt at all. She was rested and had eaten well. Better, actually, than when she was at home.

Just surviving had taken all her strength but now? Now she was ready to fight back. Go on the offensive. Darin DNA was courageous DNA. Her father had managed to escape from a totalitarian government. She was not going to play the victim.

She wasn't a warrior like Metal. But she was smart.

"Yes," she said. "Take the call and let's go."

NINE

METAL ANSWERED HIS cell with one hand while holding on to Felicity's waist with the other.

"Metal." *Midnight.*

"Sir."

"Come in to HQ. We have airport footage." Metal felt a savage rush of pleasure course through his system. Footage. Footage meant a visual. A visual meant step one in catching the fucker who'd hurt Felicity.

"There in twenty, sir."

"Wait." He heard what sounded like a growl at the other end of the line. "It's snowing, Metal. I want you and Ms. Ward there in one piece. There's no ticking bomb on this. Drive like someone normal."

"Normal?" Metal asked philosophically. "What's normal? Psychologists say—" but he was talking to air. Midnight had hung up.

"So what's up?" she asked, picking out an outfit from the clothes Lauren had brought over.

Metal watched with sorrow as Felicity dressed, covering up that lovely body. But they had to go out and she had to be dressed to do that. He observed her carefully as he helped her put on a turquoise sweater and black pants. Her movements were smooth and seemed pain-free.

Lauren had packed several changes of clothes in the suitcase. The two were more or less the same size, except Felicity was perhaps two inches taller. The clothes fit. She looked like a million dollars.

Even better, she dressed without wincing once.

"Okay, like I said, we're going into my company's headquarters. My bosses will be there and I think Jacko will be there too. We've got that footage from the airport—legally—and we're hoping you can pick the guy out."

"There will be hospital footage too," she said, pulling all that long, lovely blond hair up in a ponytail. She looked like a college student just out of high school. Fresh and bright and shiny. And determined.

Miles away from the wounded, panicked woman who'd fallen through Lauren's door three days ago.

She looked so beautiful. So smart and determined. This was a woman worth saving. Worth protecting. Nobody would ever hurt her again. He was a warrior and he worked for a company of warriors. Together with his team at ASI they were going to find this guy, figure out what he wanted and either waste him or hand him over to the cops.

Metal would rather just waste the fuck, but Bud might not approve.

"I don't know if they've got the hospital footage yet. We'll go with what we've got and start to track this fu—this guy down."

She gave him a funny look then put on the coat Lauren had brought over. Her own coat was bloody and torn. Metal frowned. The coat was pretty but looked thin. And he didn't have anything that wouldn't float on her. "You going to be okay with that coat? Doesn't look to warm to me. It's snowing outside."

She smiled. "I'm 100 percent Russian. Snow is my natural habitat. I'd die in Texas or Florida."

Well, maybe. But Metal reached into the hall closet and pulled out a long black scarf, sniffing it surreptitiously. It passed the sniff test so he wrapped it around her neck about ten times then tied the ends together. He stepped back to admire his handiwork and kissed her on the nose. "You look fabulous."

"Thanks, Dad." She scrunched her nose up at him. "I'm not sure I can move. I feel like Iron Man in his suit."

Metal frowned at her. Something was missing. "Gloves! God, I hope Lauren included gloves in her care package." He rummaged around and found a pair of cashmere-lined black leather gloves. Bless Lauren. "None of my gloves would even remotely fit you."

He put them on Felicity himself and it pleased him on some deep and complicated level that he was making sure she would be warm and comfortable on their way to finding and wasting the fuckhead who'd attacked her.

But she needed to be not just warm and comfortable—she needed to be unrecognizable.

He dressed for the outdoors then grabbed her by the shoulders. She realized this was serious by the expression on his face. "Metal?"

"This is the way it's going to work." He pulled a fold of the scarf up over her mouth and nose and pulled on a black wool watch cap, completely covering her hair and pulling it down to her eyebrows. He grunted with satisfaction. Only her eyes showed. Then he put a pair of his winter goggles on her. Nothing of her face or body was identifiable. Even a full face photograph wouldn't help anyone in identifying her. "From the moment you step outside my house until we're inside my headquarters,

you're going to have the scarf around your lower face,
the watch cap pulled down over your forehead and you're
going to wear those goggles. It's going to be uncomfortable in my SUV. Are you okay with that?"

Her gaze was steady. "Of course."

His heart swelled. His scarf was itchy and though
it passed the sniff test it sure didn't smell like roses.
Ditto the watch cap. She was going to be uncomfortable the entire way but she wasn't complaining in any
way. Good girl.

"Jacko's more paranoid than I am. He's got this film
he found on the internet and he coated the windows of
his vehicle with it. It's perfectly transparent to the naked
eye from inside the vehicle. From the outside looking in,
you look a little indistinct. But the great thing is that the
windows are impenetrable to cameras. I have no idea
how it works but I do know it works."

"Probably the film induces pixilation," Felicity said.
"Pretty neat."

"Well, that film is going onto the windows of my
SUV and the house as soon as I can manage it. In the
meantime—" he pointed his finger at his scarf and the
cap, "—you're going to have to make with the impro-
vised burka. Sorry."

"It's in a good cause." She took his hand and his heart
swelled again. She shouldered her laptop backpack and
turned to the door. "Let's go."

FELICITY HAD NO idea what to expect on reaching Alpha
Security International, where Metal and Jacko worked.
She knew it was a security company, of course. The Security in the title was clear. They declared up-front exactly what they were. Totally unlike most IT companies

that made a point of hiding what they did in the title. They had fun muddying the waters, calling their company Xanadoo or Purple Hat or EonWonk.

She had an idea of what a security company did, of course. God knows she'd been around enough U.S. Marshals and FBI agents.

Security companies provided security and the people who worked there were no-nonsense people and she imagined they worked in no-nonsense surroundings.

Boy, was she wrong about ASI.

When Metal drove them through gates set in eight-foot concrete walls in what looked like a rough part of town she was expecting industrial flooring and the smell of sweat and leather. Not that different from a start-up IT company. Maybe without the lollipops in big glass jars, skateboards and Foosball. These would be serious adults, after all.

Metal himself had undergone a metamorphosis from really nice super sexy teddy bear to badass Captain America the instant they walked out his door. Some kind of switch in his head had flipped and he was like a robot that had three hundred sixty degree situational awareness and was absolutely ready for anything. She'd watched without saying anything while he put on a shoulder holster under his parka. Driving, he constantly checked rearview mirror, sideview mirrors and out both windows in a regular pattern. It would have been absolutely impossible for anyone to take them by surprise. He was silent as they drove, which didn't surprise her. It was snowing and if she drove in this kind of weather while watching out for bad guys she'd be in a nervous sweat.

Metal relaxed marginally once they were inside what turned out to be a compound.

As soon as the gates rolled back together behind them, and Metal helped her down from his vehicle which wouldn't have been out of place patrolling in Iraq during the war, they entered coolly elegant and perfumed premises, about a billion miles from what she'd been expecting.

They entered a long corridor with terra-cotta tiling and terra-cotta sconces, lined with huge enameled planters full of thriving ferns interspersed with lemon trees. As someone with a black thumb, Felicity appreciated what it took to keep plants alive. A lot.

There were several doors along the corridor but Metal went straight for the central door on the left-hand side.

A discreet brass plaque was to the right with ASI in black italics. Metal didn't knock or do anything. The door slid open of its own accord as soon as they were close, which was pretty neat. Had they simply been following the video cameras from inside or was it a facial recognition program?

She was running through what kind of software would be necessary for a facial recognition program for a company that had a wide clientele when she stepped through and barely stopped from gasping.

The lobby looked like a movie set for a sci-fi film, *Minority Report* maybe. Deep earth tones with neutral accents, dark wood and brass, a smooth flow to the furniture, so that it took a moment to realize this was business premises. The actual reception area was such an integral part of the look that she started when someone behind a space-age desk stood. It was a young guy, very fit, friendly looking.

"Hey, Metal," he said, "both bosses are waiting in the main office." He nodded at her. "Ma'am."

"Great, thanks, Ron." Metal had his hand at her back and escorted her through three sets of glass doors then stood for an instant in front of a big smooth wooden door with no insignia until it, too, slid open.

The main office was vast and that amazing decor continued here, too, though the look had been melded with utility. High-end monitors everywhere and the familiar ozoney smell of electronics. The room was colder than the rest of the building. Of course. There must have been at least three hundred thousand dollars worth of electronics in that room and they had to be kept cool.

"Felicity!" Lauren jumped up from a chair in the immense room, ran to her and hugged her. "I'm so glad you see you looking so well! So I guess Metal's been taking good care of you, huh?"

The tone was warm, caring, absolutely not suggestive but Felicity lit up like a stoplight at the memory of Metal's tender loving care. Lauren held her shoulders and stepped back, eyes widening at Felicity's megablush.

"Oh." Lauren blinked. "Oh!" Her eyes rounded and her jaw dropped. She whirled to Jacko but he was busy conferring with two older guys. They both had "boss" stamped on their foreheads in invisible ink.

One handsome, one ugly, both scary-looking. Definitely guys you wanted on your side. Felicity hoped with all her heart that they *were* on her side. Jacko was on her side because of Lauren and Metal was definitely on her side because…well.

But these two?

Her heart was beating a little faster. These guys could help or not. She'd called in a bomb alert in a major airport and she'd stolen an ambulance. Who knew how they'd react to that?

Well, maybe she could soften them up with her thank-you gift.

"Honey." Metal bent low and murmured in her ear, exerting a little pressure to the small of her back with his huge hand. He hadn't stopped touching her since their arrival through the back entrance of his work premises. Even now, he stood so close behind her she could feel his body heat. Living reassurance.

Felicity would have thought that he would want to keep things discreet, for professional reasons, and was perfectly prepared to have him treat her like a stranger. But no. His entire body language proclaimed that they were a couple.

The two scary guys behind the two huge desks stood up and walked around to her. "John Huntington," the good-looking scary guy said and shook her hand gently.

"Douglas Kowalski," the ugly, scarred scary guy said and, alarmingly, held out his hand. Felicity looked at it for a second. It was huge, scarred like his face, raised veins on the back. She needed her hands for keyboarding. If he squeezed her hand it would take a month to get the hand back to normal.

But he, too, held her hand in a gentle grip for a few seconds then gave it back to her.

"Nice to meet you," she said to both. They were really hard to read, not that she was an expert in male psychology. Or even female psychology, for that matter.

Still, most people either wore their emotions on their face or it was clear they were hiding something. Not Huntington and Kowalski. Their faces simply gave absolutely nothing away.

There was a silence that would have been awkward if anyone showed awkwardness, but no one did. Except for her. She was cringing inside.

"So, um." She fidgeted, met Lauren's eyes. Lauren gave her a sweet smile. Okay. "I, um, I understand that you have footage for me to go over. More than that, I, um, I understand, or rather Metal told me that, um, you guys are willing to help me." Her voice went up, as if it was a question, even though Metal had made it clear that this wasn't in doubt. The entire resources of his company, and apparently they were considerable, were going to be used to help her figure out why she'd been attacked and above all, to track the man down and bring him to justice. And it was all free of charge. She was a hacker and she often worked free, like all hackers, but more for the thrill of a new problem than anything else. This wasn't a new problem, this was the oldest problem on earth. A woman in trouble.

"That's right, Ms. Ward," the ugly one—Douglas— said. "We're here to help and we're going to be Skyping with a close friend who works at the Portland PD. So why don't you sit down and we can get started."

She hoped with all her heart that the Portland PD guy didn't want to slap handcuffs on her.

"I'd say I don't know how to thank you—" She held up her hand when both John and Douglas opened their mouths. "But actually I do."

Felicity handed John the thumb drive she pulled out of her pocket. He took it, looked it over curiously, handed it over to Douglas, who looked it over carefully too.

Felicity pointed to the drive. "That's a little program I wrote." Actually, it was a *great* program and worth a lot of money if she wanted to monetize it, which she didn't. "Do you guys have an IT tech you trust? One who is really good?"

John nodded. "We outsource our IT. We use Rajiv Anand of XTY."

That lobe in her head where geekhood reigned lit up like a Christmas tree. "Oh great! He is really, *really* good. So…I just gave you a security program. Tell him I'll buy him a vintage 1977 Pac-Man machine in pristine condition if he can break into it. If he can't, then that program is yours. And your in-house computer security will be completely impenetrable."

The two men looked at each other, then Douglas left the room with the thumb drive.

"So, Ms. Ward—"

"Felicity, please." Felicity was her name of the heart. The name she'd chosen for herself. Ward had been picked by the government computers.

John nodded soberly. He was really quite handsome if you overlooked the fact that he could probably kill you with his pinkie. He looked like a pirate with good teeth. Of course Metal could probably kill you with his pinkie too. She leaned back a little and smiled inwardly to feel his solid bulk behind her. He didn't want to kill her with his pinkie.

"Felicity." John swept Metal and Jacko with his glance. "Let's look at the footage from the airport. It just arrived and we got it only through a friend of a friend. They're still really pissed at the false bomb alert."

She froze just as she started sitting down in front of a monitor and keyboard. Three men were looking at her. Lauren had disappeared somewhere. "Uh. Sorry. I couldn't think of anything else to do."

"Oh!" John scowled. "Good God, don't misunderstand me. That was really quick thinking. I wasn't blaming you, I was just saying why it took us a while to get the footage. Actually you were amazingly quick-witted. You saved your own life. That's worth a little chaos at the airport. So let's look at it. We're expecting the hospital footage any moment."

Any moment? If she hadn't been recovering and, um, otherwise engaged with Metal, she'd have had that footage yesterday.

The screen in front of her—all sixty inches of it—came alive and the three men leaned forward. The screen was split into six sections, obviously the six security cameras that had been on in the concourse. The footage was dated and timed. Three days ago at 3:20 p.m. Her flight had landed at 3:05. The screen was chaotic, a sea of bobbing heads. It was impossible to make out faces.

"Wait a second," she said. "Can I enter your system?"

John nodded.

Felicity took a quick snapshot of herself full face with the screen's camera, entered the code for her super secure cloud server and pulled out her facial recognition software. The software took the coordinates of her facial features, made a dataprint, matched it against the images from the concourse and isolated her face in the crowd. A faint pink square highlighted her face as she moved so she couldn't be lost again.

She checked her second hand. The whole process had taken twenty seconds. Not bad. Not *great* but not bad.

There was a weird quality to the silence and she swiveled left and right. "What?"

Metal cleared his throat. "We, uh, we don't have facial recognition software."

Well, duh. "I know, I checked. So I used mine." She focused back on the screen.

Okay, there she was, before the world crashed down on her. She was smiling as she moved past the purse shop, the shoe shop, the cosmetics shop. Oh man. The emotions swept over her. She'd felt so free. So light and hopeful. She'd even felt…young. Young and carefree and about to embark on a visit to a new city with a new friend. And minutes later, the whole thing crashed.

"Sorry to interrupt but—" John took a deep breath. "You, ah, checked our computer system for facial recognition software?"

Well, *yeah*. She'd said that, hadn't she? Felicity nodded.

"So when did you do that?" There was a slightly choked quality to his voice.

"When I sat down." Metal, Jacko and John all looked at her as if she had suddenly been beamed into the chair from space, à la *Star Trek*. "What? I did a quick check of your system. Facial recognition software has distinct features and your system didn't have them. So I pulled my own program, loaded it and searched. Don't worry, I'll remove the program later, unless you want me to leave it in?"

Silence.

"Okay, guys, this is creepy. What's wrong?"

Metal put a big hand on her shoulder, squeezed gently. "I think we're in awe of what you just did. It would have taken me an entire morning to check to see if a system had a specific program, then find my own, load it and do a search. If I could do it at all. You did it in seconds."

There was a strangled quality to his voice too.

She was about to answer when she saw him. Oh God,

a shudder went through her as she remembered her happiness, then this man behind her with the guttural voice, threatening her. Wanting to kidnap her.

She froze the video, feeling that panic and terror all over again.

Metal was talking to Jacko, something about the hospital footage. Her voice wasn't working so she grabbed his hand. She was shaking.

Metal stopped talking immediately and placed her cold hand between his two warm ones. "Honey? Honey, what's wrong?"

She couldn't catch her breath. All she could do was place the locator box around the man's head and point.

All three men understood immediately, leaning forward.

"That the guy?" Metal said. It wasn't really a question. He tapped the screen over her attacker's head and the screen zoomed. "He's threatening you right now, isn't he?"

She nodded. She could almost feel the sharp bite of the knife in her side.

Metal's nose was practically pressed against the screen, eyes narrowed, a fierce expression on his face. "Enlarge the frame again."

She pressed a key and there he was, three-quarters profile, hat low over his eyes. This was going to be a problem because eyes were important to a faceprint, which measured the exact distance between pupils, the vertical distance between forehead and cheekbones, depth of eye sockets. Nodal points, measurable and indispensable.

"Gotcha," Metal whispered.

"Not quite." Felicity's hands left the keyboard and

twisted together in her lap. Her hands were shaking and she didn't want anyone to see. "I don't think I'm going to have enough data points for a faceprint, not unless he looks up. I think he knew what he was doing with that hat. Let's watch the footage in real time and see if his face shows up more clearly. Then we'll go through that sector frame by frame."

The three men grunted, eyes glued to the screen.

So she watched it all over again, living it all over again. Hands trembling as she watched a man try to kidnap her.

She saw herself pull away, stumble because she'd been sliced. Moving fast through the crowd, disappearing into the bathroom. A few minutes later the bomb alert. She'd been in the bathroom so she hadn't seen this. There was no sound. One minute the concourse was filled with passengers walking, shopping, eating, talking. Then everyone froze to listen to the announcement and at the exact same moment, like starlings in flight, mouths opened in silent screams and they started rushing the stairs and the escalators, pushing and jostling. The only people who remained still were foreigners, who were watching everyone go crazy.

Instant panic, as if someone had stirred a stick in an anthill.

"Go over the attack again, but start earlier, and track both faces," Metal said and she clicked back.

They watched on two screens from two different angles. She saw herself walk past the long lines waiting to go through security and into the arrivals area together with some of the other passengers on her flight.

The cameras switched to the street level.

"See that?" Metal pointed. Her attacker walked into

the airport from outside, shaking snow off his coat. A few clicks later he had made his way upstairs. He positioned himself to one side, carefully watching the passengers as they passed by security and into the open area. Only this time her face and the attacker's face were outlined. As she watched herself bebopping down the concourse like a puppy let off the leash, he followed. "He knew everything," Metal said.

"Timed it just right too." John frowned. "Didn't spend a moment more than he had to in the airport in full view of the security cams. So he knew what flight she was on and timed it to be there when she exited." He turned to Felicity. "Was your flight on time?"

"No, it was twenty minutes late. Pilot said he ran into head winds."

"You didn't have a suitcase with you so you didn't check any luggage."

"No. I just had my carry-on. When we landed I walked straight out of the plane."

"Do you think he could have hacked into the system to see if the plane was late?" Metal asked her.

Felicity snorted. A chipmunk could have hacked into the system to see if the plane was late, let alone a human with half a brain.

"I'll take that as a yes." Metal was biting his lips as if holding back a smile. "So what we know is that your attacker didn't spend an extra second getting himself to where he could cross your path. He knew your flight was late so waited somewhere outside. He was smooth and efficient and wasn't hanging around getting himself noticed. Which means he had intel on you."

This was sort of scary. She nodded.

"Fast-forward it to where you get out of the bathroom and then slow it to real time and keep both of you on the screen."

They watched as pandemonium broke out and she peeped her head out from the little bathroom atrium. It was weird watching the same thing from two entirely different points of view. The system kept them both in view but from two different cameras. When she made her way toward the stairs, cap on and head low, her attacker was in the center, fighting the tide of panicked passengers, head swiveling to look for her.

She'd felt it. Even wounded and scared out of her mind she'd felt him seeking her out. But on the screen she could clearly see that he was never looking in the right direction as she made it down to street level and out the doors.

Outside, the cameras weren't so well situated. She caught a glimpse of herself, huddled over in pain, staggering toward one of the ambulances. Then the attacker showed up on the other monitor, a real full face shot since in his frustration he lifted his face, forgetting the cameras.

"Freeze!" Metal shouted and her finger tapped to freeze, then zoom in. Instantly her program found the essential data points, a grid mapping his face. It looked like a veil with tiny lights where the threads of the veil had been dropped over his face, molding itself to him.

"Cool," Jacko said admiringly.

"Never seen that actually done before," John admitted.

Yeah, they had his face. Step one. Step two was finding out who the hell he was.

Felicity's fingers hovered over the keyboard. "Okay. We can put in a request to send this faceprint to the proper authorities. Either the FBI whose ViCAP records are pretty extensive. Or maybe the CIA or NSA—they keep a good biometrics database. I can almost guarantee you that the answer will be no, we cannot use their system, that the answer will be weeks coming and that the very question will put ASI on some kind of watch list."

"Or?" Metal asked, watching her closely.

"Or I hack," she said simply. "And get the answer fast."

"Hack," Metal said decisively.

"Hack," Jacko said.

John shook his head and smiled wryly. "Hack." His eyes closed in what looked like pain.

"I'll need my computer. No offense, guys, but your system is as leaky as the *Titanic*. Just about as old too."

Again John shook his head. "No offense taken. Do you have your computer with you?"

She shot him a *get real* look and he raised his hands.

Felicity opened her laptop and flicked away a tiny mote of dust. The laptop had a dull surface and no logo. It wasn't for sale anywhere in the world and its insides could send a man to the moon and back while hacking into Amazon. Completely untraceably too.

"Gentlemen, please," she murmured and they turned their heads away as she entered the password and brought up a special program she'd written. It took a little concentration and about five minutes but at the end, she brought up an internal FBI page. It had the dark blue stripe across the top with faded stars marching across horizontally and the gold-and-blue FBI logo in the center. Below, NGI. Next Generation Identifier. The new FBI facial recognition database.

"You can turn your heads back now," she said and the three homed in on her laptop screen.

"Christ!" For the first time she saw John drop his worldly CEO expression. "Did you just hack into the FBI computer system in a few minutes?"

"They have crap security," she said as she imported the biometrics of her attacker into the system and let it run. "Actually, I could have used my own ID as a freelance service provider to the FBI but it would never have let me get this far into the system and it sure wouldn't let me run FR. This is much easier and faster."

"You're scary," Jacko said, but he was smiling.

She rolled her eyes. Jacko had piercings, a giant tribal tattoo visible under his thin T-shirt, and he was as big as a refrigerator. You could probably hit him with a baseball bat and the bat would break. And *she* was scary?

"Okay, here we go." Thousands and thousands of faces flickered on the monitor, faces flying by under the data point template she'd established.

After ten minutes Felicity sat back. It usually didn't take this long. FR software was pretty advanced and the newest generations eliminated obvious non matches and only brought possible matches into the system.

Douglas came back into the room and jerked his thumb at John. "You're going to get a call—"

John's cell pinged and everyone turned to him as he looked at his screen. "It's Rajiv," he said, raising his eyebrows to her. "Can I put him on speakerphone?"

Felicity shrugged. "Sure."

Metal put his hand on her shoulder again, as reassurance, though she didn't need it. She was lacking in many, many things and wasn't too good in the real world, but in all things computer-related she felt strong and secure. Whatever Rajiv had to say wasn't going to hurt her.

John pressed a button and lay the cell down. "Rajiv, my man. What's your opinion of the software?"

"I want to hire this guy, John. Have him send his rèsumè stat and he can start work next Monday. I'd hire him sooner but I'm going to be at a security conference in Hong Kong. It's like that software casts an invisibility cloak around your computer system. It was closed up tighter than a virgin's—"

Metal leaned forward. "Rajiv—this is Metal. There's a lady here."

"Oops, sorry."

Felicity smiled. "That's okay. I'm the one who wrote the program so I won't take offence."

"Wow." Silence from Rajiv. "A nerdette. The cool factor just went up, like, a billion points. Will you marry me, lady, whoever you are? In California, so your program goes into our joint property?"

Metal rolled his eyes. "No, she's not going to marry you, Rajiv."

"And she's not going to work for you, either," John added. "She's going to work for us. And you can consult with us instead of the other way around from now on."

Felicity stared at John but he just held up a long finger. *Wait*, he mouthed.

"Hmm. So what's your name, mystery coder? And Metal, I haven't ruled out marriage yet. Even if she is seventy years old with warts."

"No warts, Rajiv," Felicity said. "I'm glad you found the code interesting."

"Frightening, more like it. So you used IEEE 802.1x? But it was an unusual variant."

Felicity smiled. He was testing her. He had no idea what the program was based on. "Figure it out for yourself. Tool around with it a bit more, test it, see if you can crack it. You won't but you might get some insights."

Silence.

"Stanford?"

She shook her head, though he couldn't see her. John had made sure the video camera was on him. It was very thoughtful of him.

"MIT."

Rajiv moaned. "Oh God. I can't believe you won't marry me or work for me. John, treat her well because she's going to make you a billion dollars. When the cyber apocalypse comes, your computer system will be the last thing standing."

"Thanks, Raj." When the call was over, John turned to her. "That's a real offer, Felicity. We desperately need someone with your skills in the company and I think we can make you a very competitive offer. But I want you to understand something, and I need to make this perfectly clear." He pointed a finger at her. "This job offer has nothing whatsoever to do with the fact that you are in trouble. This company will work to find your attacker and the reason behind the attack and will protect you in the meantime. We would do it anyway because of Lauren."

"And me," Metal growled. His presence beside her was almost overwhelming. He was, yes, big and broad and strong but above all he gave the impression of his strength at her service. An impression so intense she felt as if she was being protected by an army, his army, conjured up for her.

"And Metal." John nodded. "This company protects

those close to us. So don't think that you have to come to work for us as payment because that's not how it works."

"That's not how what works?" a woman's voice asked.

Felicity happened to be watching John's face, and the change when he heard the woman was astonishing. John was a formidable figure, physically and mentally. She wouldn't want him as an enemy. He was visibly a hard man, all business, and yet when he looked toward the door his face changed, softened.

The reason why was obvious. The woman walking toward them, arm in arm with Lauren, was an astonishing beauty, like something out of *Vogue*. She had a Grace Kelly kind of beauty and poise. Incredibly elegant and graceful. She was exactly the kind of woman who had tormented Felicity all her life. Felicity had been the kind of girl whose hair was always mussed and whose cotton socks fell down around her ankles and the popular girls had always made her pay for being so good in school. Not to mention the fact that she was a late developer and was contemplating a trainer bra when every other girl had mastered makeup and boys.

Things had been completely different at MIT, geek central, but Felicity was very aware of the fact that she lacked elegance and, really, social graces too. Most elegant women looked at her through a faint veil of contempt, as if she was somehow lacking in something essential to womanhood. Or even personhood. It was the reason she frequented nerds who didn't give a damn what she was wearing or what designer purse she had or if her hair was combed or even if she was a Martian. She could have two heads and they wouldn't notice.

So she instinctively prepared herself as the woman came closer but it turned out she didn't need to brace or defend herself at all. The woman rushed to her and embraced her warmly. Felicity was so surprised it took her a moment to embrace her back, holding on to the incredibly soft, expensive material of her pastel-colored suit.

The woman pulled back and smiled at Felicity, her eyes wet. "Felicity. I finally have a chance to thank you for helping Lauren. She told me what you did for her. Any friend of Lauren's is a friend of mine. I am so glad to meet you." She bent to kiss Felicity's cheek, soft, perfumed, real. "Thank you so much." Her voice choked. Beside her, Lauren sniffed back a tear.

Whoa. "That's really nice of you, ah—"

"Suzanne. Suzanne Huntington. John's wife." Well, Felicity didn't need to be told that. John was looking at her as if she were sunshine itself after a long, cold winter.

"Nice to meet you, Suzanne. But I didn't really do all that much for Lauren—"

Lauren shrugged. "Just saved my life. No big deal." She reached out for a hug too. Felicity hugged her back. She'd hugged more people in the past three days than she'd done in the past three years. Not to mention, um, hugging Metal.

She turned bright red at the thought of how much she'd hugged Metal and he'd, um, hugged her. Thank God no one noticed.

"I understand you're in some kind of trouble." Suzanne shot her husband a hard look. "We're going to help you. John and his company are going to help you, aren't you, John?"

"Already there, darling," he said, smiling.

"So, Felicity." Suzanne turned to her with a soft smile. "As the guys would say, we have your back. You've got quite a team here on your side."

"And me." Metal put a heavy arm around her shoulder and squeezed so hard she was nearly pulled off her feet. "She's got me."

Suzanne's eyes widened as she took in what Metal was saying. Lauren was beaming. Felicity was as red as Hellboy. Argh.

Just so no one was in doubt, Metal pulled her even closer and kissed her forehead.

And then, something weird happened. Something that was completely new to her. Instead of feeling awkward and embarrassed and the perpetual outsider, some kind of switch was thrown and she suddenly felt like an *insider*. Which was nuts because she'd only been in Portland for a few days and most of that time she'd been asleep. She and Metal had had sex or...whatever they'd had, once. But somehow that didn't make any difference. She felt a part of something bigger than her for the first time in her life, and she liked it. It was an odd feeling, but not. Actually, it felt natural, as if she'd stepped into the natural world from her virtual world and things were slotting into place.

There was Lauren, definitely a friend. Their friendship had been forged in trouble and danger and it was real. Suzanne—her friendliness was genuine, the warmth in her eyes was real too. The guys—John and Douglas and Jacko—they were on her side and John had offered her a job and it hadn't sounded like a fake offer at all.

And Metal. Wow. Metal. Metal was giving off definite vibes that they were together. Most of her fleeting sexual encounters had ended with both of them backing away as fast as possible. Metal wasn't backing away. He

had his arm around her in front of his friends, his teammates, and he wasn't backward about it either.

She leaned against him, just a little. He was a man
made to lean against. Even knowing nothing about her,
he'd leaped to her aid immediately. She didn't remember
too much about when she'd landed on Lauren's doorstep
but she remembered that. Remembered this big, rough
man rushing to her, catching her, easing her gently down.
Remembered the incredible care, the instant acceptance
of the fact that she couldn't go to the hospital.

He was attracted to her but beyond that he was a
genuinely kind man. Sort of like Al Goodkind. A good
heart in a tough man.

And he was hers. For the moment, yeah. It could end
tomorrow. But that was true for everything. Right now,
this guy was hers and she was very lucky.

"Thanks, guys," she said and to her horror her voice
broke. Something happened to her chest and she couldn't
get words out. Something heavy and waterlogged was
lodged in her throat.

Metal pulled her into a full frontal embrace and she
found herself with her face against a thick warm neck
and a big hand cupping the back of her head. She drew
in a deep breath and smelled him, smelled Metal. That
scent was now buried permanently in some deep part
of her brain that was an unknown pleasure center that
pinged to life when Metal was near, like a Pavlovian
response. Sex and security, what a potent combination.

Being held by him steadied her. She'd had a weepy
moment born of stress and maybe physical weakness,
but it didn't matter that she was still physically weak.
She had Metal.

And the rest of the team.

And she felt much better.

"Okay?" Metal whispered in her ear. She nodded.

"Sorry." She lifted her head from his shoulder. "Had a little moment there."

"Had a few myself," Suzanne said and put a steaming cup of tea beside her on the desktop. She touched Felicity's shoulder gently. "Hot tea definitely helps."

Suzanne seemed so magical that for a second Felicity thought she'd simply conjured a cup of tea out of thin air like a magic fairy, but no. There was a Thermos sitting on another desk.

But if there was anyone in the world who looked as if she could make a cup of hot tea instantly appear, it was Suzanne.

Felicity jumped at the sound of a soft beep and turned to the main monitor. They all stared at it, frowning.

NO MATCH FOUND.

"That's not right," she said.

"How big is the FBI's database?" Metal asked.

"About seventy-two million faces. Maybe more." Felicity couldn't figure this out.

Four male frowns. "*What?* There are seventy-two million criminal suspects in the US?" John asked, looking appalled.

She shook her head. "No, it's not like that. They start with mug shots, of course. From every level of law enforcement. But most of the faces in the database are noncriminals. A law was recently passed whereby anyone anywhere who applies for a job that requires a photo, that photo goes into the NGI database, together with your biographic data. When the database was set up, it included shots from what they called 'civil images' but those were never defined. There are other categories too that aren't defined. There's a 'Special Population Cognizant' category and a 'New Repository' category. Personally, I suspect they dip into Facebook too. Exclude kids under the age of fifteen and maybe seniors over the age of sixty and housewives and homeless people and illegals, and I suspect this database more or less covers everyone in the US."

There was a stunned silence.

"Son of a bitch," Jacko said. He turned to Lauren. "You're wearing your special hat when you go outside. I don't want you ending up in anyone's database. I've been in the military so I'm there, but you…"

"Absolutely." Lauren was looking shaken too. "Wow." Suzanne was frowning and looking at her husband.

Metal rapped his knuckles on the desktop. "Whatever. This guy isn't in the largest database of faceprints in the world, so we're fucking nowhere."

Felicity hesitated for a second. Because they could get somewhere, but it would be, um, illegal. Really illegal.

"Well, that's not *quite* true." She cleared her throat delicately. "There was this guy who gave a paper at the last Black Hat conference. It was a highly technical paper on collation of faceprint datapoints but if you knew how to understand the subtext you could tell that he's hacked into every single facial recognition database in the world. Including North Korea. Of course that would be, um, technically illegal. But still, doable. But before I ask him to do that, and I'd have to promise him something in return like my cyber security system or my firstborn, let me try something else."

In a few seconds she had a screen up.

Metal peered at the Cyrillic letters up top. "Is that Russian or Bulgarian?"

"Russian." She was digging, digging. "The guy who attacked me spoke with what sounded like a slight Russian accent. I grew up with my mother who had that accent, only stronger. So he might be Russian or Ukrainian. But this database will pick up both."

She pasted in the faceprint and started the system. "This might take a while and of course it's probably a wild-goose chase, but—"

The computer beeped. *They had a match!*

Everyone leaned forward, including Suzanne who kept a hand on her shoulder. Without thinking about it, Felicity reached up and squeezed her hand. Suzanne squeezed back.

Up on the screen was the faceprint of her attacker and a couple of photos underneath.

"Gotcha," Felicity whispered.

The first one was a shot of the guy in some kind of graduation ceremony. She peered more closely. There were four men in the shot, arms over each other's shoulders. They looked happy. And drunk.

"INSEAD," Metal read. "What's INSEAD?"

"An international business management school outside Paris. Our guy got himself an MBA in 2010. And his name is…" Felicity pulled up some more data. "Anatoli Lagoshin. Anatoli, what were you doing at the Portland Airport trying to kidnap me?"

"This other shot," John said, pointing at the monitor. "Formal thumbnail portrait. I can't read the writing but it looks like a business brochure to me. And the guy's on the organization chart."

"It is. A prospectus." There was a tiny British flag on the upper right-hand side. She clicked on it and the entire prospectus switched to English. She scrolled to the top.

"Oh my gosh! It's Intergaz! One of the largest corpora-tions in the world! It's a Russian natural gas company and half of Europe gets its gas from it. It's immensely powerful and rich. What on earth would one of its of-ficers want with *me*?"

Metal's finger hovered over the image of Lagoshin. "First thing we do is canvas all the hotels and motels in the area with a photograph of the prick."

"I'll get two of our men on that." Midnight spoke qui-etly into the interoffice intercom.

"Now, let's find out who runs it," Metal said grimly. He used the wireless mouse and came to a stop at a sin-gle photograph, at the top of a series of photographs. Even without reading the text, from the look of the face this was the top dog. "Vladimir Borodin," he read. He turned to her. "Name mean anything to you?"

"Vaguely, I guess. I mean I've heard it before. I read Russian but I don't keep up with the news there or any-thing. Let's see what his background is." She read, click-ing through, then froze. Metal had placed his hand on her other shoulder and he must have felt her tension.

"What, honey?" he said, his voice low.

A chill had invaded her, penetrated her very core. She was freezing. Her parents had warned her thousands of times about them.

"His name is Vladimir Borodin." Her voice shook. "Former *Colonel* Vladimir Borodin of the *Komitét Gos-udàrstvennoj Bezopàsnosti*. Under the Soviet Union."

"The KGB," Metal breathed.

She nodded miserably, looking up at him. "My father and mother risked their lives to escape from the KGB and now someone from the KGB is after me."

TEN

IN THE SUV going back home, Metal went into warrior mode again. The smiling guy at ASI disappeared and super spy took his place. He was quiet as he drove quickly back to his house in the worsening weather. The snow had never really stopped all day but now there were flurries. He was a superb driver, though fast. With anyone else she'd be a little scared of this speed in icy conditions but the vehicle felt solid and safe under her at all times.

He only spoke when they were close to his house. Ordinarily she didn't pay much attention to geography when someone else was driving but they passed that pretty park with the fountain and the statue—the fountain was frozen and the statue dusted with snow—and she knew they were near.

The trip was hazy, since she had so much to think about. It still seemed absurd, that a former colonel in the KGB could be after her, but for her parents it wouldn't have been absurd. They'd been terrified all their lives, even after the KGB was disbanded. The KGB had been a historical artifact for her, dead before she was a year old. Given her parent's penchant for talking around things elliptically instead of imparting information, she'd simply taken the letters as a stand-in for some mythical monster like the boogeyman.

She remembered Googling the initials when she was

twelve and being surprised that the KGB had been an actual *thing*.

It had scared her that, though tossed on the dustheap of history, part of a country that didn't exist anymore and was, in any event, on the other side of the world, the initials could still make her mother pale.

She didn't have enough data to make any meaningful assessment of this and she wanted to avoid the fog of panic that had surrounded her parents. She was *not* her parents. She had spent her entire life not being her parents. Sometimes she thought she had immersed herself in the tech world, with its young geeks who thought the world began the year they were born and knew no history at all, so that she could escape her parent's nebulous world of unspoken and unseen terrors, all from the past. Since she discovered computers at age seven she'd simply dived right in and disassociated herself from their world as much as possible.

They had anxieties she couldn't understand and that had clearly wrecked their lives. She hadn't wanted that for herself. Still didn't want that for herself.

And anyway her attacker wasn't KGB. He couldn't have been much over thirty. He, too, had been a kid when the KGB had disbanded. He was an executive at Intergaz. Which could mean anything but didn't necessarily entail the CEO knew anything about his extracurricular activities. Borodin hadn't been an active member of any secret service for nearly a generation. That atavistic stab of terror had been a reflex, more her parents' fear from beyond the grave than her own.

Anatoli Lagoshin was the man to be worried about, and he was an MBA, not a former member of Spetsnaz.

The farther away she got from the situation the crazier it was. Nothing made any sense at all.

It was easier to focus on a problem that she could meaningfully assess. John's job offer. She could assess it, but she didn't know how to think about it. As a principle, Felicity was really happy freelancing and being her own boss. She'd had a brief unhappy stint in a corporate job and had realized within the first month, when she'd been gently chided for not following the dress code, that it wasn't for her.

She liked making her own hours and rising or falling on her own work ethic.

But…there'd been something really nice in the air at ASI. A sense of comradeship. Of close team work. They also had a really cool sort of no bullshit thing going on. Certainly there wasn't a dress code. Coming out, Metal had greeted two guys who looked like they'd just been sprung from jail. He'd introduced them to her and the two guys had been super polite and so friendly she forgot immediately that they looked like they could slit her throat with no trouble. They listened to the same music she did, she discovered as they chatted.

Having John and Douglas as bosses didn't seem like such a bad thing. Working in that office…well it beat working in her dusty little house. They did exciting stuff. And presumably they'd take care of billing and filling out the endless paperwork for taxes and business compliance she found so tedious and baffling, so she could concentrate on her work.

And living in Portland… It was cold here, so that was good. She didn't think she could do Miami. She had Lauren here, who'd showed over and over that she was a true friend. And Suzanne very definitely could become a friend. Lauren talked often with warmth of Claire and Allegra. Two potential friends right there and she wouldn't have to do anything but sit back and be liked.

Jacko…Jacko tolerated her, for Lauren's sake. Though at times she thought she saw a smile lurking in his dark eyes when he talked to her.

And there was Metal. Yeah…

As if thoughts were tangible, he turned to her.

"So," he said, his voice expressionless. "MIT, huh?" It was the first thing he'd said to her in the SUV.

He gave her nothing by which she could read his mood. Not his face, not his voice.

Only one answer.

"Yes." Was this going to be a problem?

"Goddamn." He shook his head. He was smiling now. "A brainiac. Do you know I never went to college? Enrolled in the navy right out of high school."

"In September, 2001," Felicity said softly. "After your entire family died. Lauren told me. And I know you became a medic. She said Jacko said you know as much as any trauma surgeon."

"Lauren talks too much. What was it like graduating from a place like MIT?" His voice was cautious.

"Okay," she said. "It was okay." Though to tell the truth, she'd barely noticed the campus and spent the entire time at MIT in the underground computer lab.

"So…I guess you're smarter than me."

"Probably." She kept a poker face. "But you can shoot better than I can."

"Damn straight." A corner of his mouth turned up. "Cook better too. So I guess we're even."

She was smiling too. "Not quite. I'm still prettier than you are."

"No contest. We're home." Metal turned and drove up the driveway. The garage door rolled up and rolled back down when they entered the garage. She barely had time to unbuckle herself before he was at her door, helping her down. She needed the help. Her side was sore but more than that, she was tired.

She had a sedentary job and didn't go out much. Her only exercise was halfheartedly following yoga tutorials on YouTube and she wasn't assiduous about it. At the end of the day she could be mentally tired but rarely physically tired.

Now she felt physically tired for the first time in years. Exhausted, actually.

Metal put an arm around her waist and as they walked into his house from the garage she was grateful for the support.

The house was warm and welcoming, and she smiled as she crossed the threshold. When she returned home after going out her own house felt stale, as if even the dust motes hadn't moved in her absence. Metal's house somehow felt alive, embracing them, saying—*welcome back*.

Which was insane, of course. She must be really tired if she thought Metal's house was talking to her.

"How about we mix things up?" Metal asked. "Instead of tea how about I make you some hot milk with honey and then feed you dinner and you make it an early night?"

"I feel like a two-year-old," she complained. And yawned.

"Uh-huh." Metal walked her into the bedroom, turned

down the covers, helped her out of her coat and boots. It felt familiar. Hadn't they done this already a couple of times?

"It seems like you're always putting me to bed like a sick child. I'm sorry. That's not very sexy, is it?"

Metal froze. His big body simply stopped moving but it looked like a nuclear explosion had gone off inside his head. "You think I don't find you sexy? Is that what you think?" he asked hoarsely.

"Well…"

His face was stretched tight with tension. He took her hand and, shockingly, placed it on his groin. Oh man. Either he was really excited or he'd put a big steel tube down his pants when she wasn't looking.

"Feel that?"

Felicity couldn't answer because the instant her hand touched him, his penis moved. A strong surge of blood— that was the mechanism, wasn't it? Because it sort of felt like magic—pulsed through him and the steel tube grew longer and harder. He placed his hand over hers to keep it there though, really? It was so fascinating she couldn't force herself to pry her hand away.

His penis was hard but also hot. She could feel heat through his briefs and jeans. Man, it was like a furnace. And just like that, heat coursed through her, too, just from touching him. He was watching her closely, eyes slitted. Under his hand, she tightened her grip around him and his eyes closed briefly. He looked like he was in pain but when he opened his eyes again, he said, "Do it again."

She didn't have to ask what. She knew. Pleasure was coursing back and forth between them and she could almost see the lines of it, as if it was a physical thing. Her hand tightened and his penis surged again.

Oh man. Amazing.

Metal put a big hand to the back of her head and took a step closer. Her hand was trapped between their bodies.

All that tiredness? Gone, as if it had never been. Energy pulsed throughout her body, head to toe, down to her fingertips. Particularly the fingertips of the hand that curled around his penis. That hand felt zapped by some energy beam.

Metal brought his forehead down to hers. "That feels so good," he whispered.

"Yeah," she whispered back. It did. It felt really good. She remembered with intense clarity when his hand had been on, been in, her sex. That had felt like pleasure central.

This was just so *amazing*. Nothing like this had ever happened to her before, ever. With hindsight, sex had been a lukewarm thing, when it hadn't actually been downright chilly. Sex before Metal had been a simulacrum of this, like eating wax food instead of the real deal. Just being near Metal, near all that male power and his intense focus on her, was better than any sex she'd ever had.

She ran her hand along his hot, hard length and Metal gave a sigh that sounded like pain. Only it wasn't pain because his penis did that jumping thing again. She was tempted to conduct a little experiment—to see what happened if she continued holding him. Every time her hand moved he seemed to become harder, longer. Was there an end point? Maybe it would explode.

Be fun to find out.

And then a thought jolted her. For the first time in

her life she had a whack at a relationship. A real one. Maybe. Not with a nerd but with a man. He'd seemed really happy at John's job offer. He seemed really happy being here with her. He wasn't looking for the exit and he wanted her close.

There might be more of this in her future. Lots more. Wow.

"I think I should see about getting you fed. You must be very tired." His face was so close she could feel the puffs of breath as he spoke.

There might be lots of this on offer in the future, cuddling and kisses and rainbows and unicorns, but sex was on offer right now. She wasn't tired anymore, not at all. Her stitches didn't hurt and anyway she trusted Metal to be really careful.

"Felicity?" There was a load of meaning in the word. "You're tired, right?"

She lifted her head back, looked him straight in the eyes. "Not that tired," she whispered.

ELEVEN

OH MAN. *NOT that tired.* That was an invitation. Definitely an invitation. Wasn't it? True, he wasn't thinking too straight because all the blood was gone from his head but even he could tell that she wasn't saying no. And if the words weren't enough, her face told him yes too.

She was bright pink, her sky-blue eyes were glowing. Her lips looked a little swollen as if they'd kissed, even though they hadn't.

Well, that was easy enough to remedy. Metal bent and touched his mouth to hers. It seemed as though static electricity sparked between them when their lips met. They both drew in their breaths.

His mouth settled on hers again, tongue stroking hers and he felt heat surge through him at her every touch. Come on, they were just kissing and he felt like the top of his head was about to blow off. He'd kissed a million times before—though he couldn't quite remember the women he'd kissed. They were like fuzzy background images and Felicity was sharply detailed, full-color, high-def.

Everything crystal clear even with his eyes closed. Each touch of her fingers felt like fire, burning him without hurting him. This wasn't pain, no.

He lifted his head. They were holding tightly to each other. With her head tipped back over his arm he was able to look down at her and see every feature clearly.

God, she was beautiful. He kept finding new ways she was beautiful, every time he looked at her. Her straight little nose, the platinum fuzz around her temples, her deep pink mouth. The most beautiful woman he'd ever held in his arms. The smartest woman he'd ever held in his arms too.

And she had this incredible sweetness tempering the smarts. Metal had once dated an international banker. God knows why he'd thought that a good idea. Lee. She'd been ferociously smart too, but it was all in the service of proving herself better than anyone else. She had a burning need to be the smartest person in the room and wasn't shy about letting people know about it. She was competitive and used language as a tool to hurt.

Felicity wasn't like that. There was nothing sharp-edged about her, nothing there that wanted to hurt.

He bent down for another kiss and she closed her eyes, smiling. He kissed her again. He knew how she liked being kissed. She liked it the way he did, long and languorous.

It hit him like a hammer blow to the heart that…he was going to learn everything about her. Learn all her pleasure points. Learn how to make her come every single way there was.

She was going to stay here, in Portland. He wasn't going to accept anything else. He was going to find the fucker who was after her, eliminate him and keep Felicity close. This was it. She was the one.

She was going to accept John's offer. Wasn't she?

John was a great boss and he liked Metal. Metal and Jacko got great Christmas bonuses and Midnight and Senior both said they were deserved. But Midnight was a hard-ass. He didn't offer jobs out of a soft heart or because he liked the boyfriend. He'd offered Felicity a job because she was really good at what she did.

Felicity. Living here in Portland. Maybe…living with him?

The thought shook him. Felicity pulled away a little and looked up at him puzzled. She'd felt something. Had she actually felt the thought? She was so smart maybe she could do that. Read thoughts or something. It should scare him but it didn't.

"Metal?"

He didn't say anything, just looked down into her lovely face.

He opened his mouth then closed it. Because…well, it was too soon. Wasn't it? She'd only been here in Portland for…he couldn't count the hours because his brain was blasted. But not long. She'd been weak and wounded for a lot of that time.

She had someone after her. She wasn't in any position to think about the future.

They hadn't actually even had sex, though what they had had was the best sex of his life.

So he should shut up, enjoy the moment, protect her until they found the fuck, give her time and space. Make sure she liked it here. Let her breathe.

But the connection between his brain and mouth had been severed.

"Are you going to accept John's offer?"

She'd been expecting a kiss, her face lifted to his, eyes closing. They popped back open again. "What?"

Shit shit shit.

But he'd said it and he couldn't unsay it.

"John made you a job offer. Are you going to accept it?" Damn. His voice came out rough, demanding. He couldn't modulate it. What the fuck was *wrong* with him?

"I—" She looked confused. "I don't know."

Of course she doesn't know, you asshole.

Lighten up.

He kissed her then lifted his head and used his mouth for something else. He knew better, he did, he really did. But he couldn't help himself. "Midnight and the Senior—John and Douglas—they're really good bosses. Really good. They are results-oriented and as long as you know what you're doing—and you do—they won't bug you. The pay is generous and you saw the premises—it's a great place to work. The guys are great too. The whole place is…" He faltered because she was simply staring at him. He swallowed. "Great," he finished lamely.

"Metal, I—" There was a little frown between her eyebrows. He didn't want that frown there. Only one way to get rid of that frown. He bent and kissed her again. Longer, deeper, hotter.

"Never mind," he said hoarsely.

Turned out his head only had room for one idea at a time. The job offer was pushed out by the next thought.

Sex.

Then that thought was shoved out by another. Sex in a way that wouldn't hurt her.

Metal placed little biting kisses on that luscious mouth as he pulled her sweater up over her head and ran his hand over her narrow back to unhook her bra. She was there with him every step of the way. She lifted her hands so he could get rid of the sweater then placed her hands on the bottom of his sweatshirt, pausing a second.

Was she waiting for *permission?*

"God, yeah," Metal muttered against her mouth and felt her mouth smile under his.

"Going to need your cooperation," she said, a little breathlessly.

It was hard, but *do the hard thing* was the unofficial SEAL motto. Letting go of her was hard. Metal stepped back so she was no longer in his arms and bent down so she could slide the sweatshirt off him. He didn't have a bra she had to fiddle with. He didn't even have briefs. All that was left for her to do was unzip his jeans and take off boots and socks.

Which she did. When she'd finished they both looked down at him, her eyes a wide pool of blue.

Man, it didn't look like a human organ, it looked like a tool. Something you broke down doors with. Metal shrugged. "I'm really, really excited."

She was bright red now, fighting a smile. "I can tell."

"How about you?" Metal's rough voice was hard. He smiled at her. Tried to smile at her but the smile didn't stick on his face. He was feeling too...*something* to smile. Emotions were boiling inside him, clanging around, and he felt like he was going to explode. Words wouldn't form in his head and if they did he wasn't sure he could get out what he wanted to say.

Lots of things he wanted to say. *Stay* being uppermost. But it was as if he'd had a seizure or something and bits of his body and head were not connected. And his dick was on a mission of its own without any command and control function at all.

"Me?" Felicity lifted her eyes from his dick to his face and maybe his face was as frightening as his dick because they grew wide and the smile disappeared.

This was all wrong. Metal wanted lightness here in

the room with them. She'd been through so much and through all of it she'd been a real trouper. Someone had tried to kidnap her, that someone might be connected to the KGB, the same KGB her parents had escaped from. And her story—fuck. A lifetime under cover, hunching to avoid attention.

She didn't deserve that. She was beautiful, bright, kindhearted. She deserved a life in the light instead of in the shadows.

She certainly deserved better than a man who could barely talk and whose dick was flying in her face, dark red, shiny at the tip, just about ready to blow.

She deserved soft words and softer kisses and gentleness and romanticism.

What she had, instead, was him.

"Let's see. See what point you're at." His voice had gone guttural and her eyes widened. God, he had to get himself under control.

At least he could keep his touch soft. He stepped closer to her, slid his hand over her belly, down between her legs. Automatically, she opened her legs for him and he wanted to weep in gratitude. Particularly when he stroked her and found her wet. For him.

Other signs too. Bright pink, down to her breasts. The nipples were a darker pink and hard. The left breast was trembling from her rapid heartbeat. He could probably guage her pulse from the beat in her breast if he was capable of counting above three.

He hated it but he probably even looked a little threatening. God, please no. But right now, though he'd been in control of himself all his life, he felt that control fraying, slipping through his fingers.

She didn't look frightened of him, though. Thank

God. Like he'd done, she laid her hand on his chest and slid it down. She didn't have far to slide, because just below his belly button, there he was. Stiff as steel.

She opened her hand and grasped him and the pleasure was so great it was almost pain. She must have felt him pulsing in her hand because she tightened it. His lungs and voice weren't working because if they were, he'd tell her to stop. Or something. Because he was a second from shooting his wad and embarrassing them both.

Words weren't going to do it, actions were.

She had on what Lauren had called yoga pants but were really sex pants because they had an elastic waist and just slid down her legs, easy as you please.

Yes. Now he was working really fast. Socks, boots, off. Pants off, panties off and holy hell there she was, naked.

You are so incredibly beautiful. I can't believe you're here. I feel like I have been waiting for you all my life. Please stay here, with me.

Those were the words he wanted to say but his throat simply closed up.

She looked up at him, a little shy, a little uncertain. What a fuckhead he was.

Well, no one had ever called him a man of words. He was an action-oriented guy. Maybe he could show her.

He gently pulled the elastic thingie—girls had a name for it but he couldn't remember it—out of Felicity's ponytail and let her hair fall down over her shoulders. God, it was so beautiful, soft and honey-toned, with little platinum streaks and that almost white fluffy stuff at her temples. He cupped her head between his palms, letting all that softness fall over his hands and wrists. It was like plunging into a waterfall.

He bent but she met him halfway, rising up on her toes, hanging on to his wrists and oh, man. She stepped forward and there she was, right up against him, breasts against his chest, belly against his hard-on.

Blood surged through his dick again at the feel of her and she sighed into his mouth, rubbing her belly against him.

"Now," he muttered. "It has to be now." Otherwise he'd just make a mess all over her belly and embarrass them both.

"Yes," she sighed.

"Say it in Russian."

"Da." She smiled under his mouth.

Da. Damned straight.

Metal put an arm under her and lowered her to the bed, gently and carefully, still kissing her. He was blasted, but not so blasted he didn't remember she was wounded. Some remote, dusty part of his brain was still firing so he remembered to scrabble in his jeans for a condom. The way he was feeling he'd need a couple of pounds of condoms but for the moment one would do.

He angled his body so that his torso wasn't on hers. He kept his hand on the edge of the gauze as a reminder that this area was off-limits. He needed it because, man. She wasn't remembering it for him. No, she was twisting in his arms, trying to get as close to him as she could, winding her arms around his neck, trying to hook her legs around his. Trying to bring him on top of her because for this first time, it should be missionary position all the way. The most basic position of all because these were basic feelings.

That wasn't going to fly, though. Before he forgot himself, before he slid over to lie on her just like she wanted, he lifted his mouth, licked her behind the ear, then whispered into it. "Turn over." His voice sounded cracked, as if he'd been screaming in the wind for hours.

"Turn over?" She didn't understand. Yeah, it went against his instincts too. This first time of theirs should be wrapped in each other's arms.

Before he changed his mind and did something stupid, he eased her gently over onto her uninjured side. God, she was beautiful no matter what the angle. Narrow back, small waist, gently rounded hips. All pale ivory-colored skin, shiny blond hair swirling around her shoulders. Her face was in profile as she turned to him.

"Metal?"

"Shh." Metal fitted himself against her back. He was much taller than she was; her feet reached his shins.

He nudged that glorious pale fall of hair away from her neck with his nose. "It has to be this way. I don't want to hurt you."

Good. He had more control over his voice now, it sounded less cracked, less deranged. Maybe because he was very close to sliding into her and frustration wasn't eating him up from the inside.

He licked the soft skin underneath her ear, kissed it, bit it. She shivered and sighed as he fit himself against her back, touching as much of her with as much of him as possible. No pressure on the wound, no pain, just pleasure.

He cupped her breast, rubbing his thumb over her hard little nipple and she shivered again. Pleasure, oh yeah.

He nipped her a little harder and growled against her ear. "This isn't so bad, is it?"

She had goose bumps on her forearms. He only had one huge goose bump and it was poking her in the back.

"No, not bad at all."

He pulled her even closer to him, and slid his hand down between her legs. Yup, still wet, still soft. He pulled her leg up, hooked it over his and oh God, she was open to him. Completely open. He drew in a deep shuddering breath as he slid his fingers around her opening, sliding in and out. She felt like heaven, so incredibly soft. Her breathing sped up and she put her hand over his.

With his mouth on her neck, Metal got a good look down her body and it was hands down the most erotic thing he'd ever seen. Her slender pale torso intersected by his tanned forearm, his hand disappearing between her legs and her artist's long-fingered hand on his. His big hairy thigh between hers. Man.

He stroked deep inside her, soft and hot, and circled his thumb over her clitoris. Against the inside of his arm he could feel her stomach muscles pull just as she clenched around his finger. Again. Again. Again.

The leg thrown over his trembled.

It was time. He bit down a little on her earlobe, not enough to hurt, just enough for her to feel it. Sliding another finger into her he separated his fingers, holding her open, and fit himself against her. "Okay?" he whispered right against her ear and she nodded. He slid just a little inside. "More?"

"More." It was like a whispered moan, as if she didn't have the strength to say more.

He wanted her to feel everything. Reversing their hands, he put her hand down to where he was entering her, just barely inside, and pressed her hand against him.

He was torturing himself. The stimulus was almost

too much. The soft heat of her where he penetrated and her hand around him where he was still outside.

She was shaking all over, her thigh over his, her hand under his. She clenched around him and softly exhaled. Holding her hand against him, Metal tightened his buttocks and slid all the way inside her, exhaling heavily when he was solidly in.

He was shaking a little too. It was like sliding his dick into an electricial socket, this incredibly exquisite painless shock. Metal held her hips still as he pulled slowly out, slid slowly back in. Felicity gave a little cry and he stopped, shocked.

"Did I hurt you?" He'd been careful not to touch the gauze or even near the wound. But in holding her hips had he pulled the stitches? Fuck. He started pulling out when she slapped her hands over his.

"No!"

Metal froze, barely breathing. "No?"

She turned her head, kissed him on the cheek. "Don't stop, please." She shifted, pushed herself against him, pressing him deeper inside her. "Don't stop," she repeated.

Fuck no. He wasn't going to stop. If he wasn't hurting her, if she was getting one-billionth the pleasure out of this as he was…he couldn't stop even if a gun was held to his head.

He was covered in sweat, a trickle ran down his shoulders onto his bed. "Honey…"

He stopped. She'd clenched around him at the word and a pulse of blood ran through his dick.

"Honey, I don't think I can go slow. Not this time." Maybe after the hundredth time, but not now. "I'm going to have to go fast but I don't want to hurt you."

She twisted her face so she could see him and smiled. She was flushed, blue eyes impossibly bright, mouth soft and red. He had a flash of that mouth on him, his dick pumping into her mouth and the image made him groan and swell even further. He pushed forward with his hips helplessly and it set her off.

"Oh!" She made a low, pleased sound.

"That's it, honey," he said, holding tightly. "Let go."

Her eyes closed, her head tilted back against his shoulder and she started coming, clenching convulsively around him, hips undulating against him. He didn't even dare move, holding his breath as he watched her, watched his beautiful woman take pleasure from him. She shook, mouth open, tightening around his dick in powerful convulsions, twining her fingers around his, as if needing him to ground her.

He held himself still, letting her grind herself against him until she slowed, relaxed, glowing in his arms.

Now. Now it was his turn. Metal gripped her as hard as he dared, pulled almost all the way out, then slid back in, hard. Her breathing changed, sped up again. He wasn't hurting her, she was rocking back against him, moving in rhythm with him, small sounds of pleasure coming from her.

Metal thrust hard, thrust hard again and started coming when he felt her convulse around him. He was known for his stamina but he simply lost all control when he felt her trembling on the edge and then falling back into orgasm, making soft panting sounds.

Too much. It was simply too much and he held her tightly against him as it all came roaring out of him in huge spurts so hard he hoped he wouldn't punch through the condom. He was jerking and sweating, completely out of control, the relief of the orgasm nearly electric in its intensity.

He came and came, hips circling as he stayed inside her until finally the storm abated. His muscles relaxed and he embraced her, instead of holding on to her. He crossed his arms beneath her breasts, pulling his thighs up under hers until she was almost completely enfolded in his embrace.

He could feel her rapid heartbeat against his chest and knew she could probably feel his. Their hearts slowed at the same rate, as if they were an organism with one heart.

"Whoa," she finally said.

"I don't have the energy to look at you," he grumbled. "I hope that was *whoa* in the good sense."

"Oh yeah." Felicity folded her arms over his and settled even more deeply against him. God, it felt good. Not as good as the sex, but a real close second.

"Good," he said and nudged her with his hips. "Let's do it again."

Her hair made a little rasping noise against the pillow as she shook her head. "I am so wiped out."

Shit. He was still hopefully semierect inside her and with any kind of encouragement he'd be ready for Round Two in about five minutes. It didn't feel like he was a thirty-two-year-old man. It felt like he was sixteen again. He remembered sixteen. The notion of "too much sex" had been utterly foreign in his teens.

He sighed and she laughed. He liked that feeling. Her laughing in his arms. He liked it a lot. He hooked his chin on her shoulder and kissed the side of her face. She smiled and looked at him over her shoulder. That was a very special kind of smile. He'd never actually seen it on her face. He liked that too. He liked just about everything that was happening.

His cell rang, spoiling the moment. He reached down, scrabbled and pulled his cell out. He wasn't answering unless it was Jacko or Midnight or Senior with news.

It wasn't. It was a poker buddy looking to set something up for their regular last weekend of the month game. He cut off the ringing. He didn't want to talk to anyone except Felicity or someone who had news about her situation.

"Gosh!" Felicity sat bolt upright in the bed, blankets around her waist. Metal's hand itched to cup that perfect little breast. He reached out but was too late. She'd slid out of bed, grabbing one of his T-shirts. It floated down onto her, hiding more or less everything he was interested in at the moment. "I forgot about my cell! I took the battery out two days ago."

Metal frowned. "You can't answer your cell. If this Lagoshin has any computer skills he'll trace it."

Felicity tugged on his T-shirt until it covered her thighs and smiled gently at him. "This won't be traced, guaranteed. But first I think I want to wash up. And before we, um—" She turned bright pink, which was fast becoming Metal's favorite color. "Before. There was talk of food. Was that true or were you blowing smoke?"

"True, scout's honor. And yes, I was a scout." Metal rose up on his elbow, full of hope. "Do you need help washing? Because I can give a hand, absolutely."

She glanced at his groin where his dick was lengthening. "I think you want to give more than a hand. And thanks, but no. I'm good."

She certainly was.

She disappeared into the bathroom, grabbing some clothes from the carry-on Lauren had brought on the way.

Well, looked like sex was off the table, for now. But not for long. Metal contemplated a future in which the kind of sex he'd just had would be available, always. Wow. Days with Felicity, maybe working in the same office, seeing her. A lot. Nights with Felicity doing what they'd just done, only without the bandage getting in the way.

Honing his computer skills with her. Cooking for her. Maybe teaching her how to shoot. Watching TV together, going out together. Just being together.

Maybe that was in his future, in their future. It felt so good that the very idea of a Felicity-less future seemed like a cold, dark place. He couldn't even contemplate it.

Having Felicity around made him feel…complete. Whole, in a way he hadn't felt since that day in September when the world stopped and then broke. Being in the navy, serving in the SEALs teams had helped. They'd become a surrogate family for him but it was a limited kind of family. Being with Felicity felt like something else entirely. He felt whole with her, a man with something close to him to defend.

He shook his head. Instead of philosophizing, he needed to start cooking. He got out of bed, dressed and made his way to the kitchen. He pulled some focaccia out of the freezer, washed some lettuce and left it to drain while making a ham-and-cheese omelet. He made really good omelets. He'd just flipped his—pretty spectacularly too, even if he did say so himself—when a disturbance in the Force made him turn around.

She was smiling at him, leaning against the door frame, barefoot, unspeakably beautiful, dressed in another sweater and another set of yoga pants that would be easy to pull down. He'd buy her a hundred pairs of yoga pants and they'd have sex everywhere.

That was his dick talking, which was what he usually listened to.

But something in his chest thumped hard when he saw her standing there, watching him with a half smile on her face. She was incredibly beautiful, yes. But intelligence shone out of her eyes, and humor too.

She didn't have any of the complex ego issues beautiful women had. She wasn't coy or vain and she didn't play those female games he hated. It was incredibly easy being around her. She'd been wounded and hurt and she hadn't complained, not once.

She was a keeper, definitely.

She pushed off from the doorjamb and walked toward him. His clinical medic's eyes noticed the high color in her face, the clear white of her eyes, her easy gait. His dick noticed the soft high breasts under the sweater— was she wearing a bra? God, if she wasn't wearing a bra he was a dead man because touching her breasts was really easy if the only thing he had to do was reach under the sweater. His dick also noticed the long slender legs under the loose material of the pants. His dick was really glad to see her.

He was glad to see her.

Sizzling and the smell of something burning… He turned the gas off just in time. Another few seconds and the omelet would be burned beyond eating.

Felicity smiled up at him. "A sex god and he cooks."

A grin spread across his face. What his teammates would undoubtedly call a shit-eating grin. "I have other tricks too."

"That's good to know."

"Didn't you want to check your phone?"

"Email too. I've got a little app for that." She moved past him and started setting the table. "But first food. I'm starving and can't think straight when I'm this hungry. And the food in this place is fantastic."

"Glad you think so." Metal slid the omelet onto a serving plate and dressed the salad. "Are you sure you can do that safely? Check your phone?"

She smiled secretively. "Yes. And I'll teach you how to do it too."

"Sounds good." More than good. Being able to check cell messages untraceably would be very useful. She probably used some kind of a mask, but those sometimes leaked.

She wasn't joking when she said she was hungry. She ate elegantly but fast. Metal ate less elegantly but fast too.

Felicity put down her fork. "I want to help clean up but right now I want to check my messages. I've been out of touch for days. I've never done that before."

They moved into the living room where she set up her laptop. It was completely unlike any laptop Metal had ever seen. He had a MacBook Air, brushed aluminum, lightweight. Hers was heavier, dark, with a dull matte finish, a super clear screen and barely raised letters on the keyboard. He didn't recognize anything when she powered it up. No familiar programs, no familiar chimes as programs came on. The screen was black then was lit with with brilliant icons he didn't recognize, going from black to HD icons in less than a second.

"I've never seen a laptop like that before? What make is it?"

She was typing faster than he'd ever seen anyone type. The shallow keys allowed her fingers to float over the keyboard rather than keying in the letters.

"Not a make," she said absently, totally absorbed. The bright colors of the screen reflected off her pale skin. "It's a prototype, still in beta. There are probably around a hundred of them in existence. Right now the market price would be about fifty thousand dollars. Okay." She sat back. "I have several of my own domain email addresses. One is the one I used with Lauren. It's been a quiet few days, nothing particular. My work email—" Her fingers blurred on the keyboard. "Hmm. Four hundred messages."

Metal paused with two mugs of coffee in his hand. "What? Four hundred messages?"

She shrugged, scrolling down fast. "I'm a freelancer. I get a lot of offers of work. But I'm selective. They have to be interesting or pay well. Preferably both. Okay. Nothing that can't wait. Now I have to check my cell."

Alarmed, Metal stood behind her. If the bad guy was looking, and presumably he would be, her cell would ping somewhere where he could triangulate. Felicity knew what she was doing, but still.

But Felicity didn't put the battery back in her cell. As a matter of fact she didn't pull out her phone at all. Her fingers blurred again and then a list appeared.

"What did you just do?" Metal asked. If she'd replied *called the cell phone fairies* he wouldn't have been surprised.

"I, um, accessed the cell phone service provider's servers."

"You mean hacked?"

"Okay, if you want to get technical. Hacked." She shrugged.

Man, she'd hacked into one of the nation's largest cell phone providers in less time that it took him to take a sip of coffee. She was scary good. "Remind me to treat you extra special well."

She smiled then frowned.

"What?" Metal leaned forward.

She swiveled in her chair to face him. "Several phone calls from Kay Hudson. She rarely calls. She called eight times in a couple of hours." Her face pulled tight. "I hope nothing has happened to Al."

"Al?"

"Al Goodkind. Special Agent Al Goodkind before he retired from the FBI. I guess you could call him my mentor. I'm not too sure what the timeline is but I think he handled my father's case before the Marshals took over. Whatever. He and my dad were friends, or as much friends as they could be considering the circumstances. He was like an uncle to me growing up. A very distant uncle, but still. He's the one who offered me the Felicity Ward name so I could start with a clean slate."

"Are you in touch with him a lot?"

"I guess. We email or Skype a couple of times a month. Why would his granddaughter be calling me? We've spoken just a few times and I've never actually met her."

"Do you want to call from my cell? Or we can go buy a burner phone," Metal offered.

"No." Her fingers were blurring over the keyboard again. "Never go out when you can do something in the comfort of your own home. My motto."

She pressed Enter and a phone started ringing. "VoIP. Untraceable. And to make sure, I ran it through Untrakr."

Metal understood about half of that sentence, but he trusted Felicity.

"Hello?" a female voice said.

Felicity straightened in her seat. "Kay? This is Felicity."

They heard a sigh of relief. "Felicity! I've been calling and calling!"

"I've, uh, been out of town," Felicity said. "Am still out of town. Sorry not to return your calls. Is something up? Something wrong with Al? Listen, does your cell have a video function?"

"Yes, it does," the woman said. An image blossomed on Felicity's super sharp screen. A very pretty redhead in an airport terminal. In the background a robotic woman's voice announced a flight to St. Louis, departure immediate. "There. Is it working?"

"I see you." Felicity pressed a button. "Do you see me? Are you at an airport?"

"Yeah, JFK." She frowned. "Listen, Felicity, I've been trying to call Grandpa and he's not answering his cell. We had a Skype date last night and he missed it. He has never done that. He's never been out of touch like this before. I know it's early to be worried but this is just not like him."

Felicity was frowning too. "No, it's not like him," she agreed. "I've never known Al to miss an appointment of any kind."

"I was hoping that he'd at least been in touch with you. I know you guys touch base. I've been out of the country and in places where there's very little cell reception, so I wasn't worried that I didn't hear from him. But

I landed in New York last night and he didn't keep our Skype date and he was supposed to meet me here today and he didn't show up. I'm really worried."

"Ask if she has contacted his neighbors," Metal said in a low murmur. Whispers carried more than a low voice.

"Have you contacted the neighbors?"

"I only know one neighbor, a retired State Department officer. He rang Grandpa's bell but no one answered. Felicity, he just wouldn't behave like this. I've booked a flight to DC and I'm going to go directly to his house." She swallowed heavily. "God, I just hope I don't find him—"

Felicity now looked as worried as the woman. "Me too. Listen, call me when you get to Al's place."

All of this had Metal's Spidey sense tingling. He bent down to Felicity's ear. "Can I talk to her?" he asked.

She looked up at him, startled. "Sure."

Metal moved to where the screen's camera could see him. "Hello, Ms. Hudson."

The woman's eyes rounded. "Who are you?"

"My name is Sean O'Brien," he said. "I'm a friend of Felicity's and I work for a security company. Felicity was attacked three days ago." He nodded at Kay Hudson's gasp. "We have no information at all who her attacker was but we can only assume he is still looking for her and he might contact people close to her. Ms. Hudson, do you know anyone in DC who could go with you to your grandfather's house? Someone like a police officer or soldier?"

"No." She shook her head. "Sorry."

"Okay. Can we contact you in about ten minutes? What's your flight number and when are you landing?"

She swallowed again. Metal understood exactly what

she was going through. This was a new world for her, as if she'd plunged down a rabbit hole. By contrast, he realized that Felicity had lived with a subtext of intrigue and even violence all her life. She had never shown that moment of cognitive dissonance. Not once.

"Flight 4512. Landing at Reagan at 5:15."

"Okay. We'll contact you again immediately."

She nodded and Felicity blanked the screen. "Okay, she's deaf and blind but we're still connected. What are you going to do?"

"Contact a friend in Washington. He's FBI Hostage Rescue Team and if he's free, I'll have him meet Hudson's flight and accompany her. He owes me a big favor. If he can, he'll do this. And if there's any funny business he'll know what to do."

Felicity nodded. "Hostage Rescue. Yeah, he'll definitely know what to do."

Metal gave a half smile as he tapped a number on speed dial. "Nah. Not because he's an FBI weenie. Because he's a former SEAL. We were trained for everything."

She smiled back. "Including leaping tall buildings in a single bound."

He winked at her. "You got it, honey."

"Mancino." Nick Mancino's deep voice came on. Metal put his cell on speakerphone.

"Hey, Nick, howzzit hanging?"

"Metal, my man! To the left, as always. You?"

"That's classified. Look, I'm putting you on video." He held the cell so Felicity could see it too.

"Fine," Nick answered then whistled. "Hey, who's the babe?"

"Babe's mine, Nick. Hands-off. We have a situation here and we need your help."

Nick's grin disappeared and the operator came on-line. "Shoot. Anything you need, big guy. I owe you."

Metal nodded and put his hand on Felicity's shoulder. "This is Felicity Ward. She's a freelance service provider for the FBI."

Nick nodded. "Felicity. Any friend of Metal's is a friend of mine."

"Nick. Ditto." Felicity hadn't smiled at their banter. She was too worried about her friend.

"Nick, Felicity was attacked at the Portland airport. We haven't found her attacker though we've been looking. It's possible that the attack has something to do with Felicity's family's background. She's friends with a retired FBI special agent, Al Goodkind."

"I know Al," Nick said. "He's a good guy."

"He is," Felicity whispered. Her eyes were wet. She hadn't cried for herself, not once. But at the thought of danger to her friend…

"Al seems to be missing. He had a Skype appointment with his granddaughter which he missed. And he was supposed to meet her in New York today and he's not there. His granddaughter is really worried and she's catching a flight to DC right now. But we're worried—"

"You're worried something might have happened to Goodkind and you don't want her walking into trouble." Nick's face had changed completely. Felicity recognized that look from Metal and Jacko. And John and Douglas. "Gotcha."

"Nick." She leaned forward. "It's probably nothing, but it's not like Al to miss an appointment, particularly with his granddaughter. I can't think of anything that would make him do that. We're—we're really worried. Do you think you can go with her to Al's place? It would make me feel a lot better. There's something going on and I don't want Kay to be caught in the middle of it."

"No problem." On the video feed he was shrugging on a jacket. "I was scheduled to run a training session but I can get a teammate to cover for me. Give me details."

Metal gave him Kay's name and phone number, which Felicity had written down for him, the flight number and arrival time. "Thanks, Nick. I owe you one."

"No," Nick said. "You don't. Al's a friend. I'll get in touch when we get to Al's house. I'll make sure his granddaughter is safe. I'd go myself but she'll know the house better. Catch you later, then."

Felicity got Kay back online. "Kay, We've got an agent of the FBI coming to pick you up at the airport. I'm sending you a photo so you recognize him, but he'll have his badge."

"Why?" Kay looked frightened. "Do you think something has happened to my grandfather?"

"It's just a precaution," Metal said. "Trust me when I say your grandfather would want someone with you."

"Okay." She shifted her gaze to Felicity. "I'm scared something has happened to him."

Felicity nodded. "We'll know in a while. And if something has happened to him, the FBI will be on it right away. Let me know what's going on as soon as you get there."

Kay nodded and her image disappeared.

Metal put a hand on Felicity's shoulder. "Nick's really good. He'll make sure Kay is safe."

Felicity put her hand over his and shook her head. "I have a bad feeling about this, Metal."

TWELVE

An hour and a half later, Felicity and Metal joined Jacko, John and Douglas back at headquarters.

It was Metal's suggestion and she was quick to agree. It was miserable weather, but she wanted to be at Metal's company—maybe her company one day. Used to fighting her own battles, it comforted her to know that many heads were working together.

"Any pings on hotels?" was the first thing Metal asked. Via their Portland PD homicide detective friend an APB had been put out against Anatoli Lagoshin checking into any hotel in the area.

John Huntington shook his head. "Nope. And we widened it to include motels and boardinghouses and B and Bs within a thirty-mile radius. We figured he'd want to stick close to Portland."

"Did you check Airbnb?" Felicity asked as she drew her coat together. Metal had taken his parka and hoodie off and was only in a T-shirt, as was Jacko. As if they were perpetually hot. She knew the premises were heated but she felt cold. The cold of fear and anxiety.

"Check what?" John asked. Metal and Jacko looked at her with a question in their eyes too.

"Airbnb. It's a service where you can rent a room or an entire apartment, anywhere in the world. Never mind, I'll check."

She'd brought her laptop and opened it. Maybe

doing some proactive detecting would help her forget her worries. She dug around a little in the Portland section. She glanced up at the three men then back again at the screen. Her fingers hovered over the keyboard, unmoving.

"These aren't technically commercial establishments, they're private homes. And the site is arranged as a series of exchanges, not rentals. The owners of the rooms or apartments don't have a legal obligation to report arrivals. Renting an apartment through the service would be a good way to avoid scrutiny. However, there's no way I can check without hacking into the service."

Silence.

"Guys?"

"Hack," Metal growled. John didn't look happy but he nodded.

She entered the Airbnb back office and probed, delicately. She didn't want to leave any trace of intrusion. Finally, she sat back, disappointed. "Nothing. It's been a slow period for tourism. There are only seven apartments rented out tonight, all by families. And I checked the past two nights which were even slower. Three families and two women. I don't know—"

Metal's cell rang. He checked the screen and glanced at her. "Nick," he said.

Felicity's heart thumped as she moved closer to him. He put the cell down and put it on video and speakerphone. Jacko and John moved close too.

His friend Nick was on-screen next to Kay, white as ice. Behind them a living room. Felicity leaned closer and recognized a series of photographs of seasides and the corner of a bookcase. Al's home. She'd visited him several times while being interviewed by the FBI for the freelance work. It looked as if he had changed nothing in his living room over the past five years.

"Sitrep!" Metal barked.

Nick's face was grim. He looked to his left at a clearly distraught Kay and appeared to weigh his words. "There are signs of a struggle and—blood."

Kay's face was shiny with tear tracks. She nodded. "There was a broken lamp and a chair on the floor. There was blood on the floor and the walls. Oh God!" She buried her face in her hands. Nick hooked an arm around her shoulders as she broke into sobs.

He looked straight into his cell phone. "I called it in and forensics will be arriving soon. Goodkind's DNA is on record and we'll do a match. Goodkind's not a pushover, though. And there's no body, so we can assume he's been taken. This is a federal crime and the FBI and local LEOs are going to pull out all the stops."

Felicity leaned forward. "Did you find his cell?"

"No. Presumably he has it with him."

"Can you trace it? Or I can?"

Nick grimaced. "He was given one of our new Spec-Phones. Untraceable unless you switch the transponder on. I already checked. His transponder is off. Which would make sense if he was taken by surprise and had his hands cuffed."

Next to him, Kay gave a brief sob, then covered her mouth with her hand. Nick held the phone away from him and whispered something to her. She nodded, eyes closed.

Felicity wanted to sob too. Whatever had happened to Al, it was connected to her. She was responsible for this.

"What do they *want?*" she asked. "What could possibly be worth attacking me and kidnapping a retired FBI

special agent?" If they hadn't killed him. And maybe
they hadn't been attempting to kidnap her. Maybe it was
a murder attempt. Take her outside the airport to do the
deed. She looked up at the men around her. "I can't understand what this is about. None of it makes sense."

"Well, it makes sense to somebody," Metal growled.
"Or we wouldn't be here. I vote we catch the fuckers
and find out why later."

John and Douglas nodded. Jacko mumbled something profane.

It all made her feel better. These were proactive men.
Her specialty was analysis. They all looked perfectly
capable of analytical thinking but more than that, they
were men of action.

Still, she had her own contributions to make. "Uh,
guys? You know what Nick said about Al's cell being
untraceable if the transponder isn't turned on?"

"Yeah?" Metal looked at her with slitted eyes. "I think
I know where you're going with this. Is it illegal?"

Felicity thought. "Well, 'illegal' is a fluid concept.
It's a new system and presumably the laws—"

"Do it." John nodded decisively. "We're not federal
agents like Nick is. He'd probably have to leave the room
if he were here, though I don't doubt that if you have a
way of tracking Goodkind, he'd say go for it. He was a
Navy SEAL before he was a special agent. As SEALs,
we used whatever got the job done. So do it."

She entered the code for her cell phone servers, automatically checking for incoming calls. She froze.
"Guys?" she whispered. "Metal?"

Four male heads swiveled to her. Metal put a big hand
on her shoulder. "What is it, honey?"

"The nightmare's over." She looked up at him and

drew in a deep breath. "It's Al. He just called me a few minutes ago. Thank God!"

They weren't looking relieved. As a matter of fact, the four men looked grimmer than ever. "What? What's wrong?"

"When you call back, put him on speakerphone," John ordered.

"Okay." She used VoIP. Finding her cell, putting in the battery, switching it on—it would all take too much time. She put through the call and sighed when it made a connection on the other end. "Al! I'm so glad—"

"Not Goodkind," a male voice answered, in Russian. "But no need to worry about where he is. We have your friend."

It was Al's kidnapper. Another Russian. Metal and the others needed to understand what he was saying.

"I'm sorry," she said coolly in English. "I don't understand you. You'll have to speak English."

He answered in Russian. "You understand me well enough, Darinova. Listen carefully, because I won't repeat myself."

The voice was cool, calm, deep. Elegant Russian, the kind her mother had spoken. The voice of a man used to command. Definitely not the man who'd attacked her. Felicity chanced it.

She kept her own voice cool though her heart was racing. "How did you get Al Goodkind's cell phone, *Gospodin* Borodin?"

He didn't miss a beat. "Very clever. You are definitely your father's daughter. But at this very moment Vladimir Borodin is in Moscow, attending business meetings late in the night. There are twenty people willing to swear to that. In answer to your question, I have Goodkind's cell phone because he gave it to me."

"He didn't give it to you, you took it!" Suddenly the coolness was gone and white-hot rage flashed through her. "And how dare you even mention my father? He risked his life to get away from men just like you, *Colonel*. You aren't fit to talk about him. And you aren't fit to tie Al Goodkind's shoelaces."

She paused, gasping, trembling. A lifetime of repressed words geysering up.

The sound of hands clapping came over the speaker. "Bravo, Darinova. But you have your facts wrong. Your father didn't risk his life, he *defected*. He betrayed his country! He was a traitor! He should have been found and executed!"

The voice wasn't so cold and calm anymore. Metal and the others felt that, too, even though they couldn't understand what he was saying. They were leaning tensely forward. John had pressed something the instant Borodin had come online. The conversation was being recorded.

"But enough of that." The deep voice became calm again. Now that he was quiet again Felicity could hear something, some kind of dull noise in the background, growing in intensity. "All of that is in the past. But in the present, my dear Darinova, we have someone you might be interested in speaking to. Do you have videophone capabilities?"

A small square appeared on the screen. She could see him when he switched his system on but she wasn't about to let him see her. "Yes."

"Look at your friend," he commanded and Felicity suppressed a gasp. Al Goodkind, duct-taped to a chair.

One eye was swollen shut. The side of his face was bloody and there was blood on his white dress shirt. His mouth was duct-taped too.

He was in some kind of upholstered office chair with a white sheet behind him.

Metal made a low rumbling sound in his throat.

"Al!" Her heart broke at seeing her dear friend trussed up like an animal. A wounded animal.

"As you see, my dear, your friend is fine," Borodin said, indifference in his voice.

"He's bleeding, you monster!" Felicity bunched her fist, wanting to punch Borodin in the mouth.

She remembered the photo she'd seen in the Intergaz brochure. Hair just turning gray, strong, confident features. Handsome, in command. He'd be a man used to command all his life. First in the KGB and then as head of a multibillion dollar enterprise.

"Nothing. It's nothing." The cultivated voice was dismissive. "He probably received worse in training in Quantico. Now enough of this nonsense. All I want is to talk to you, face-to-face. I sent someone to pick you up at the Portland airport—"

"Pick me up!" Felicity spat. "He nearly sliced me in two!"

"What an exaggeration, my dear. No, he was just offering an incentive for you to follow him while making sure you didn't scream and attract attention. But I saw that stronger measures were necessary to attract your attention. Hence, Special Agent Goodkind. All I want is to talk. Your friend will be released and no harm will come to you. I want half an hour of your time."

On-screen, Al was shaking his head wildly, eyes wide and desperate, sweat trickling down his face to become bloody by the time it reached his chin. He was making muffled sounds behind the tape.

A fist came from the side and hit him on the temple. Al's head hung down, bloody sweat dripping onto his thights.

"You monster!" Felicity cried.

"Just a tap," Borodin assured her. "I have no desire whatsoever to kill a United States federal agent, believe me. Much more trouble than it is worth. As a matter of fact, when we meet and you talk to me, that is when I release him. Very happy to do so. He has been most troublesome."

Good! Felicity thought.

"I am not going to put myself in your hands," she said.

"Ah, my dear," he said, voice like velvet. "I think you will. You will have to if you wish to save your friend Mr. Goodkind. And I repeat, I have no desire, nor any interest, in killing either of you. I need to talk to you because I have reason to believe you have information that will prove useful to me. Then I will disappear. You will never see me again."

"What kind of proof would I have that what you say is true?"

"None, Darinova. None. But what choice do you have? So—" the voice turned brisk and businesslike, "—this is how it will work. Give me the name of the place where you want to meet."

"I—" Give him a place? That startled her. "I don't know Portland." The four men's attention sharpened at the name of the city.

"Neither do I. So we're even. Just name a place and I'll be there with your friend. I'm giving you the power to choose." Another of those dull rumbles.

"Ah—" She really didn't know Portland. She'd only seen a documentary once on its light-rail urban transportation system on the Net one rainy afternoon when she'd been very bored. One place stuck in her head. "Pioneer Courthouse Square."

"Pioneer Courthouse Square, then. In one hour's time, at 7:00 p.m. exactly, you will be at Pioneer Courthouse Square, close to a road where I can park and show you your friend. I will come alone, unarmed, and it is snowing too hard for any snipers to be deployed. You will be able to see from a distance that I am unarmed. Your friend will be in a vehicle and you will be able to see him. The vehicle will have a driver. I will stay at a distance from you at all times. Certainly beyond touching distance. Once we have spoken, I will free Special Agent Goodkind and you, of course, will be free to go. I just want to ask you a few questions. But if do not agree to see me, you will never see Goodkind again. Is that clear? Darinova, is that clear?"

Her throat was tight. "Yes."

"*Da.* See you in an hour."

"Wait!" Felicity shouted but the connection was broken. She called Al's cell again but it went to voice mail.

"WHAT THE FUCK was that about?" Metal demanded.

Felicity pushed herself away from the desk and swiveled to meet his eyes. "That was Borodin. He pretended he wasn't but that was more for show than anything else. He wants me to meet him in Pioneer Courthouse Square in an hour."

"Fuck no," Metal growled.

Metal's eyes widened like that of a spooked horse. John, Douglas and Jacko looked at him in surprise. They weren't used to seeing him agitated. He didn't do agitation, not even in firefights. But the idea of Felicity walking into a trap. Into a trap set by the fucking KGB—his nervous system simply couldn't handle it.

"I agree with Metal, Felicity," John said. "It's too dangerous. But we'll be there for the meet, no question. And I'm going to tell our friend in the Portland PD that a criminal will be in Pioneer Courthouse Square. A man who kidnapped a federal agent. And I should probably call the local FBI office too. We can do this, there's no need for you to get involved in any way."

Thank God Midnight had put this into words. Metal simply couldn't do it, couldn't reason. All he could do was shout no at the thought of Felicity walking into danger.

And thank God, too, that Felicity wasn't the kind to get her back up. Lots of women—and he'd dated plenty of them—would have bristled and gone out of principle. This wasn't Metal laying down the law, though. It was simply Metal terrified that something would happen to her.

She put her hand on his, looking sad. "I am so sorry, Metal. You're right but you're wrong. I don't have any training to do this but—we'll never see Al again if I don't show up in Pioneer Courthouse Square. He made that clear. And he also said he only wanted to talk."

John frowned. "Tell us exactly what he said. Listen to the recording and translate everything exactly. Let's get a picture of what we're up against."

They listened to the tape and Felicity gave a word-for-word translation. Metal hated every word of it.

"He's lying," he said emphatically to her when she'd finished. "He's fucking lying. Can't you see that?"

"Oh, of course he's lying," Felicity said. "That goes without saying. He's former KGB. They lie every time their lips move. However, he has laid himself open. He said he'd show himself to be unarmed." She glanced out the window. "Is it true what he said? That a sniper can't operate in this snow?"

Metal jerked his thumb at Jacko, who was the expert. Plus, he couldn't stand that thoughtful expression on her face which meant she was thinking about it.

"Be hard," Jacko said, ignoring Metal's glare. Answering in a way that would only encourage her. "They'd have to use thermal scopes, which don't give as clear a sight view. And the way I understand it, you picked the venue, right?"

Felicity nodded.

Jacko turned to Metal. "No sniper can set up a nest in an hour in a foreign city. Pioneer Courthouse Square has high-rises around it. They don't have time to figure out the best angle and get rid of the inhabitants of the space. As a matter of fact, I can't figure out this guy's angle if he lets her pick the venue."

"There's something definitely nefarious," Felicity said firmly and Metal wanted to kiss her. "It's the KGB. He has something up his sleeve. But if he is unarmed and I am near to you guys, maybe we can save Al." Now Metal didn't want to kiss her. He wanted to tie her down and not in a good way.

"There's something I need to figure out too. How long will it take us to get to Pioneer Courthouse Square from here?" Felicity asked.

"Five hours," Metal said. "Pointless going."

"About twenty minutes." John looked out the window. "Maybe half an hour in this weather. Men, start suiting up."

Everyone headed for an innocuous section of wall, undistinguishable except for the fact that it didn't have artwork. John placed his palm against the wall and the whole section slid away to reveal their armory.

Felicity peeked in. She saw an amazing amount of gear including¾ "Are those hazmat suits? We're not going to need hazmat suits."

"Yeah. We're prepared for more or less everything," Metal answered, teeth clenched. Everyone was moving forward as if this crazy scheme was a go. He could object all he wanted but short of shooting them all in the leg, there was no stopping them. So he was suiting up too.

"While you guys do your thing, I'll do mine," Felicity said mysteriously and sat back down at her computer.

Metal put on his vest. He, Jacko and Senior had had to have custom-made vests ordered. Vest, Glock 19 in a side holster. Taser. They all decided against rifles, except for Jacko, who was the best shot of the four of them. Particularly Metal didn't want a rifle. He had no intention of being far enough away from Felicity to need one. He looked around. Everyone was ready to go.

Four tough guys prepared for anything.

Something felt tight in his throat.

This was *his* battle, not theirs. And yet here they were, putting their lives on the line for him and for Felicity. Though they were tough and trained and well-equipped…well, shit happens. A lot. And it can happen to the smartest, best-equipped son of a bitch around.

Jacko and Midnight and Senior were backing him up because that's what they did. They were a team and it was why he loved working for ASI so much.

And when he emerged from their armory his throat tightened again because there she was—another teammate. Beautiful and smart and brave, her fingers blurring at the keyboard, weird noises coming from the computer.

She was going to become an ASI teammate, he could feel it, like something inevitable, something that simply had to be. Some force in the universe had brought her to them.

To *him*. Because she was his teammate, his special one. The one he'd been waiting for all his life. The one who'd become his family after losing his other one.

She was so focused that she didn't even look up when they emerged. Of course they'd all been trained to move quietly even in full battle rattle and ready for action. Nothing jingled when they moved, they made sure of it.

"Honey?" Metal said finally.

She looked up, eyes with that glazed look of someone who was concentrating furiously. She saw him and her face softened and something went thump really hard in his chest. "Metal," she said and smiled.

Oh God. They were about to embark on a mission, and though they were going to make sure nothing happened to her, nothing was certain. She could be hurt. He couldn't stand the thought.

She motioned for them to come over. "Come look. Or rather listen."

When they were behind her chair, staring at the monitor that showed the last frame of a beaten Goodkind, head hanging, knocked unconscious, she pressed a key.

"Before we go, I want you guys to listen to this. I ran the recording through a special program that isolates background noise." She pressed another key and they listened carefully. Borodin's voice had disappeared and they listened to a background rumbling, which now sounded familiar.

"Man," Metal said. "That sounds like…like planes taking off."

"Yes," she said. "It does, and it is. Look. I hacked—er, consulted with the Portland International control tower and watch."

On the screen, instead of Goodkind, were two timelines. The first of the recording and the second—

She pointed at it. "Now watch. Below is a time plot of the background noises. Above is the exact moment three planes took off from Portland International."

The two timelines coincided perfectly. "Al is being held at the Portland airport. I don't think he could possibly be held hostage in a commercial airliner so in all likelihood he's being held in a private jet. Borodin promised he'd let me see Al but I don't know if he will. Right this moment, unless he's being transported to Pioneer Square, he's there."

John had his cell out. "Nick? Advise the Portland office that Goodkind is possibly being held on a private plane in the General Aviation section of Portland International. Activate your HRT guys here. There's also the possibility that he's being transported via vehicle to Pioneer Courthouse Square, so contact the airport authorities, see if you can intercept the vehicle. It will probably be a van. Be advised that this is being managed by a former colonel of the KGB." He listened for a second. "Yeah, I know. At any rate, in an hour we'll have him. I'll be in touch."

Metal could only imagine what was being set in motion in the FBI. The Portland office, of course, but also in DC. The FBI was good at what they did and they protected their own ferociously. Borodin had messed with the wrong guys.

And the wrong girl, he thought, as he helped Felicity put on her coat. She was as brave as any warrior and sure as hell smarter.

Midnight tapped the screen and pulled on a parka. "Okay," he said, twirling his finger. "Heading out."

"I won't be more than five feet from you," Metal repeated for the fiftieth time. They were sitting in the back of an SUV. Jacko was driving. John and Douglas were in a second SUV. An FBI team was on its way to the airport.

Felicity shivered and Metal's arm around her shoulders tightened. Jacko, John and Douglas had looked completely expressionless as they got into the vehicles, men on a mission. She understood they had done this a thousand times before.

Metal looked pissed. And though she was rarely acute about anyone's psychological state, she understood that Metal's anger covered fear. He wasn't afraid for himself. He was afraid for her.

She was afraid for herself too. It was insane to go meet Borodin, a former *colonel of the KGB*. Her parents would have been appalled. They'd defected to a country two continents and an ocean away to get away from the KGB.

But what else could she do? What was the alternative? Not show up? Maybe Borodin would have Al shot on the spot, out of spite and because he wasn't useful anymore. Al was a good guy. He'd always been kind to her, in his gruff way. To tell the truth, he'd almost been more of a father to her than her own father had been.

She knew her father loved her but he'd been a remote figure all her life. Al was a warmer man, and he'd done nothing but help her.

She loved him like a father though she'd never told him.

She could never live with herself if something happened to him that she could have prevented. If he died because she was too scared to meet with Borodin, she'd be heartsick the rest of her life.

She couldn't abandon Al, simply couldn't.

But she was scared.

It was dark now and snow was falling wildly, the wind scattering flakes in every direction. How Jacko could see to drive was beyond her, but he seemed to have no difficulties. This was the kind of weather where she'd lock herself in the house for a week.

Instead, she was going to meet a monster, unarmed. That wasn't quite true. She did have weapons. John and Douglas and Jacko. And Metal, of course. Who was going to be as close to her as he could, despite the advice of his teammates.

Metal brought out his tablet and ran through it with her once again. "You are going to stand here—" He stabbed the glass screen with a thick figure. They had worked out hiding places and fields of fire—which she understood to be a way to avoid shooting each other—and what they called comms. Each had an earpiece in his right ear. She had one too. They were on a frequency only they could hear. Metal wasn't done with his briefing. His tenth. "And I will be here. Behind this." He stabbed again, at a concrete plinth. "Do you understand me, honey? I'll be five feet from you and I'll have my gun out."

Felicity turned toward him with difficulty. She had on a vest too, only it was several sizes too big. Luckily she was also wearing a big down coat that had been lent to her, which hid the fact that she was wearing a vest under it. Damn, it was uncomfortable. How could law enforcement officers wear one for hours? The thing rubbed against her breasts. Did female officers have a molded vest to accommodate breasts?

But her discomfort was nothing compared to what Metal was feeling.

"Yes," she said gently. Metal looked like his head was ready to explode. "I understand. I'll make my way to the corner and stand ten feet away from the curb. I don't move and if I hear a whistle, I drop to the ground immediately." She cupped his big hand with hers.

He grunted, as if something hurt.

"Get your fucking head back in the game, man," Jacko said from the driver's seat. He glanced in the rearview mirror. "You're behaving like a fuckhead and you're scaring her."

Metal ran a big hand down his face and drew a deep breath. "I'm sorry, honey. I don't want to scare you. I just want to know that you're on board with the plan."

"Yes," she said, and squeezed his hand. "I am. It's a great plan. And basically all I have to do is stand there, far enough away that he can't grab me. And if he does, you guys come out firing."

"Damn straight," Metal said fervently. "Be easier just to waste the guy the instant he shows his face."

"But then Al might pay the consequences." They'd been over this.

Metal opened his mouth but Jacko said, "We're here."

The plan was for Jacko and John to park on the other

side of the square and the ASI guys would quietly move toward prearranged stations. Metal would make his way to the plinth and she would slowly walk across the square to the corner where she'd meet Borodin.

Through their comms system they'd heard that the FBI HRT had reached the airport.

One way or another they'd find Al.

It was freezing cold when she emerged from Jacko's vehicle. A gust of wind nearly knocked her off her feet. Metal held her elbow and murmured, "Easy now."

She nodded at him and he nodded back and…disappeared. Amazing. He was a huge man and yet he seemed to simply melt away.

Five minutes to deadline.

Felicity faced the street where Borodin would park, took a deep breath and began walking. The wind was at her back so she didn't have the snow blowing in her eyes. It was below freezing. She didn't dare cry. Her mother had told her stories of tears freezing in the depths of Russian winters.

The square was lit but the lights seemed weak, somehow, never penetrating more than a few feet. It was a pretty square, with an amphitheater to her right and some low concrete buildings to her left. She'd seen the aerial photographs and knew that the terra-cotta bricks were inscribed with names but the snow was too heavy on the ground to see them, even if she could in the dim light.

Three minutes to deadline.

"That's right, honey." Metal's deep voice sounded in her ear. "Just keep walking. We all have a visual on you and we're not going to let anything happen to you."

"We're alone in the park," John said in her ear. He was holding a tablet that gave thermal images. "But there's a vehicle coming up. Parking…it's parked on the next block. Someone is getting out. A tall man. He's alone, moving toward the RP." Rendezvous point. They'd also given her a crash course in the military slang they'd be using.

"Anyone else in the vehicle?" Jacko asked. He was the only one with a long gun. He had a thermal scope. If another sniper was in the area, Jacko would see him.

"Can't tell," John said.

She was more than halfway across the square now.

Two minutes to deadline.

She was alone in the middle of the snowy square. Metal and his teammates were all around her, observing her every move, but she couldn't see them. All she could see was the expanse of snow-covered brick, some trees and a few blocky buildings. Across the street was a lit building, looking warm and welcoming. For a second she longed to be in that building. Inside was her place, not out in the blowing wind.

One minute to deadline.

But she was here now and Al's fate was in her hands. She wasn't going to let him down. Not now, not ever.

Thirty seconds.

A gust of wind blew snow in her eyes and she closed them for a moment and continued walking. She didn't want to give Borodin even the faintest excuse to bail.

Or shoot.

Deadline.

"Stop, honey," Metal said in her ear. She stopped, far from the curb.

A man walked out of the misty snow. Tall, elegant, an *ushanka*, a fur hat with fur flaps over the ears, on his head. The man in the brochure. The CEO of Intergaz. Vladimir Borodin.

"Tell him to show he is unarmed."

"Show me that you come unarmed, as you promised," she said in English.

"But of course, Darinova," he answered in Russian. He took off his elegant topcoat, folded it neatly over his arms. Underneath he was wearing a black sweater which fit tightly enough to show that he wasn't carrying a weapon. To her untrained eyes it looked as if he didn't have a bulletproof vest, either. Reaching slowly, he put his hands in his pockets and pulled them inside out, so that they hung from his hips. He held his arms high as he turned slowly around.

"Ankles," Metal said.

"Ankles," she repeated.

With a slow dip of his head, he lifted first one pant leg then another.

"Hat," Metal said.

"Ushanka," Felicity repeated and Borodin doffed his hat, showing her the empty interior.

"May I put my coat and hat back on?" he asked politely. "This isn't as cold as Moscow in winter but still, I am uncomfortable."

A shot of rage went through her. "I don't care if you are uncomfortable," she said. "Where is Al Goodkind?"

"Special Agent Goodkind?" Borodin lifted a sardonic brow. "He is well."

"You beat him half to death!"

Borodin chuckled. "Hardly, *duschka.* Clearly you have led a sheltered life. He is fine. And he is close."

"Don't you dare call me sweetheart! You're a monster!"

They were close now, five feet apart. Borodin took a step forward.

Without Metal saying anything she stepped back. "Don't come near me."

Borodin tilted his head. "Fine. I've stopped, see?" He was standing with his feet braced, unmoving. "So, do you want to see your dear friend?"

"Yes."

Borodin suddenly lifted his right hand, fist clenched. A sign. If his men saw that through the snow they were using binoculars. Or maybe they had thermal imagers like Metal's team had. "I am sure you are surrounded by men. Armed men. My vehicle is coming and inside is Special Agent Goodkind. So please do not shoot."

Felicity didn't bother denying that she had men behind her. Out of the corner of her eye she could see a vehicle slowly making its way down the street.

"All I want is to ask you a few questions, Darinova." He had his coat and hat back on and stood relaxed, open hands by his side. He didn't have gloves on. Neither did she and she was starting to regret that. In the rush she hadn't even thought of gloves. Or a hat.

Borodin stared at her, then he lifted his hand, elegant and long-fingered and curled his fingers in the universal gesture *come to me.*

He wasn't threatening in any way but she felt her chest tighten, panic reaching its fingers into her. Dread consumed her and she felt as if one step forward would seal her doom. "What do you want from me?" Her voice was weak. She found it hard to breathe. "I don't know anything. What could I possibly tell you?"

Borodin shrugged and took a step forward, as if to hear her better. He glanced sharply to his left, where the van was arriving, slowly, rolling to a stop more than braking to a stop.

"There you are wrong, *duschka*. There is much you can tell me. And, of course, you will."

Oddly, he brought something out of the top pocket of his elegant overcoat. In the snowy mist, Felicity couldn't figure out what it was. It certainly wasn't a weapon. He reached up to his head and cupped his ears. At the same time, something rose from the van fifty feet away, a flat cylinder, like a gigantic coin, with a man wearing earphones behind it. It swung around toward the square...

"LRAD!" Metal screamed in her ear and then pain gripped her entire body.

Her head pounded with the pulsing pain, her brains were beating against her skull. She fell to her knees, agony in every cell of her body, then fell to the snowy ground, curling up in the fetal position, though nothing staved off the excruciating pain. She turned and retched miserably, holding her head with her hands as if to stop her head from exploding. She'd never felt pain like this before, it took over her entire being.

Dimly, as if from some other planet, two hands gripped her arms and she was lifted up. Her legs folded under her. She couldn't stand, the pain made it impossible to move her muscles. A heave and she was tossed over a male shoulder. The man started walking quickly toward the street.

The man...she couldn't remember the name. She couldn't remember her name. All she felt was pain and overwhelming nausea. She opened her mouth and bile spilled out as she gave a little cry.

Nothing made sense, she couldn't get her bearings, she couldn't think.

Then, suddenly, the debilitating nausea stopped and whatever it was that had gripped her body eased away. But she was horribly weak. Something wet coated her neck and when she lifted her hands, they came away bloody. She was bleeding. From where?

Strong hands grabbed her and tossed her onto something. Something hard. Inside something. She could barely focus. Her head still hurt fiercely, as did her ears. With a huge effort she lifted herself up on an elbow, shaking with the strain. In a box with one side open, slanting snow blown by the wind. A figure in a dark overcoat smiling coolly.

Borodin! Some of the fog in her head cleared. She was in the back of a van and Borodin was closing the doors. But she was still horribly weak and nauseated. Her head hung down, neck muscles too weak to hold it up.

Borodin opened his arms wide to bring the doors closed when something dark slammed into him from behind and he fell face-first into the van. Felicity reached out, wanting to hurt him, hit him with something but there was nothing to grab and her muscles weren't responding. Like someone had severed the connection between mind and body.

The dark shape reared up, face a bloody mask of rage. Metal! Oh God! Metal had come for her!

But he was almost as damaged as she was. Throwing Borodin into the van nearly used up all his resources. He was staggering, head down, hands on knees. Barely upright. Borodin hit him on the side of the head with his elbow and Metal staggered even more. Before he could fall down, Borodin leaped out of the van and gave Metal a hard push into the van, lifted his legs in and closed the van door.

A second later, he climbed into the passenger seat, and turned his face to the driver. Felicity could see his lips move but heard nothing. She couldn't even hear the engine firing, taken by surprise when the van pulled away fast. Neither she nor Metal had any warning and they bounced around in the back of the van as it sped away, taking corners dangerously fast. There was nothing to hang on to in the van so they rolled with the centripetal force.

At one particularly tight corner, she slammed her head against the side of the van. Metal reached out and held her tight. He spoke but she couldn't hear him.

They were helpless. Borodin was taking them God knew where and who knew when they would get their strength back? Metal was doing better than her, but barely. At another corner he was able to hold her and brace himself against the wall with his leg but she could feel that he was straining.

No hope of taking Borodin and the driver by surprise, either, even if Metal was fully functioning. Borodin kept one hand on the back of the seat, face turned to the driver, switching his gaze to them every few seconds. He had a gun in his hand.

Felicity felt sick all over again. They were trapped. Despite all their precautions, Borodin had outwitted them with some kind of sonic cannon. Would it leave permanent hearing loss? Not that they'd live long enough to worry about that.

A biting pressure on her wrist and she looked down. Metal was holding his gun. But his hand was trembling. She looked up at his face, grim and pale. Blood stained the sides of his head.

Then—he winked.

Oh God! Yes! Maybe there was hope!

Metal brought one trembling hand up to grasp the wrist of his right hand holding the gun. Her body blocked the view so Borodin couldn't see them. Metal's left hand gripped the right so hard his knuckles whitened but the trembling stopped.

But he couldn't move fast enough. Borodin's eyes kept flicking over to them and Borodin had complete use of his senses. He'd had acoustic protection from the sonic cannon.

Metal was doing his best to be ready for any drop in attention, but it wasn't coming.

Then Borodin held a cell phone to his ear and her heart leaped in her chest. He was using Al's cell! She recognized the phone case—a gift from his granddaughter. Blue with the FBI seal in gold.

She thumped Metal on the chest to get his attention. They couldn't whisper and even if they could, they couldn't hear each other. Metal looked at her, a question in his eyes. She carefully brought out her cell and started thumbing frantically. It was an app a fellow hacker had sent her as a semijoke. Dangerous, in the wrong hands. Hers were definitely the right hands.

Metal was watching her carefully but she didn't dare try to signal anything. Sending her cell instructions with trembling hands was using up her entire hard disk. Borodin was speaking but she couldn't hear anything. Couldn't hear when he was nearing the end of the conversation. If he finished before she did, all was lost. Metal would never have his chance.

Borodin was still speaking, attention diverted from them, by the time she'd finished inputting the app. Metal was watching her carefully. Not understanding, but trusting her. She looked up into his eyes, those bright eagle eyes watching her every move. She held a finger up—*wait!*—pressed the final key and nodded.

Now!

She couldn't hear any sound at all, but she could see. A flash of brilliant light followed by a puff of smoke. Borodin reacting as if he'd received a punch to the head. Blackened flesh appearing on the side of his face. The driver turning his head, reaching out...

And Borodin's head exploded and the driver's head exploded and the van slipped in the snow, bumped over the curb and crashed into a streetlamp.

Felicity lay on her back, stunned. Everything seemed a million miles away, part of another, remote universe. Was she dead?

Metal's rough face, blood streaming from a cut in his forehead, appeared right above her, right where heaven would be. His mouth was open, lips forming a word, over and over again. Dreamily, Felicity reached up and cupped the side of his face. She smiled at him. Or did she? It was hard to tell what she was doing. And maybe it didn't make any difference, if she was dead.

She drifted off then came to again as she was violently shaken. Metal, mouth opening and closing. A faint noise came to her from a faraway place.

Her name?

Metal pulled her up and into his arms, his mouth close to her ear. She could hear a little more clearly now. He was shouting her name, but it felt like he was on another continent.

Faces appeared in the van's open doorway. Snow was blowing into the back of the van, falling on her face. Her skin felt cold.

Two men in police uniforms. Three other men, men she knew. But she couldn't remember their names. All three of the men, men she knew she knew but couldn't remember their names looked pale and battered, with trickles of blood on the sides of their faces.

Hands reached out for them, but Metal shook them off. He pulled away and held her by the shoulders so she could see his face.

He yelled something at her.

"What?"

"I love you!" he shouted, holding her tightly.

"I love you too!" she screamed back.

They toppled to the side in each other's arms.

EPILOGUE

Portland Memorial Hospital

THE NEXT DAY, Kay peeked into the room then pulled her head back. "He's awake!" she said excitedly to Felicity.

Metal had his arm around Felicity's shoulder and they both shuffled forward. They'd spent the night in the hospital and had been released an hour ago. They hadn't left the hospital yet, just traveled up two floors.

The police had sequestered the LRAD, the Long Range Acoustic Device mounted to the roof of the van. It had beamed over 160 dB at them, well over the threshold of pain. Felicity and Metal would suffer slight but permanent hearing loss. Jacko, John and Douglas had been far enough away to feel the pain but would have no long-lasting effects.

They were all a little dinged but Felicity knew they were fortunate to be alive.

Borodin and his driver were dead and the FBI had found Al in a private jet, duct-taped to a chair, watched over by three guards who were never going to see the light of day ever again.

One of them was the man who had attacked her at the airport and it pleased her no end to know that he would be jailed for the rest of his natural life.

What the CEO of Intergaz wanted with her was still a mystery.

However, they were all alive. Big plus.

Al was sitting up in bed, a huge lopsided grin on his face. One side of his face was relatively normal, the other side swollen and discolored. The bruises on his face were turning yellow and green and he looked awful, but he was smiling at them. He hugged Kay, kissed the side of her face, then held his hand out to Felicity.

She rushed to hug him. "Oh, Al! I'm so glad you're alive!" Tears welled in her eyes. "I'm so very sorry. This is all because of me. I have no idea what that man wanted but I am so sorry you were caught in the middle."

He hugged her back. He smelled of disinfectant and soap and old man and he felt absolutely wonderful.

Al glanced at the other man in the room, standing discreetly in a corner, hands folded over his crotch. He wore an ill-fitting black suit, white shirt, black tie and a curly wire running from his ear down into his collar. He had FBI practically tattooed on his forehead and he was there to protect Al. Felicity would have kissed him, except his head would probably explode.

"Any news?" he asked the man.

"No, sir." The man shook his head. "But there is a lot of diplomatic maneuvering because Russia cannot explain how it is that one of their leading businessmen found himself in Portland with a team of former Spetsnaz soldiers kidnapping an American woman and a federal agent. Lot of fallout, none of it good for them."

Al nodded sharply, then winced.

Metal grabbed a chair, placed it close to Al's bedside and practically carried Felicity to it. "Sit," he said. She took off her backpack, set it on the floor and plopped down in the chair. She would have bristled at his commanding tone, but it felt really good to sit down. The doctors said it was going to take some time for her to completely recover. For both of them to. Maddeningly, though, Metal showed very few signs of strain. She on the other hand looked like she'd just come back from a particularly long and vexing war.

She'd have time to recover, all the time she wanted. And as of today, she was on ASI's payroll with a fabulous salary and benefits and strict instructions not to put her nose in the office for another month.

Al held her hand and looked at them. At her, Kay, Metal and FBI guy in the corner.

"I have an idea what they were looking for," he said softly.

Electricity crackled in the air.

"What?" Metal asked.

Felicity opened her mouth and closed it. Looked at Al's kindly, lived-in face. A face that had known sorrow and that knew how to keep secrets. She looked deeply into his sad brown eyes and knew.

There were secrets there. Her life was one long secret. She'd grown up in the shadows of so much kept hidden, so much unspoken. Hidden things poisoning her family, casting long shadows.

"Al?" she whispered.

Understanding that something was happening, Metal placed himself right behind her chair and put a hand on her shoulder. She reached up to touch his hand. Knowing in a deep part of her that she would always have that hand on her shoulder from now on.

Al fidgeted, trying to change the position of his pillows. Metal left her side, arranged the pillows and lifted Al bodily so he could sit comfortably. Then Metal came back to her, standing behind her, strong and solid.

"Thanks," Al said wryly. "Time was when I could do that for myself."

"Al." Felicity's throat was suddenly tight. "Is there something I should know?"

He sighed. "I don't quite know. It all comes back to your family. Your father was a brilliant man, Felicity. But complicated."

She nodded.

"When he defected, there were rumors he was working on something brand-new. Something revolutionary for the time."

"In terms of nuclear weapons?" Felicity's heart was pounding. Metal's fingers tightened on her shoulder.

"Yes. There were a lot of rumors in the community of physicists that your father had made a breakthrough. But that he was conflicted about it."

"Breakthrough?"

Al nodded. "That he had managed to miniaturize many of the components of a nuclear bomb while using very lightweight materials. That—well, that he had developed or was in the process of developing man-portable nuclear bombs."

"Jesus," Metal muttered.

Al met Metal's eyes over her head. "Yeah."

"Scary shit."

"Very scary," Al said.

"I don't understand." Felicity looked back over her shoulder at Metal, then at Al. "Man-portable bombs?"

"I thought that was just an urban legend," Metal said.

"Maybe. Maybe not." Al drew in a deep breath then winced and held his side. "Sorry. Nobody really knows if it is an urban legend or not. Or rather Nikolai Darin would know, except he's dead. At the time he defected, the Soviet Union was losing the Cold War. For those with eyes to see, the end was near and a lot of people in the security apparatus were very anxious. They weren't going to go down with the ship. A lot of wild-eyed ideas were green-lighted. Weaponized smallpox. Poisoning major waterways. And very small nuclear weapons that didn't require missiles. They had a name for them too. Deti."

"The little ones," Felicity whispered.

Al nodded. "Yeah. The little ones. Rumor was that they could be carried in a backpack." He looked at Metal. "Smaller and lighter than the kind SEALs carry into battle. Place one in every major city, blow them up and you've won the Cold War. Because who would know who placed them, set them off? Moscow would deny it vehemently while mopping up the rest of the world. With no proof, what was left of the United States wouldn't retaliate. It was supposed to be a last-ditch plan if Moscow ever fell, as it did in 1991. By then if the Deti ever existed, no one could find them."

"They *lost* nuclear weapons?" Felicity asked, appalled. "How can you do that? As if misplacing a pen? That's insane."

Metal gave a harsh laugh. "Entire arsenals were lost when the Soviet Union fell. For a few years it was absolute chaos. We had to send over inspectors at our expense to start to do an inventory. The office that kept track of their nuclear arsenal was disbanded and the files lost. We were looking at an entire arsenal that the Russians—most of them ex-KGB—were trying to sell to the mob and to terrorists. It was wild. They ransacked a whole country."

"Was that what Borodin wanted from me? The location of the Deti? That's—that's crazy. I'd never even heard of this until now. My father never said anything to me. Nothing at all. Why would Borodin think I knew anything?"

Silence.

"Al?" Her voice rose because Al winced again, but it wasn't because of a cracked rib. "Al? What do you know?"

"Nothing, honey." He shook his head. "I don't know anything. But you—you might know."

"No." Felicity shook her head decisively. "I don't know anything about this. Nothing at all."

"Your father and I got drunk together once," Al mused.

Felicity's mouth fell open. "*Drunk? My father?*" Her sober, serious, unsmiling father? The only Russian in the history of the country to have never developed a taste for vodka? "Never."

Al smiled faintly. "Oh yes. Just the once. You must have been, oh, eleven? Twelve? Back in Russia the Mafiya had taken over. The whole country was a huge criminal enterprise. Your father was in Washington for some reason and he called and came over with two bottles of the best vodka I have ever had, bar none."

"You guys drank two bottles of vodka?"

Al shook his head. "Not quite, but almost. I had an epic hangover the next day. The next three days, actually. Vomited my guts out. Anyway, deep in the night we started talking about regrets. He said there was something he deeply regretted doing. I looked at him and knew. And he knew I knew. I asked him where they were."

"The Deti?"

Al nodded. "Yes, honey. The Deti. Bombs that could have changed the course of the world."

"And what did he say?"

"He said you'd know where they were," Al answered, gray eyes watching her so carefully. "He said he left everything with you."

It was almost as bad as being hit by the sonic boom. Felicity felt nausea rise and her head pound. "But… that's insane. I don't know. How could I? This is the first I ever heard of even the existence of the Deti. How could my father have said that when he never told me anything? And how could he say I knew when I was just a little girl?"

"Your father's English wasn't perfect. He chose his words carefully. He said you would know. As if he hadn't told you yet, but would."

Felicity sighed sadly. "He died without telling me. You must believe that."

"Wait." Metal turned to Al. "He said he left everything with Felicity?"

"Yes. He said that. He left everything with his daughter."

"He didn't leave anything with me! Not that I know of. When they died so suddenly, I sold the house and all its contents. If he left information on the bombs in…I don't know. A book, in a piece of furniture, behind a painting, it's gone. But he wouldn't do that, would he? Leave something of importance to me without telling me?"

"But he did," Metal said softly. "He did leave something of importance to you and he told you to always keep it with you." He bent and picked up her backpack. "And you do. You always have it with you."

Felicity gasped.

Metal zipped open the top of the backpack and pulled out the soft leather carrying case. "Your father's Nobel

Prize. Check it carefully, honey." He opened the case and carefully handed the medallion to her.

Felicity took it with numb fingers. She held it in the palm of her left hand. She'd seen it a million times. She looked up at Metal then at Al. "It's the genuine medallion. There aren't any extra letters or numerals. There's nothing here." She turned it over and looked at it, seeing nothing she hadn't seen a million times before.

"Let me see," Metal said gently and she handed it over. He brought it close to his eyes and carefully studied it. Then he reached down and slid a knife from his boot. A knife she'd had no idea he was carrying. It was thin, razor sharp, pointed. Holding it by the black handle, Metal put the pointed end against the face of the medallion and worked the knife. Felicity watched uneasily. That medallion was very precious to her. She was about to say something about being careful when Metal gave a grunt of satisfaction and held his broad palm out.

Felicity and Al peered down at the tiny dot in the palm of his hand.

"A microdot," Al murmured. "Fairly high tech for the time. Now we'll have to find a forensic IT specialist to find the equipment to read it."

Felicity sat, stunned. "What do you think is on the microdot?"

"Coordinates," Metal said. "Coordinates to hidden atomic bombs."

Portland, Oregon
Three weeks later

SHE CAME IN LAUGHING, waving goodbye to Lauren, who waited in the car until she was in the house before driving off.

"Hey," Metal said.

"Hey." She looked so incredibly beautiful, color high from the cold, eyes bright bright blue. Weighed down by about a ton of bags.

"I see you've been shopping," he said mildly. Apparently she'd just discovered it as a recreational activity. She now made regular forays and came back with booty, filled with delight. She shopped with Lauren, she shopped with Suzanne and Allegra and had started an entire new chapter of shopping with Claire, Bud's wife. Metal didn't care. She sometimes came home with amazing underwear in every color of the rainbow. Yeah.

"God, yes. Lauren and I discovered this amazing shoe shop, outlet really. Fifty percent off your fifth purchase. Incredible quality."

"You happy with what you bought?" he asked.

"Absolutely." She smiled a secret smile. "Particularly happy. I got you a present."

"Yeah?" God, she was irresistible. And he never resisted her. Couldn't.

She'd gone to work at ASI almost immediately, notwithstanding Midnight's and Senior's protests. In only a few weeks she had become indispensable to the company. Metal was under strict orders never to leave her.

God, no. Why would he do that when she made him so happy? As a matter of fact…

But first some news. Metal had no idea how she was going to take it.

Felicity was unwinding his long ratty black scarf from around her neck when she froze. "What's wrong?"

Damn. For a self-professed nerd she was getting really good at reading people. Or at least reading him.

"Let's sit down," he said. When she sat, he took both her hands.

Her eyes searched his, back and forth, those incredibly perceptive bright blue eyes that saw through him. That saw *him*.

"They found them, didn't they?" she whispered. "The Deti."

Metal nodded. "Six of them. Exactly where the coordinates said they'd be."

"I thought we were never supposed to know. That it was a state secret. At least that's what Al said. That I'd never have closure."

Well, it turned out Al loved her too much to leave her hanging.

"I found out through a roundabout way and we are to forget this forever. Do you understand me, Felicity? We must never talk about this."

She nodded, face sober. "Never. I have Russian blood. We keep secrets for generations."

"Okay. They went immediately to the site of the coordinates. The FBI and a NEST team. NEST is—"

"Nuclear Emergency Support Team. Yes. Where did they find the Deti?"

"On an old farm, near Merritt, Minnesota. Just a few acres and an abandoned clapboard house. Merritt is—"

"Merritt was our first home." Her face was pale. "I barely remember it. We left when I was four. I never saw it again."

"It was bought by a corporation whose owner we can't track down. But the important thing is that the land belonged to no one and your father made sure it would never belong to anyone. They found them exactly at the coordinates—buried six feet underground in a special casing."

Al had no idea how Darin had managed to smuggle the Deti in, but they were small. An ordinary trunk would contain them.

"Why now? Why let us know now? I'll bet they found them immediately."

Yes, they had. Now, because Al had been debriefed for a full week and had waited another two weeks to casually get to a pay phone and call him. Risking big too. It was a measure of Al's love for Felicity, that he was willing to risk jail to get her closure.

"It was the first chance he got," Metal said simply.

"So." Felicity clung to his hands. "It's over."

"It's over," he agreed. "No old business. Not anymore. Just new business. Just us, together. And our future." *And our family*, he thought.

More than anything in the world he wanted a family with Felicity.

"Our future." She smiled. "I like the sound of that."

"Me too."

The future. Felcity's entire life had revolved around the past, around the choices made by her parents. Around her mother's unhappiness and her father's guilt. One evening after making love, she'd confessed to him that she felt light now, as if a terrible burden had been lifted.

Well, it had. No burdens now.

He had his own past to bury. He'd loved his family fiercely. But they were gone now. Had been gone for almost seventeen years. He had never really laid his grief to rest. But in these weeks with Felicity, he'd spent hours, even days, without thinking of them. They had loved him. They wouldn't have wanted him to feel such grief that he couldn't get on with his life.

Both of them were free now.

"I want my present," Metal announced. "Right now. And then I want to give you mine."

Rising, she went to one of the bags and brought out a tartan-wrapped package. He recognized it as from a Scottish store in the center of town. She placed the package solemnly in his hands.

He tore the wrapping paper open and pulled out a long cashmere scarf. "This is beautiful but it's the Black Watch tartan," he said. "Honey, I'm Irish, not Scottish."

"Not today you're not. Today you are a Scotsman." She wrapped it around his neck and he fingered the material. It was incredibly soft. "I'm going to burn this old black one of yours I've been wearing. Now." She sat back down, folding her hands in her lap. "My present. I want it."

Metal's palms suddenly started sweating. Oh God. He had an entire speech ready. Had been practicing it too. Now he couldn't remember a word. The only thing in his head was a bright keening panic. What if it wasn't the right time? What if she missed Vermont?

What if she said *no?*

He brought the small package out of his pocket. He didn't have the nerve to say he'd bought it three weeks ago because she'd think he was insane. He was, but not about this. He was absolutely certain about this.

This was right, this was meant to be. He felt it in his bones.

His panic stopped, just like that.

He held the package out in the palm of his hand. Felicity picked it up with her delicate fingers, turned it over. He'd simply ripped the wrapping paper off the scarf but she picked hers apart carefully. Untying the bow of the ribbon. Gently opening the wrapping paper.

A small intake of breath.

She opened the jewelry box and stared.

Metal had gone straight to the source for all things beautiful and elegant. Suzanne Huntington. She had approved and so Metal knew, beyond a shadow of a doubt, that it was a ring that would be pleasing to a woman.

The central stone was a sapphire, a little darker than her eyes. There was an intricate setting and Suzanne had told him the name of the setting and told him the cut of the sapphire but he couldn't remember any of that now.

She held the ring in her hand, then put it on. A band Metal hadn't noticed around his chest suddenly eased.

"I, um." His mouth was suddenly dry. God, where was a beer when you needed one? "I thought that since you've had so many names, you wouldn't mind one more change."

"Yeah?" Her tone was dry but her eyes were wet.

"Felicity O'Brien. Sounds good. Don't you think?" He'd tried for casual but his voice broke on the last word.

She was admiring the ring and was smiling when she lifted her head. "Felicity O'Brien," she said softly. "Sounds great."

* * * * *

To purchase and read more books by
Lisa Marie Rice, please visit Lisa's website
at lisamariericebooks.com/books.